It was a chilling moment; Ensign Lahira Ocean was about to see her first response from an alien life form! Replacing the old Aricebo message on the screen came a series of fuzzy symbols, along with a myriad of different letters from every language Humanity had ever encountered, foreign or domestic. When a match was found, it was automatically added to the fleet's database and they were one step closer to mastering the alien language - in digital form, at any rate.

They could have gotten a response from the foreigners in Human tongue, but that would have been little use - it would have almost certainly been in a bastardized form of the language, and far less clear-cut. Furthermore, while an unintelligible message would only take seconds to decode, it would take much longer for the aliens to slap together a passable Human-spoken packet.

"We are processing," the message read. It was a message of ambiguity, a state of limbo that would not last very long.

More data streamed across the screen. This was a side-by-side comparison of genetic markers and features, and the calculations were automatically forced into a corner of the screen so as to avoid obscuring any views of the stationary green ships. The information was, as hoped for, clear-cut; this species was vastly different from the Humans and their two organic allies. They were based on silicon, not carbon. This little fact helped make the next bit of transmission ever so slightly more understandable.

"Processing complete."
"You cannot help us find our creators."
"You must be purged."

The message from the aliens was stunning. Lahira felt nauseous. For a moment, there was silence. It was a tense span of time, one where every Human in the fleet with access to a television screen stared at it in concern. Was it a mistranslation? A bad joke? Or was it what Humanity had long dreaded?

I0537423

Protostar: Memoirs of the Messenger

A Novel

By Jesse Pohlman
http://www.jessepohlman.com

Pohlman Press
Freeport, NY

This is a novel by Jesse Pohlman, Copyright 2012-2013. It is *Independently* published by Pohlman Press, an entirely mandatory creation. All rights are reserved. Thank *you* for your purchase!

Cover art by Rick J. Avolin; colored by Jesse Pohlman (www.jessepohlman.com).
Lettering and additional touch-ups by Katherine Anguera (www.kanguera.com)

This book is dedicated to my grandmother, Lucille Pohlman;
You've seen and done so much that defines the Human
experience.

Chapter One
Symphonies at Light Speed

Ensign Lahira Ocean might have made her living as the chief navigator aboard the *George Washington*, but she held a secret lust for history. It didn't have the same taste as plotting astronomical courses, or the same tingling as the avoidance of asteroids, but the subject held a subtle whiff of enlightenment as well as just a glimpse of arrogance. "*If history is written by winners*," she often mused, "*then the victors naturally come off better than the vanquished.*"

That's how it was on Earth in the early twenty first century, one of her favorite eras to study. In this case, the vanquished had been the fossil fuel industry. Most people had, at the time, imagined that the world they knew would end in disaster; either by nuclear fire, a worldwide pandemic, or through the simple decay of society. To many, society was condemned to stagnation and eventually deterioration. Some even embraced the pending demise of humanity, seeking to find beauty in the destruction of all they understood. The writers at the time talked about zombies, quite possibly as a metaphor for masses of unskilled laborers; or, they created tales about vampires who sucked the blood from the living, a comparison to the so-called "fat-cats" who were so heavily protested at the turn of the millennium.

It turned out that sometimes destruction could be beautiful for the *right* reasons.

Change began with the emergence of a new power source. Instead of burning dead plants and animals to obtain energy at the cost of environmental destruction, the revolution of power came when Thorium, a nuclear fuel, achieved recognition as a (mostly) safe source of energy. It had risks attached to its use, but its acceptance yielded an end to "energy wars" as people knew them. It was plentiful in the Earth's crust and difficult to transform into the much-feared weapons of mass destruction. It was never a sole source of power, not even in the year 2483 in which Ensign Ocean lived, but it was certainly a predominant one. Once its abundance in the galaxy was discovered, there was little question on how the future of Human expansion would be fueled.

Even more than just eliminating conflicts over energy, Thorium powered other ambitious projects to improve mankind. Energy wars in desert nations might have ended, but water wars loomed as the effects of global warming, a mild disturbance in Earth's overall climate, caused in large part by Humanity's earlier technological development, became apparent. The plentiful and cost-efficient fuel that science had happily conjured up allowed for man to begin removing the salt from its bountiful ocean water at an economically viable rate. The world's thirst was quenched for the immediate future, while simultaneously providing water for growing crops to feed the world's poor, and all without overarching political demands on peoples' freedoms.

Were there still conflicts? Yes; religion, in its most fanatic forms, remained been a major problem for politicians. In pre-industrial history it's impact was universal, with crusades and witch-hunts and Human sacrifices generally grazing the lives of every person on Earth. It had sent out new roots as a galvanizing factor during the end of the 20th century, providing clear delineations between an "us" and a "them." Even once the underlying societal problems of scarcity were solved, obsessive amounts of faith remained a thorn in man's collective side. Over the centuries, however, the more virulent ideologies had been all but stamped out - scant few persisted, let alone acted openly to disrupt the order that had developed. To this day, with so much moderation in the stars, it was impossible to know how many tiny, fractional cults existed with violent underpinnings, but none of them were a threat. It was similar to the anarchist movements in nations such as Greece - and the socialist ones, for that matter. Crushed because their root causes had been solved, but not entirely forgotten as occasional dissidents among the stars railed against the less convenient parts of a free society.

She sighed and unplugged her neural cable from the small slot in the back of her head. Taking the cord in her hand, she withdrew it from the data terminal she'd been accessing and looked about her quarters. They were spartan enough at first glance, with a scant few books, disk-cases and hard-drives on a shelf; a bunk with generic blue blankets and pillows; a retro-style tourism poster featuring the planet Magellan. "Warm Up On Circumnavigation Beach!"

Her quarters had a tiny kitchenette with utensils, a small sink, and a refrigerator holding, so far as she could recall, basic essentials such as milk, cereals, eggs, and beer. She normally ate breakfast alone, but indulged in her other meals in the *George Washington's* mess hall. A small end-table with a picture of herself as a child, alongside both of her parents - a dark-skinned female and a light-skinned male - rested near the head of her bed.

Aside from her data terminal, there was a view-screen in her room in case she was needed, one that was currently turned off. In the dark plasti-glass she could make out her reflection; she was of medium height, almost 5'6, with short and closely cropped black hair. She had faintly tanned skin, a byproduct of her upbringing on Magellan. Her brown eyes were accentuated by a tiny, dark mole on her left cheek; it was a mark she'd often considered removing, but had been assured was not as hideous as it sometimes felt.

Stretching, she looked at her clock; it was nearly time to turn in, with her next shift roughly eight hours from the Earthen midnight that the ship's clock was set to. She sat down on her bed and removed her uniform piece by piece; from the dark blue overcoat to the brown undershirt she chose to wear. Her medals and ranking insignias were quickly removed from their resting places, and she rose briefly just to place them on the small end-table, next to her younger self.

She reached into a tiny closet and withdrew another outfit - a blue overcoat with a lighter blue-tinted undershirt - and set about affixing her tiny metallic devices to it. Once she was satisfied that the prizes were in the proper order, she returned to the seat and gazed at the clock again. It had advanced an entire five minutes. She set an alarm on it; that, and she programmed some Beethoven on her view-screen while setting a sleep-timer for twenty minutes. The orchestra picked up and began to play, soothing her nerves. With a sigh she laid down and rested her head, imagining that she were back on her home-world - or any world, for that matter!

As Lahira rested in her bed, waiting to fall asleep and contemplating the course she'd steered to reach her position as chief navigator on the *George Washington.* Magellan, the planet she called home, had been the fourth extra-solar planet colonized by man, a world only sixty light-years away from Earth and its Sol system. Settled in 2143 and named - as all Human planets, save within Sol, were - after former explorers, her's was a world that almost wasn't. Considered a sub-prime place to build a home due to its long summers and short, yet brutal winters, it was a struggle for the early governors to attract investment credits and workers alike. Without money, it was hard to pay employees; without employees, it was impossible to produce anything! Thus, it's intrinsic value was limited.

Then, the rovers and impactors revealed extensive Thorium and Iron deposits. This, coupled with its blessings of both a near-Earth gravity and day/night cycle, and it was only a matter of time (and fund-raising) until Geo-engineers could moderate the harsh climate of Magellan. Venture capitalists saw the world's long-term potential and developed resource gathering crews; while some of the earliest failed, the survivors of that difficult era managed to grow into planet-sprawling mineral powers. While the planet wasn't granted a stupendous bounty of other "Rare Earth" minerals, it quickly developed into the Human race's primary source of fuel and simple construction materials.

The exploitation of mineral resources alone might have ensured Magellan's future, but Lahira's ancestors had emigrated to that world for another reason - trade. With the species' greatest reserve of fuel, Magellan was destined to become a pit stop on Humanity's road towards more colonies. Add to it that her home star system's neighbors had three fairly habitable moons (albeit no worthy planets), and suddenly Magellan was comparable in function to a major metropolitan city, while its neighbors were akin to suburbs. True, the drive was longer than twenty minutes! But trade was more than reasonable in that area, and with trade came profit. Where profit went, the Oceans (or, as her mother had been, the Samsons) pursued it. As co-owners of a fairly substantial shipping company called (fittingly) Interstellar Oceans, the Oceans made their money by handling freight-forwarding and exports between Earth and its territories.

Lahira was the exception; her family had always been excellent at arranging transportation, but she herself wanted to do more than just coordinate shipments. No, she wanted adventure. She wanted hands-on experience. Her parents weren't thrilled with the concept of her joining the navy, but they didn't object, either. They were fully capable of looking at the big picture - when the navigator finished her tour of duty, she'd have built up a sizable network of contacts that would heavily reward her in the business world.

Would she ever retire? She'd thought about that for some time! She'd spent five years (one less than normal) earning a Master's Degree in Interstellar Navigation at the Maritime School of Applied Physics, Earth's most prestigious military academy, located within New York City itself. It was a military school and had been throughout its history. She graduated first in her class; with a rather annoying girl named Kelly Grant hot on her heels. Once she was propositioned to take a role in the Human armed forces she couldn't pass it up. Not only would she get to see all of the worlds belonging to Humanity, but she might even get to help settle new ones! Add to it that her parents ultimately conceded to her desires for adventure and approved of her taking on a six-year tour of duty, and she was in!

From a low-level scanner operator, she'd worked her way up to the night command and, finally, to her current job as a navigational lead. There weren't many more places she could go, unfortunately. Either she could take charge of a smaller ship when its Captain was promoted, or she could hope for a position in the bureaucratic side of the military, coordinating missions with Earth's government. Both options made the prospect of an honorable discharge seem welcome; but the command of a real naval vessel? That sounded enjoyable, if only it wouldn't be a tiny, undignified one.

She would have ruminated on her upbringing and dreams some more, but drifted into sleep as the music cut off.

*****

She awoke to the sound of birds chirping. They were quiet, at first, penetrating into her subconscious and causing her to imagine she were in a forest surrounded by avian creatures. Then the sound grew louder, and as she began to stir it seemed like the birds were growing closer; they were friendly enough, for the chirping was fortunately not of the shrill sort, and they worked collectively to scoop her up and lift her away. She rolled over and opened her eyes, soaring high above the clouds.

And suddenly she was back in the belly of the *George Washington*. The chirping continued to grow louder, becoming mildly irritating before Lahira stood and placed a hand on her alarm clock, silencing it. She yawned and stretched, walking to her refrigerator and withdrawing a small vial of orange juice, one of milk, and a small ready-to-serve bowl of cereal. She looked down at the breakfast choice she'd made; Apple Bits. It was a lucky draw - to the left of the Apple Bits had been Frosted Oats (passable) and to the right? Corn Bits, a sister cereal to the Apple Bits and one that the Ensign was in no mood for.

She poured the milk into the cereal and withdrew a plastic, yet sturdy spoon from her kitchenette. Sitting on her bed, she stirred the tiny bits of apple-shaped, cinnamon-flavored food and took a bite. Then, she took a sip of her orange juice; tangy and with heavy pulp, exactly the way she liked it. Breakfast took her approximately five minutes to wolf down; a brief shower and shaving touch-up took twelve. Thanks to her preparations the previous night, dressing up took just a scant three. By the time her shift was going to start at 8:00 AM sharp, she was fed, clean and clothed, ready for a day of work.

She exited her hole-in-the-wall apartment in the Officers' Quarters and made her way down the hall. The interior of this area looked about as well as any Human military vessel ever could; it had linoleum walls and faux-marble floors which resembled, poorly, a college dormitory. This was a stark improvement over the interior of smaller ships, which were typically made of unmitigated sheet metal with perhaps some paint covering them. Those in the Human fleet were hard pressed to find comforts, even in the most advanced of their vessels.

Then again, the human fleet wasn't exactly massive - in fact, it had just four *Alexander*-class battleships: The titular *Alexander the Great,* the *George Washington*, the *Ghengis Khan*, and the newest addition to their number, the *William the Conqueror.* These battleships were named after the greatest generals in Humanity's history, and were hardly useful to the bulk of Humanity's masses; they were built primarily as a safeguard against any potential threat from a foreign aggressor. Their predicted usage was minimal, for a myriad of reasons, not least of which being that no foreign power yet encountered had a desire for bloodshed.

The smallest, perhaps most rickety military-grade vessels were labeled under the *Bantam*-class. As with the *Alexander* order, the first of these ships took on the name of their entire class. Just slightly larger than what Ensign Ocean had learned were called the *Wickes*-class vessels (300 feet in length, but increased to one hundred in width counting engines) fielded primarily between the first and second "World Wars" during the 1900's, the *Bantam*-class ship was designed for two main purposes. Their first task was the service of any orbital or otherwise-established facilities of the Human military. Secondly, and perhaps more importantly, was that it was armed and capable of dealing with any rebellious or lawbreaking citizens that might cause trouble; pirates, for example, frequently used commandeered freighter vessels with ad-hoc armaments to hold up legitimate transports. There were easily forty of these in service at any time, with at least half a dozen in reserve while undergoing maintenance.

Following the *Bantam*, the next larger class of ship was the *Destroyer*-class. The Human fleet contained twenty of these vessels; each was nearly three times as long as the *Bantam*-class vessels and easily thrice as equipped. The *Bantam* might have only held a crew of one hundred and twenty, whereas the *Destroyer* could carry one and a half thousand easily - more if configured to carry cargo and troops as opposed to smaller ship-to-ship fighters, transport planes, or other equipment. These gargantuan vessels were the size of post-Second-World-War aircraft carriers, albeit some of the smaller ones; Lahira had even found a close structural match in the French *Clemenceau*-class aircraft carrier, though the *Destroyers* were substantially larger in width to account for armor and life-support systems. Roughly measured, they were almost 300 feet in diameter! Their purposes were simple - if *Bantam* vessels couldn't take care of some sort of military conflict, *Destroyers* were called in. They sorted it out, usually with overwhelming firepower. Pirates knew better than to stand their ground.

Even these *Destroyer*-class vessels bore little comparison to the *Cruiser*-class. Only eight currently served in the Human navy with at least one more slated to be completed in the immediate future, and they were named after the simple concept of communication; monikers such as *Courier* and *Telegraph*. These beasts were substantially larger than the early 20th century Triple-E Maersk container ships - over 1,600 feet long and one hundred and nearly five hundred feet wide, they sported more than a heavy compliment of artillery. Their exact armaments were hard for Lahira to know for sure, as each one had it's own role; some were designed for launching interceptors, some for launching missiles, and some were armed to the teeth with point defense and long range direct fire cannons. If, in all the stars, there were some crisis that demanded more attention than the

Destroyer-classes could provide, a *Cruiser* would, well, deliver the point home.

But then there were the *Alexander*-class ships. They were, to put it bluntly, unfathomably powerful. It took until the mid 2080's to develop a vessel on Earth even close to its size, and only after Thorium had been widely commercialized and after the third Lunar colony was operational. If a *Cruiser*-class vessel could support an average-sized town, an *Alexander*-class ship was an entire city. These behemoths were built exclusively in space, and easily measured three and a third thousand feet in length; they could actually fit more than four Cruisers inside of them! They were, of course, recent inventions, and sported all of the latest technology in both communications and destructive capacities. As the planets Mankind had colonized were worthy of no less than the name of the greatest explorers of history, so too were these ships deserving of only the greatest names of military history. It was aboard the second of these, the *George Washington*, that Lahira Ocean served.

It was 7:52. She stepped onto an elevator with a number of other crewmen and headed toward the ship's control room. She had a date, so to speak; a date with her crew rotation and, furthermore, with her Commander.

Lahira stepped off of the elevator and made her way toward the bridge. Walking down the corridor, she passed by a fellow, though junior officer; his name was Gavin Trusant, and he was a fellow Magellaner. He was tall and dark skinned, with a shaved head and sharp, keen eyes that seemed to take in every detail. From what Lahira could recall, he was an entirely average officer when it came to weaponry, but he had a keen eye for doctrine - and, according to the rumor mill, debating it with superior officers to a fault. She wasn't an expert in combat, so she just accepted her associates' words at face-value; but she had an appreciation for opinion that exceeded her respect for aim.

She made her way toward the door to the bridge. As she approached, she took note of the two guards; Bryan and Joanna, their names were, and they were a fixture of her daily routine.

She showed them her identification and offered them a good morning - they saluted, she returned it, then she looked toward a computer terminal just outside of the heavy blast doors that she intended to pass through. A beam of blue light emerged and scanned her eyes and face, detecting whether any modifications had been made since she'd last checked in and determining whether or not further identification was necessary.

The hissing sound of the door's hydraulic servos opening the multi-centimeter thick doorway was the only answer she needed. Her heels clicked as she entered the well adorned, well cared for bridge.

The *George Washington*'s control center was not, as so often guessed at in 1900's science fiction, located in the very front of the ship. There *was* an observatory there, but it was mostly for on-vessel rest and relaxation as opposed to the actual command of the ship. Instead, the star-ship's bridge relied upon externally mounted cameras, sensors, and information inputs in order to tell what was taking place outside of it. This data was piped into the command and control room, interpreted by the officers running the show, and acted upon by its leadership.

No, the *George Washington* was controlled from the very inner-most area of the ship, heavily protected by blast doors and capable of surviving even if the vessel was heavily damaged and had experienced multiple hull breaches. It made no difference to the command staff if the meter-thick layers of armor had been punctured and half of the warship had been exposed to the cold void of space; its leadership could continue on, giving any survivors their best shot at getting away alive - even victorious!

Once the thick blast doors protecting the control room had opened, Lahira strolled inside. She looked up toward her commander and saluted; he returned the gesture, then smiled at her with a genuine warmth; a sincere attachment.

"Ensign Ocean," the heavily decorated commander offered politely. Once upon a time, her rank may have been named differently; the Human navy had simplified them for reasons that she had never quite understood. "How are you, today?"

It was this personal leadership that Lahira admired the most; not the dozens of medals on the man's chest, the mission patches he'd earned, or the fact that he could have retired years ago but had chosen to keep serving out of a true love for humanity.

"Commander Owens," she returned gracefully, not stumbling for the slightest over the fact that her name and his were so phonetically similar. "I'm doing well, sir. Yourself?"

The five foot nine, bald-headed man nodded firmly; he wasn't ever a quick man, even in his youth, but instead took his time and deliberated. It was whispered that at one point he had hair - *a* hair, perhaps, seemed more the likely case in Lahira's mind. He might also once had been handsome, but now he resembled a grandfather far more than an older/sexier man-motif. Barely visible underneath his uniform was a small, silver chain that only a select few would have known ended with a tiny, wooden-and-metal cross - a symbol of religion that so many officers had foregone.

It wasn't that faith-based trait he was known for, however; he was known, instead, for being both a decisive figure and a decidedly "unplugged" one. Whereas Lahira and most other officers had agreed to have implants in their bodies, augmentations which allowed them to mentally access data and other features of 2400's convenience, the commander refused, instead relying on his officers to feed him information or, at most, placing a comparatively archaic network of electrodes and neural scanners over his shining head and inputting his commands in a less direct manner. "I am doing well, today; I'm looking forward to being productive. Ready to guide us through the stars?"

She bowed her head slightly. "Of course, sir!" Lahira answered warmly, walking over toward her seat. Its occupant, a junior officer as she had once been, removed the wires from his head, stood and saluted - and she returned it. The navigator nestled down into her seat and relaxed, exhaling gently as she slipped one end of her own cable into the computer terminal before her. "I'm always ready," she declared before she reached behind her own head, to the base of her skull, and plugged herself in.

Once upon a time, the navigator suffered from the same disorientation that all others did when accessing a computer network with her brain. Despite the evolution brought about through science, Humanity's biological adaptation to the changing environment had been at a snail's pace. No matter how well-bred the trait, and no matter how young the first exposure of a child had been, there was just no way that the psyche of a novice computer user was going to naturally anticipate and adjust for the sensory overload that came with computing in 2483.

That had been a long time ago. Today, Lahira hardly had to concentrate to bring herself into and out of "cyberspace," an archaic yet oddly appropriate term for where she found herself, now. She stared at the *George Washington*'s computer network, a massive and heavily fire-walled contraption. The "hard" - as opposed to wireless - connection to the system bypassed her instantly through any external-access defensive concerns; one didn't get on the bridge without either brute force or recognition by that same computer's physical security, thus the counter-intrusion programs knew not to immediately challenge her access.

Now, the navigator had only to authenticate herself to view the information that was appropriate for her rank - and the information that Commander Owens authorized her to see. Mentally communicating her first series of access codes, she willed into view a visual representation of the ship's computing power. She could see all of the primary departments: Defense, Engineering, Navigation and Communication. Moreover, she could see how each department was drawing from the vessel's processing power.

Defense typically utilized a steady 12% of the *George Washington*'s resources, unless it was running a drill or under an actual attack. Fortunately, Lahira had yet to see the latter; but in drills, she'd seen the numbers spike to 25%. She wasn't an expert on weapons, but she had learned something about them in basic training. The *George Washington*'s primary armaments were a collection of six heavy rail-guns. The technology to use magnetic fields to launch heavy, metallic objects at high velocity wasn't new - it existed even in the late 1900's! Fortunately, physics allowed for a nifty advantage; the more speed a projectile had and the heavier it was, the more damage it would do to its unfortunate target. Without so much as a few atoms between a rail-gun round and its target, each kinetic impacter could do catastrophic damage to whatever poor souls were in its way.

Aside from that, the ship had four other weapons it utilized. The simplest of them were conventional, shaped-charge, high explosive rockets that could wreak some serious havoc upon their targets. Secondly, there were small, heavy-caliber machine guns that could shred incoming threats quickly and could even fire flak rounds; shells that would explode before reaching an incoming threat, allowing the intruder to waltz right into heavy shards of metal that would reduce it to ribbons. Third, the *George Washington* had eight, one-dozen member interceptor squadrons that could be loaded to engage enemy planes or perform assault runs against other targets.

But the final weapon that the *George Washington* had was a rather flavorful assortment of nuclear warheads. In space, without atmospheres or gravity to restrict the many vectors of motions, these weapons weren't *quite* as impressive as they were when used on a planet's surface. A ship struck by one would suffer serious damage, of course! But physics were friendly in this case, as the potentially-devastated vessel could defray most of the damage by simply getting pushed away, as opposed to having to resist the summary force of the entire impact. They were still deadly, of course! But a victim of nuclear force would not necessarily be eliminated by just one strike, especially if it wielded modern Human technology.

More to the point, the defense section of the ship was also responsible for the *George Washington*'s anti-asteroid shields. While part of Lahira's job as a navigator was to minimize the risk of collision, between cosmic radiation and stray, pebble-sized harbingers of death that could slice steel if struck at high enough velocities, impacts occurred all the time. She didn't fully understand the science behind the projection of these force-fields, but she knew that they made most incoming objects less than threatening. An electro-magnetic matrix combined with the projection of a plasma...And she got lost, right about there. The best she could do was guess that it was similar to a solar flare.

Finally, defense was responsible for internal security, as well. Acting out of their own ready-room, Security was headed by Ken Takeda, a man from the world of Columbus, the very first extra-solar planet colonized and named after the "discoverer" of the "new world." Admittedly, it was not Columbus' discovery, but that was part of the in-joke: Columbus was not the first extrasolar territory, just the first full-fledged planet that was inhabited by mankind. Nevertheless, Takeda ran defensive protocols and prepared for firefights. Small arms, on-world combat, and tactics - they were the ones who took care of any fighting. Ordinarily, this wasn't a serious concern.

Something, today, just didn't seem right with the way the *George Washington*'s computers were assigning her access. She decided the only way to get an answer on her questions - those deeply rooted subconscious doubts that only one with a neutral implant could perceive - was to dig deeper.

*****

Ensign Ocean had a problem; with her head plugged into the *George Washington*'s computers, she could tell that her department, navigation, wasn't being given all of the processing power it required. She'd already scanned the first of the other branches of the star-ship's command chain, one dedicated to the defense of the ship.

The next department Lahira worked with was engineering, and frankly she was much worse at dealing with this subject than she was with weaponry. Weapons were simple - shoot things, and kill them. Engineering involved managing the engines of the ship, and they worked in ways she just didn't fully grasp. She knew that the first human vessels were transported by Alcubierre engines; a technology first theorized in the early 21st century but only implemented in the it's later years. She knew the basics of it; by creating a warped area of space in front of the ship and an oppositely-designed one behind it, the ship didn't actually move through space so much as space moved around it, effectively transporting its contents! There were no "jump-drives" that could effectively teleport a vessel through space, although it remained a holy grail of travel science! Humanity simply had faster-than-light speeds created through changes in space.

These changes were fickle and required constant recalibration. The engines alone consumed maybe 10% of the computer network's resources, but engineering was also responsible for any sort of technical problem one might have that didn't involve computer software. Airlock on the fritz? Life support mistaking cats for dogs? Broken water pipe? All of that and more were reserved for this department. This could consume up to another 15%, depending on how optimal the conditions aboard the ship were.

If the ships themselves could move faster than light, however, there was a simple question that Lahira could ask all day and never understand the answer to - and that, of course, was "how the hell do these ships communicate?" The answer to this, provided to her by her colleagues in the communications section of the ship, always involved neutrinos being received in certain orders that indicated certain assignments. The navigator was at a loss for productively grasping how it worked. After all, information wasn't supposed to move faster than the speed of light; but then again, neither was any form of mass.

The communications department also managed computer security, networking problems, and the physical maintenance of most of the vessel's sensors. They naturally sought to monopolize the *George Washington*'s processing power, seeing as they were in charge of doling it out, and they normally consumed 30% - mostly for legitimate reasons, including the management of all fleet communications, although there were always rumors of the younger officers sneaking in some video game time on the clock. This was A-OK with Earthling Lucas Traveras, the Ensign in charge of that department, so long as - of course - their job got done.

In Lahira's department, she had a number of officers working directly under her. The majority of her task was to ensure that the *George Washington* didn't fly face-first into a star; she plotted courses around comets, ensured that she avoided gravity wells, and otherwise kept the ship out of trouble. In most circumstances it was a relatively easy job; true, she and her subordinates were responsible for scanning the skies for threats, either from other vessels or from nature itself, but modern day scanning equipment could pick up pebbles thousands of lunar distances in advance.

Star charts were another aspect of space-faring she had to be familiar with, but ultimately they weren't overwhelming. She knew the Human territories like the back of her hand, knew where the borders of her species lay, and knew the fastest lanes from one side of that region to the next. Around Earth, much like a tree, the Human star maps expanded in branches; a main planet might have as many as seven or eight colonized moons. She kept her subordinates in a relatively relaxed order, and viewed herself more as a teacher than a commanding officer. As long as there was no difficulties, no emergencies, it was a fairly easy, if technical job.

In combat, well, that was another story. Navigation was responsible for tracking enemy targets just as it was responsible for evading threats. Defensive tactics and dodging missiles were a major part of the job, just as much as sitting around at a scanner and hoping not to hear an asteroid had come within a light-year of the vessel. She was particularly good at those circumstances, although she was good at just about all of them. Her department used maybe 20% of the computer resources on an average day.

In total, about 12% normally went to defense, 20% went to navigation, 30% to communications, and 25% was employed by engineering. The remaining 13% were ordinarily left for officers to use the galactic-net, work on personal projects, and the like; that, or were called into use by the defense department, sometimes at the expensive of communications' less noble projects.

And that's why it was so alarming that, at the moment, defense was in the 20% area while 50% was going toward communications. Engineering and, of course, her own department were getting hosed! That could only spell trouble.

As Lahira fidgeted in the computer-chair, her restless mind currently interfaced with the computer system of the *George Washington*, she heard the faint beginnings of viola strings. It was Pachibel, this time, that arose to help relax the navigator as she assessed those power inequalities. She couldn't believe that communications and defense would suck up so much of the resources that she was going to need to lay out today's travel plans!

While staring, disembodied as a phantom, at the green and blue lines of ink-like threads that made up the *George Washington*'s virtual computer resource distribution displays. It was like watching various colored river flowing into lakes; but the usual river flow was hardly recognizable and, more to the point, the usual depth of her department's lake was incredibly reduced. It would make any operations requiring this water - including the piloting of her vessel through the stars - just about impossible.

She removed herself from the virtual world and unplugged her head from the wire; but, by leaving the wire in, made clear that she was planning to return. She stood and rose to Commander Owens; his chin dipped as he looked her over. "Any news?" Lahira's boss asked, studying her in a patient, warm manner. It wasn't as though he seemed worried by her behavior, although it was unusual for officers to plug in and out so quickly.

"Well, sir," she whispered cautiously, "and believe me when I say I don't particularly have a problem with it, but the computer resource allocations are *really* strange." Her statement was accompanied by a perfectly casual, concrete, factual tone. There was no pleading, no complaining, and no anger. She made it clear she was presenting facts she knew nothing about.

"Yes, yes," the Commander answered, nodding his head gravely. "Right now we are in the process of evaluating some rather important data. Ensign Travares is actually working with Ensign Takeda on a very important inventory update requested by Earth about thirty minutes ago." He sighed, and spoke in a demure tone that underscored this task's importance. "It's of substantial importance."

She widened her eyes, slightly. "I'm curious," she admitted; and he smiled in response. A welcoming. "What's going on?" The other officers on the bridge all belonged there, all had authority to be briefed on matters of Mankind's survival. It was perfectly reasonable for the Commander to disclose his greatest concerns, as necessary.

He regarded her curiosity with a gentle nod, but as his elderly eyes gazed away Lahira knew she wasn't going to like the answer. "About an hour ago, maybe less, Hudson received some fairly unsettling news. I actually called Ensign Travares up as he slept and asked him to do his best to crunch the numbers they provided. We're not entirely sure what the data means"

Lahira was puzzled. Hudson was a world she wasn't exactly familiar with, but it was an important one; after all, it was named after the famed explorer of the New York region in America. "Can I see a read-out of what you're looking at, sir?"

Now, oddly enough, the *George Washington's* head officer gazed upon his subordinate with a sense of pride. "As a matter of fact, we *do* have exactly that need from you." He moved over to the bulky communications and information display hub on the bridge and stood near the soldiers plugged into their networking nodes. "Ensign Travares? May I trouble you for a minute?"

It took merely a second for the dark skinned descendent of the "Hispanic" culture of 21st century Earth to gaze upward and answer in a balanced, slightly spicy flavored tongue. "Commander?" Disorientation was evident; Lahira had never seen him work so hard as to wake from his cybernetic dream with a hang-over! "Hello, yes, what may I do for you?"

"I'm sorry to bother you while you're working, Lucas."
Lahira's eyes jumped - informality was rare on Owens' bridge.
"But I would like for you to forward your latest copy of the files
we received from planet Hudson, as well as any fleet-wide
updates on it, to Ensign Ocean at once. She is our best chance at
determining what we are seeing."

Lahira was stunned; information coming throughout the
entire fleet had to be of great importance - great enough that
multiple updates from dozens of sources and scanning devices
were possible. "Yes, sir, I'd be happy to!" the Ensign stated,
nodding his head to the commander and closing his eyes as he
slipped back into digital space.

The navigator performed a similar ritual, moving back into
her seat and re-attaching her cord to her skull. With a soft click
that resonated from her cranium all the way to the tiny bones of
her ears, she was again floating above those many colorful rivers.
This time, a few droplets of that liquid formed up, flowed above
her head, and formed into unrestricted, un-confined data. With an
exhalation and a touch toward the fluid, she forced it to process
according to navigational protocols that were standard in the
Human fleet.

With a blink of her virtual (and physical, though she
couldn't know it) eyes, she studied the information; there were
images, there were charts, and there were velocity readings. She
had seen read-outs like this hundreds of times in her training; it
was a roster of star-ship routes, and it included their anticipated
arrival points as well as anticipated destinations. The only
problem with the numbers were that they were impossible, and
downright fraudulent. It wasn't a meteorite swarm - that was
certain, since celestial bodies operated according to predictable
laws of physics, unless sentient forces tampered with them. It
wasn't any registered Human vessel or convoy heading toward
Hudson. It was, however, something on its way to the Human
colony.

She jerked her body upright in the chair, removing her
head from the cable and whipping her shoulder around toward

where she'd expected Commander Owens to be. This proved to be a mistake. She nearly knocked him over, as he'd gone in close to get her opinion firsthand. He caught her, nearly fell back a step, and the two gazed at each other briefly, coughed politely, and took an appropriate distance. If there had been any actual tension between the two, it might have been disturbing.

"I was afraid you would react that way, Ensign Ocean," he stated with practiced indifference.

Lahira opened her mouth, but words took some time to form in the face of her concern. "Sir, what I'm seeing, I mean, I've only---"

Lucas grumbled, perhaps because he could hear her voice in the digital mire. The best Communications officers were quite capable of being 'half-out.' "That's...The last...One..."

Commander Owens nodded with an uncanny gravity, fully agreeing with his subordinates' assessments. "I do believe that you, and everyone here, are well briefed on Condition: Genesis?"

The Commander's words brought her eyes to a full state of wideness. "Sir, could you repeat that for me?"

Owens nodded slowly, his eyes measuring hers' - they gauged her reaction to it, and his judgment that she was stunned was absolutely correct. "Of course, Ensign. You have been been briefed on Condition: Genesis, yes?"

These very specific protocols were based upon the Judeo-Christian sacred text's opening chapter, wherein the creation of Mankind and all of the universe was described. While its namesake might have had something to do with a great cosmic anomaly that threatened to recreate the universe, it was actually far more nuanced than that. 'Condition: Genesis' was a series of procedures for dealing with a different sort of beginning - the beginning of diplomatic relations with an unknown alien contact.

Such a system had to be very specific. Even computing languages might be different between two species, making transmissions between ships difficult; never mind the fact that the means of dialogue would almost certainly be different between the Humans and their new visitors. Specific, tailor-made ships had to be deployed which were equipped with large displays that could relay visual messages - assuming, of course, that the new species could see light in order to detect the glorified documentary about 'how the Human came to be!' First contact was a tricky affair, one that was overwhelmed by unknowns.

"Sir," Lahira attempted to do the impossible - questioning the obvious facts before her. "There have only been three of them in the history of the Human race. Are we sure they aren't pirates, or maybe rebels, or at *least* foreigners we've already known?"

The Commander smiled resolutely. "I believe the data you have indicates that these ships are even larger than the *George Washington*, which is by and large one of the most massive vessels known to any species? Furthermore, the Aquarians would have told us they were coming; the Firions might not tell us, but we know they generally don't field larger vessels, and the Automatons?" He shook his head, clearly distrustful of the last group. "If they wanted to visit us, they'd have a reason."

Everything the Commander stated had been correct; indeed, the inbound ships were quite a bit more massive than the *George Washington* was. "Never mind the fact that each one of them has borders far closer to other systems in Human territory, and none would be coming to planet Hudson from this direction unless they'd gone far, far out of their way," Lahira nodded with a grim mask over her face.

It was, indeed, the use of Occam's Razor which indicated that this had to be a new species. The Aquarians were the first that Humanity had met; and, if they had met another first, the history of Mankind might have been completely different. The Aquarians happily accepted such a simplistic moniker; they were, for all intents and purposes, highly evolved fish. They had fins which had developed skeletal structures sturdy enough to hold and manipulate objects. Their home-world was an ocean-covered world with some land that, by-and-large, went unused. Oh, they had developed technology to access land if they wished, but their bones were too brittle for waltzing upon the ground over prolonged periods.

When Human and Aquarian met, it was a touchy situation. It was the first extra-Human contact, after all. Luckily, both were friendly by nature, and both had interests in trade and peace. Both also had navies, but they were small in comparison to the size of their peaceful fleets. They drew up treaties and made agreements on resource sharing. There was even one moon, just inside the Aquarian stellar border, that served as a combination trade-zone and embassy, where Humans lived upon the ground and Aquarians lived in the ocean.

The Firions were the second species that Humanity had encountered. Their home-world was a sulfurous one, a world close to its parent star and with substantial amounts of magma near its equator. They did not subscribe to the same genetic profile as the Humans and Aquarians, as they thrived on eating silicates as opposed to organic matter. As far as their demeanor, they were less friendly than the Aquarians, but they weren't particularly expansionist, either. They were in the middle; they defended their borders, they traded when it would benefit them, and they kept a very strong military posture. There was every reason to believe that they performed espionage on the Humans and their Aquarian allies, but were they a military threat?

To start with, they were locked in a seemingly-primitive mindset. Subscribing to tribal urges, the species was broken up into many two-or-three-system states, not unlike what Humankind had experienced during its earliest years. True, there was an official government that represented all Firions, but they often feuded with one another and found unified progress difficult to achieve. They certainly had a larger naval fleet than any other species, but their political difficulties kept them from having uniform technologies and doctrines, thus weakening their combat efficiency. Finally, of course, a war with any of their potential opponents would be disastrous; the Humans and Aquarians were firmly allied, whereas the Firion states were just as likely to engage one another. As for the Automatons?

Well, they were a whole different ball game.

From what Humanity had been able to piece together, they had been invented by a seperate organic race which had subsequently fallen victim to an old science-fiction horror show cliche. Through whatever malicious deeds they'd committed, these first creators had drawn the ire of the Automatons and, in a violent war, the machines eliminated their builders. It was a touchy topic one the machines did not like discussing - and Mankind made it a point not to irk them.

Unlike so many of the science-fiction writers of Lahira's favorite epoch of history, however, these metallic monstrosities did not have one omnipotent, universe-spanning artificial intelligence dominating their entire 'species.' Instead, each individual entity, be it a star-ship or a truck, of the Automatons was its own thinking, functioning creature. This was a blessing because there was indeed a productive internal debate amongst their kind, but it was also a curse because quite frankly they did not always get along and, when it came time to increase their mechanical herd, the exact nature of each new member of the society was an exercise in forcing logic routines to change and forging newer, more improved code which would be compatible with the older models still 'alive.'

As a rule, the Automatons were isolationists. They pursued their own affairs. Did they attack any foreign, organic species? No - as a matter of fact, they had established non-aggression pacts with their neighbors, as well! They even, on rare occasion, would find an invention that another species had developed useful and seek to acquire it for themselves. In situations like that, they were vastly generous. If, on the other hand, they were irked - and they often could be irritated by things which the other, organic species found unusual - they were frankly a mess to deal with. Military force wasn't a desirable option for either side. Their 'ships' didn't need to worry about life support or storing anything other than fuel and attachments for self repair, meaning they bristled with overwhelming amounts of weaponry. It was no stretch of the imagination to guess that they outgunned their enemies six to one.

As even their battle-ships were sentient and independent, they would only volunteer to put their existences in jeopardy in the direst circumstances. As their "government" seemed more geared towards representing everyone's interests, that made declaring war a serious prospect, as the ones who would do the fighting were concerned with self-preservation. This led to any incidents which occurred devolving into the task of discovering an acceptable set of terms with them - the provision of a particularly nice, mineral-rich asteroid here or there, perhaps, or simply convincing them that conflict was not going to benefit anyone.

Not one of these three species was represented by the foreign vessels now headed toward the planet Hudson, and Lahira Ocean gazed at her superior with worry in her eyes.

"You're correct, Ensign," Commander Owens agreed. If anyone would recognize the gravity of this situation, it was him; he had been part of the task force which handled the Automaton contact. "It has to be someone new. And that means I need you to chart a course to Hudson. We have a welcome party to lead; at this speed, they'll be arriving to Human space in two days."

*****

The violins of her favorite Bach song played as Lahira's conscious mind returned to her computer terminal. She seized (gently, of course) the computing power necessary to begin planning a route; to get from the service station that the *George Washington* was at to planet Hudson would require roughly three days, unless she wished to pass dangerously close to a black hole. As promptness was a matter of importance, she decided to chart something a little unusual.

With a gesture of her hand, the Ensign's eyes were filled with gravitational readings and equations. She drew her fingertip along the path between the ship's current position and the planet *Hudson*. If she took a straight line, she'd find her ship nicely swallowed up by the aforementioned singularity. That was impossible to tolerate.

A soft sigh; there was a fairly large safe distance, so with a sweeping gesture she drew a circle around the black hole's outer reaches. With a hint of willpower, she colored it green and labeled it +0, signifying that there was absolutely no change in direction to be anticipated. She bit her bottom lip, and went halfway between the green line and the hole. This was colored red and labeled +42%. It was irksome to say the least - the *George Washington* had a very high risk of inadvertently getting gobbled up.

She slowly looked around other stellar objects in the area; the nearest other star was a few hours out of the way, and would not solve the problem she was facing - traveling to one of them and utilizing it as a sling-shot was out of the question. Then, however, she cracked a grin.

"I need a simulation," she remarked, speaking over the sound of the background symphony. The computer processors whirred under the strain of her command, but it provided a model of the *George Washington* for her to play with. She placed it a third of the way in from the green line to the red and ran it for a microsecond. The ship listed, the ship began to turn, but before anything drastic could happen she had frozen it. "Bring me the magnetic and gravitational lines."

Orange and yellow streaks emerged upon it; magnetically speaking, the ship wasn't experiencing any simulated damage. Gravitationally, on the other hand, the vessel was being pulled in very gently. She canted her head to the side, studying them for a moment. "Alright. Shift 90% of our asteroid shield's power to the exterior of the circle and re-run the simulation for ten seconds. Lets move those magnetic lines a bit."

This time, instead of the vessel listing so quickly, it resisted - slightly, due to the magnetic forces of the natural enemy itself - the pull of the collapsed star. She bit her bottom lip and nodded. "I need a standard data set of outcomes, here. Give me one thousand executions. Five hundred exact copies, with plus or minus 3% variations for the other five. Run it."

It took roughly thirty seconds, during which she relaxed and listened to her music. Though she had a soft spot for hard rock, a genre that had lasted for centuries in its own right, the classics were, to her, the best. When the simulations finished, she studied the data tables. Naturally, the best outcomes were pre-ordained to rise to the surface.

"Give me two hundred and fifty at a 1% differential." Twenty more seconds, and she had more figures to study. "Alright. Chart course..." She looked through the list. "Eighty five. That's roughly sixty eight meters off of the green line, correct?" When the computer's voice confirmed this, she nodded. "Transmit this data to the big screen. I'm going to stay in and nudge the course as necessary."

The information on the screen above the apparently-comatose Lahira was, in a word, bold. She was taking the ship within the black hole's danger zone. She was depending upon a change in magnetic fields to counter the greater forces of gravity, but if it held? No, *when* it held, it would let her use the collapsed star as a force magnifier and catapult the *George Washington* forward just fast enough to make it in time to greet their new neighbors. She would have to re-run her simulations regularly, and adjust them almost minute to minute, but the actual risk of catastrophe was zero - at least, in the hands of someone as skilled as she was!

By the time that Lahira unplugged herself from the computer, she was just on the outskirts of the Hudson system. She exhaled softly, returning to reality after another long, marathon session of coordinate programming ending with ordering a full stop. She fully awoke and gazed up toward her Commander.

"We're approaching Hudson now, sir," she offered politely. Hunger only now seemed to strike her as an issue; she'd been under for hours. A slow nod acknowledged her statement as her superior officer pressed a number of buttons on his spiffy rotating, reclining command chair.

"Frontal view," he stated to himself as dozens of the

screens in the foremost part of the command center went to life with a soft thud. He nodded once again as he set his eyes upon the blue-yellow sun that hosted the planet *Hudson* and gazed toward Lahira. "Normal speed ahead. We're going to group up with the fleet just outside of the furthest-most planetoid's northern orbit."

"Aye, sir," responded Lahira, plugging her head back into the console and providing the ship with its orders - this time, she remained conscious, merely thinking the commands and watching as the stars began to move again on the screen.

The *George Washington* quickly found itself joined by another, smaller ship; the cruiser *Courier*. Three destroyers swiftly joined them, the *Entropy*, *Radiance*, and *Yamaha*. A fourth destroyer, one heavily modified with massive television screens, led the fleet forward as a number of smaller *Bantam*-class vessels joined up. By the time the Human fleet was finished forming, the *George Washington* had even been joined by the *Ghengis Khan*. They also had the Cruisers *Signal* and *Lightpost*, to accompany a total of four destroyers (plus the modified one) and eight *Bantams*, including the category's namesake.

It was just under half of the Human Star-Fleet, and Lahira smiled broadly as the force gathered up.

"Alright, everyone. We're going to activate Condition: Genesis shortly," the Commander announced over the *George Washington's* internal communications network. "Admiral Winters and the *Alexander* are too far away to command this encounter, still, so she's placed me in charge. Before I go on fleet-wide, I just want the *George Washington* to know that there is *nothing* to be afraid of. We've done this before." He twisted the truth, a tiny bit. "Some others in the fleet - besides my aged self - have even been personally involved. Just be careful, stay alert, and this will be our finest moment together."

When the applause on the bridge ceased, the Commander opened the fleet-wide channel. "Commanders, Captains, and officers; this is Commander James Owens. Under the authority of Admiral Winters, I've been placed in command of this mission.

We are going to operate under Condition: Genesis. The ship *Warm Welcome* will be in charge of handling language coordination, making sure that we can have a dialogue with the aliens."

"I'm having Ensign Travares send each of you orders under the files Contingency Alpha, Contingency Bravo, and Contingency Epsilon. Each of your bridge officers on duty should be aware of the situation, and all our crew needs to be ready to act. If you have questions, direct them to Ensign Travares and our crew, and we'll clarify. If you don't, simply acknowledge this transmission and wait. ETA for alien vessel is twelve minutes. Godspeed."

As the different vessels of the Human fleet confirmed their orders, Lahira watched two separate realities unfold. She was watching, on the big collection of data-screens, tiny flecks appear in the distance as if they were newly born stars. Even the high-resolution cameras on the *George Washington* couldn't pick up the inbound aliens' ship's shapes, yet. The navigator, on the other hand, could make an educated guess based on the travel paths that these visitors were taking.

Nevertheless, the minutes ticked along and where there were once tiny flicks, there were now silhouettes of ships that belonged to the newest alien race to be discovered. Even with superior numbers and a commander who had previously worked on first contacts, the navigator couldn't help feeling nervous about her new mission.

Chapter Two
Hearing Back From Aricebo

Much like Lahira had imagined, the inbound vessels were indeed larger than the *George Washington* she toiled within. She was somewhat surprised to find that the difference between the battleships and the new arrivals was less drastic than the density of the ships had initially led her to believe. Each of the four was made of an unusual, incredibly dense, green-shaded metal, and while the Human vessels put an emphasis on smoothness and aerodynamics (generally useless in space, but a matter of heritage to the Humans), the verdant newcomers' ships were far more like flying bricks with unusual features jutting from their sides.

She exhaled gently, rubbing the back of her neck and brushing her hair away from the cable attached to her skull. Her eyes lost their focus on the bridge's screens and brought forth an assessment of the vessels' top speeds during their journey. They were fast, alright - faster than Human ships, but not by much. That was a tactical advantage; and the heavy density of the vessels was a mystery to her - it could be any number of things, depending on exactly how useful this armor was.

"Alright, people!" the Commander shouted, shocking Lahira out of her fugue. His eyes were shining with possibilities, looking toward the display, but his lips were firmly drawn to etch determination into his face. A graphic forced its way into her field of view, and it showed a swift deceleration of the alien shifts that was reflected in the televised venting of thrusters in the front of the green star-ships.

James Owens cracked a touch of a smile. *"Warm Welcome,"* he stated as casually as possible given the gravity of the circumstances. "Set Condition: Genesis, transmit pattern Darwin." Softly, perhaps to himself, he whispered, "Do your thing, Darwin."

The viewscreen directly to the right of the fore-facing

display turned on, showing a view of everything occurring to the right of the *George Washington*. Lahira watched as a sizable vessel with awkwardly mounted, titanic screens attached to it began a showcase of various images. They included pictures of Humankind, an image of a hydrogen atom that zoomed out into a molecule of hydrogen dioxide and, further back, into a droplet of water. The water became rain falling into an ocean, and the ocean swiftly rolled back into an image of Planet Earth. Now the show focused on the Sol system, giving a relative overview of the size of the world.

Then, once again, the image showed a single hydrogen atom. It was scientifically accurate, appearing in its natural state - one proton, one electron. Underneath it, consequently, appeared the number "1." Next was helium, with its atomic mass of two - and this, naturally, had two underneath. Each atom's number was provided up to 100, enough that any sentient life smart enough to figure out space-flight might determine what numbers mankind used.

Next came letters. The number "1" then was spelled out as "one." Furthermore, the hydrogen atom gained a sub-title of "Hydrogen." Each atom was named, giving Humankind and its new neighbors a common understanding of atomic principles, as well as a system for counting what they observed. If these people were traders, they would be able to respond with their own numerical system and their own names for substances, allowing a shared perception of what matter was.

Finally, graphic depictions of radio waves were shown. First, merely the physics of the phenomenon were detailed - simplistic technology developed around the early 1900's on Earth, and key to space travel. This would ensure that the aliens knew what the *Warm Welcome* was talking about. Once this message was repeated for a second viewing, a particular radio frequency was isolated and displayed, traveling from the *Warm Welcome* to those receiving it.

"Prepare the packet," Commander Owens ordered. Lahira knew the procedure well - once both sides of the contact knew they were talking about the same thing, it was self-evident that one ship would send the other information on that particular channel. It was something of a leap of faith, as that data could - at least in some of the wildest theories she'd overheard Ensign Travares talk about - cause damage to the recipient's computer networks. Of course, the navigator had dismissed this off-hand; all the foreigners had to do was listen and, if they so chose, reply when prompted by the large TV screens.

And after a few minutes of waiting, presumably for the aliens to receive and interpret the "packet" of information about Humankind, including its language, they received one hell of a stunning response.

"Commander," came the voice of Lucas Travares, sounding more surprised than anything, *"Warm Welcome* has gotten a reply!" The bridge exploded into applause with the sole exception of the fleet's chief officer and its communication's supervisor. "Sir," Travares continued, his voice sounding far less than thrilled, "its different."

Considering the circumstances, the entire affair was different; this was first contact with an alien race and, while it wasn't the first time this had happened in Human history, it was a rare and special occurrence nonetheless. Yet when the Navigator heard her colleague's pronouncement, she immediately cast her eyes to her supervisor. Unfortunately, as she'd dreaded, Commander Owens looked concerned.

"Ensign Travares," he queried cooly, "did the *Warm Welcome* reiterate the response verbatim?"

The man's peppery accent emerged. "Aye, sir. I'll put it up on the screen." With a moment's effort, Lucas sent his thought-based commands from the implant in his skull along the wire that fed into the *George Washington*'s computer networks. An auxiliary data stream inserted itself on both sides of the fore-facing display, overlaid upon the image of the alien star-ships before the Human fleet. A scrolling pattern of binary code, 0's and 1's, was the first to grace the television.

"Can you process it, Ensign?" Commander James Owens

asked, his eyebrow furrowing.

With little more effort than a blink of an eye, a series of pixelated images emerged on the screen. At first they resembled little more than dots in a line, but suddenly they became far more unsettling; there was an image of two lines intersecting, of a large square accompanied by nine smaller ones, and - finally - a representation of a stick-figured Human being. Lahira couldn't believe her eyes.

The Commander, on the other hand, couldn't help himself as his lip twitched involuntarily. It was a recognition of something that shouldn't exist. "That's the Aricebo message, yes?"

Perhaps with a hint of surprise in his voice, the communications officer nodded. "Yes sir, our computers confirm it. Pixel for pixel." He stared blankly. "How in the world...?"

Over his communications link with the bridge, from his offices, the security chief Ken Takeda piped a question into the bridge; "What's the Aricebo message?"

"The United States beamed it into space once, during the 20th century. It was a joke," Travares clarified, "a pseudo-scientific attempt at contacting alien life." Lahira nodded her agreement; the technology available was vastly unprepared for the task of alien dialogue, and the message was merely an overblown demonstration of earthly power.

The Commander nodded. "If I recall," he put forth in a sagely tone, "it was really just a demonstration of a space-scanning array's capabilities, and wasn't even properly aimed?" At a confirmatory nod from his communications officer, Owens' lip twitched again. "I wonder what the hell this means?"

For a few moments, there was silence. Then, Travares' eyes widened. "Commander, *Warm Welcome* has a packet! We're patched in to their decoders, and I'm adding the translation to the screen."

It was a chilling moment; Ensign Lahira Ocean was about to see her first response from an alien life form! Replacing the old Aricebo message on the screen came a series of fuzzy symbols, along with a myriad of different letters from every language Humanity had ever encountered, foreign or domestic. When a match was found, it was automatically added to the fleet's database and they were one step closer to mastering the alien language - in digital form, at any rate.

They could have gotten a response from the foreigners in Human tongue, but that would have been little use - it would have almost certainly been in a bastardized form of the language, and far less clear-cut. Furthermore, while an unintelligible message would only take seconds to decode, it would take much longer for the aliens to slap together a passable Human-spoken packet.

"We are processing," the message read. It was a message of ambiguity, a state of limbo that would not last very long.

More data streamed across the screen. This was a side-by-side comparison of genetic markers and features, and the calculations were automatically forced into a corner of the screen so as to avoid obscuring any views of the stationary green ships. The information was, as hoped for, clear-cut; this species was vastly different from the Humans and their two organic allies. They were based on silicon, not carbon. This little fact helped make the next bit of transmission ever so slightly more understandable.

"Processing complete."
"You cannot help us find our creators."
"You must be purged."

The message from the aliens was stunning. Lahira felt nauseous. For a moment, there was silence. It was a tense span of time, one where every Human in the fleet with access to a television screen stared at it in concern. Was it a mistranslation? A bad joke? Or was it what Humanity had long dreaded?

Then, with no warning, four lights emerged from ridges along the hulls of each alien vessel. The illuminated nodules danced about for a moment - and then a beam of swirling red light erupted from them and began to dance along the bows of *Warm Welcome*, *Signal*, *Ghengis Khan*, and *Bantam*. Each one seemed to erupt in flames wherever the red streaks struck! There had been no mistranslation.

The latter, smallest vessel clearly couldn't endure the damage and exploded in a burst of flame. *Warm Welcome*'s screens were sliced clean off; not to mention a large hole had been punched in its exterior, one that was rapidly venting oxygen, material goods, and - most tragically - people.

The two larger ships sustained the least damage, pound-for-pound. They had far more up-to-date, combat-oriented equipment, with more shield generators per square foot to boot. Nevertheless, thick layers of titanium peeled away after the blue-green barriers of the asteroid shields proved unable to repel all of the inbound plasma fire.

Lahira gasped, whispering, "Oh my" as she inhaled in astonishment. Ensign Travares was silent. Most of the bridge gasped, and sighed, and growled. Only the Commander remained unfazed save for a slight wince and a gaze downward.

"Tell the fleet to execute Contingency Alpha, move all of our anti-asteroid shields into combat position!" declared the Commander. From that point on, a very precisely timed chain of events took place, almost as if guided by machinery more than man.

First on the *George Washington*, and then on every other ship, slots in their armor opened up two by two. With each panel that flipped back came a pair of long, cylindrical tubes which parted outward like a flower's bud opening up. Each of these tubes illuminated briefly as their contents - rockets with high-explosive warheads - erupted forth from their homes. While these first rockets were fired, a lift within the ship prepared a second duet of rockets for launching.

When the ship's anti-asteroid shield generators powered down and began to realign forward as much as possible, the gap in the *George Washington's* defenses was utilized perfectly. Thanks to computer-aided timing on behalf of the defense crews, each of the *George Washington's* heavy rail-guns fired upon the left-most alien vessel. The high-impact rounds cleared the barrier just ahead of the first salvo of rockets they sent, and just before the shields reactivated in a protective stance.

Finally, in the very rear of the ship, a pair of launch bays opened up. Tiny, streamlined, dart-like planes began to gush out of the Human vessel like rain pouring from a cloud. With all eight squadrons of twelve interceptors from the *George Washington* being joined by an identical number from the *Genghis Khan*, along with smaller numbers from the heavily damaged *Signal*, the Human fleet scrambled its deadliest weapons in its first offensive wave.

Not a bad start, for the first war that Humankind was fighting against an alien race!

In the back of his mind, Commander Owens knew what his strategy depended on. First and foremost, it was a strategy based on timing: The fleet's rockets and rail-gun rounds would slip past the shields of their launching ships just before they re-activated. The rail-gun rounds would strike first, and any shields their targets might have would be overloaded. Hopefully, there'd be little left after that, but rockets would detonate all over the remains of the enemy's ships. If the rail-guns merely pierced their targets' hulls, that was acceptable - the rockets would enter and devastate the enemy's interior! He had superior numbers, after all; and the four alien ships, especially after firing their primary (and admittedly troublesome) weapons, would have no hope of intercepting all of the inbound explosives.

Not only was he right on the money, but his plan worked better than he could have hoped! Every last Human in the fleet had expected to see some random-colored lights emerge from the alien vessel's exterior and repel the heavy metallic objects they'd fired. No such luck; every last rail-gun round collided with their target and created large holes in their hulls. Chips of armor erupted from the impact sites.

The Commander's eyes narrowed at this unexpected result. The crew of the *George Washington* didn't quite cheer, what with the gravity of their already-incurred losses, but there was a clear lifting of weight from their chests. It seemed as if this alien threat, while having caused severe casualties in an opening assault, would be eradicated quickly, because within seconds these invaders would get a taste of high explosive, shaped-charge warheads. Unfortunately for the Humans, they weren't quite as lucky as they'd initially seemed to be.

Oh, most of the missiles hit, with only a few being intercepted by either an invading vessel's point-defense weaponry or one of the dozens of small fighter planes which flooded from its aft. The intruders' hull was peppered with small red fire lotuses, each one a focused jet of searing-hot explosive force. As the flames died down, Humanity hoped for its victory. Surprisingly, however, the Human barrage didn't have quite the intended effect (that is, to say, reducing its target to ashes). In fact, very few of the impacts actually caused *mild* damage! It was as if the alien vessels were impervious to conventional weaponry.

"Just like I thought," the Commander whispered to himself.

Lahira's eyes danced up toward her boss. "Sir?" Ensign Travares, upon hearing his colleague, also turned toward him; at times like this, junior officers handled most of the charts and relays so that information could be funneled through the chiefs of each department.

The Commander was calm, but his eyes were narrowed ever so slightly. "Ensign Ocean, your assessment of the aliens indicated they appeared more massive than they are. Its their armor."

The navigator gasped, but she didn't have time to dwell on it. Before she had that chance, alarm bells entered the back of her mind, and not just through the data cable plugged into the base of her skull! Even as the *George Washington* screamed at her, she could see with her all-too-mortal eyes that the alien's main weapons were illuminating again!

"Ensign, calculate--"

The Commander's advice was unnecessary. Lahira was already slipping back into the stream of information, and as a consequence what she meant as a polite interruption emerged as a shout. "On it, sir!" she roared, numbers emerging before her eyes as she attempted to decipher which of the fleet's ships were targeted. This was a mostly automated process, though Lahira still had to judge what data was relevant and quickly add her own input on what her vessels were doing. Who was going where? Were there fighter planes in the way? Was the computer right, or wrong, in its assessment of the alien weapon ports' direction and angle? All of these facts were necessary in computing just which of her species were next in the sights of these assailants.

She bit her bottom lip - all of them were.

The navigator didn't waste time asking her Commander for permission to relay the alien's targeting information. There were two reasons for this decision; first, if the ships in the Human fleet had chief navigators half as skilled as she was, they would have deduced it for themselves and she would only be confirming or cooperatively adjusting their numbers. Secondly, even a few seconds' delay could be the difference between life and death for some of the fleet's smaller vessels.

Even as she transmitted the data to her allies by sending a simple suggestion along the cable plugged into her brain, she opened her eyes and commanded it to flood upon the *George Washington*'s screens.

Commander Owens, on the other hand, merely nodded. "Adjust our shield emitters to Ensign Ocean's---"

The bridge of the *George Washington* was shock-mounted, meaning that any impact which moved the vessel as a whole would meet with servos and inertia interrupting gels that would prevent any major disruption of the ship's command center. Even then, as the visual displays showed three beams of hot-red light slamming into the *George Washington*'s front and being intercepted by blue-green barriers meant primarily to prevent asteroids from striking it, the Commander had to reach for a safety railing to prevent himself from stumbling as the ship shuddered.

"Alright!" shouted the Commander, righting his old frame. His calm facade didn't break, but it was clear that this latest attack had tipped him over some subtle line of patience. "Engineering, pipe me in a damage control report. Defense, get ready to launch tactical nuclear weapons." He frowned as he walked over to the stereotypically magnanimous chair in the center of the bridge. He seemed calm as ever, nestling down in the chair and placing a spider-web's worth of electrodes and sensors over his head, back, and arms. It was only through foresight that he'd prepared that networking net - ordinarily it would take minutes to affix all of the interfacing, but all the Commander needed was just a few pats on the back before he was transmitting and receiving signals to the *George Washington*'s computers.

For a moment, the old man seemed to be in pain. He reached up toward his chest and patted the concealed cross he carried, but before he could clutch it as his fingers tried to, his mind left his body behind. Lahira detected a new presence in the ship's computer network, and she opened up an information link with it. He received it just as he'd attempted to retrieve his religious relic; clumsily, without a firm grasp.

While it felt like a long time, in reality Lahira only took microseconds to establish the connection. After all, by the time they'd tied things up, the Commander had information from the entire vessel pumping into his brain. "We are all plugged in," he whispered to himself; his words were echoed in the digital world, wherein his staff overheard his thoughts as a firmly-stated comment. It meant they should switch to a primarily-neural form of communication.

Lahira didn't mind - unlike the old man, she was involved in this wired world for most of her life. Her generation was practically mandated to have those implants, whereas he? He'd lived in a time when he could get a job and a first-rate education without one, although he certainly had to prove himself capable in the face of people who were in the machine, not just riding on it as he was.

"Inbound missiles," whispered a voice in the back of the navigator's head; it had a slight, subtle accent to it that was unlike Ensign Travares'; it was the voice of Ken Takeda, the defense chief. In the navigator's field of vision a data-set emerged that simply radiated, well, unusual radiation. It was an atomic outset which was completely unlike any the Humans had encountered. "Commander, they--"

He was interrupted by the Commander himself, who beamed in the same information. "It tastes like solar-burned carbon," he whispered, "like when stars enter into an Ia supernova phase."

To Lahira, who knew more than a lot about solar processes, that did not sound good.

The life-cycle of most stars ended with a helium eruption; small stars burned their hydrogen fuel up, used what helium its temperatures and gravitational pull could manage, and detonated. It wasn't pretty, and even a tiny star exploding like that could eliminate most of a solar system. Some large stars, on the other hand? They had the mass and fuel to keep climbing the atomic ladder. Carbon was denser, and it didn't like to burn. If it did? The heat of it was far, far greater than that of the hydrogen, and the explosion when all of *that* fuel disappeared?

It turns out that the spectrum of light that such a detonation emitted was a dull, smokey green. Before the Commander could relay any orders to his interceptors, one of them fired upon and detonated the alien missiles. Many lives, in that moment, flashed before the Human eyes; yet, strangely, they all lived to tell the tale! It was a large explosion, yes, and anything caught within its blast radius was vaporized; but the weapon was clearly scaled down to a size useful for naval combat.

It turns out that launching unmitigated supernovas at your enemies when you're within the same solar system is a bad idea.

The fact that this supernova missile was shrunk down to a tactical scale made the job of the Human fleet easier, at least in the sense that they weren't all dead. It also meant that the missiles could actually be intercepted with a relatively safe procedure - the radiation the warheads emitted could be recieved, and the payload of the weapons could be determined as a result, thus yielding an approximate kill zone. Unfortunately, it also meant that these aliens possessed the technology to create a supernova. Just the thought of a scaled-up version of that bomb, one that fully intended to destroy a solar system, was enough to give Lahira nightmares. Sadly, she probably wasn't alone.

The Human interceptors made it their business to pick off those missiles. At some times, this was a dangerous job; even though the navigator could cheer them on and, at times, feed them valuable information on where enemy fighters were, the truth was that many got shot down in the attempt; never mind if they accidentally set off one of the bombs. On the plus side, the enemy's rockets were either destroyed by electro-magnetic pulses, by interceptors, by the fleet's myriad point-defense weapons, and even through the simple concept of jamming their targeting equipment and generating missed shots. It cost some lives, but the ships of the Human space fleet remained intact.

Except, perhaps, for the *Genghis Khan,* which was the only ship unfortunate enough to have one of those carbon-burning missiles heading right for it! Despite all of the flak rounds that the battleship fired, one rocket slipped past its defenses. Lahira could hear the vessel's commander screaming his orders to re-align the ship's shields, to brace for impact, and - most of all - to run as far away from the port side of the ship as they could.

The success of this plan was initially hard to tell, as the green detonation made it impossible for the navigator to see, either on the *George Washington*'s monitors or on the data-feeds from the other ships, what kind of damage the *Genghis Khan* endured. After about two seconds, however, the first images came in and they were exactly as she'd feared; the ship wasn't where she'd expected it to be.

It didn't take her long for her to realize that the vessel had been blasted a good distance away from its original location! It had endured quite a lot of damage, with a massive hole in its left side reflecting just how badly it had been struck, but - perhaps due to no other force than the rage of its Commander - she could hear the orders coming down for them to fire another barrage.

Her hopes were bolstered when the voice of Commander Owens, whispered aloud as it was calmly delivered in the network, provided his own order: "Fire all guns, deliver the second salvo, and launch nuclear devices one through four, one to each."

The *George Washington's* shields receded momentarily and, roughly in tune with the other Human vessels, unleashed every weapon it had at the ready upon the alien fleet. When all was said and done, the aliens were facing two dozen rail-gun rounds, hundreds of rockets, and ten nuclear warheads. While the first barrage had been launched in haste, the second came with slightly less firepower but much better targeting.

Lahira's calculations were dead on - she cyber-psionically pumped navigational information into the computer, which fed that data into Ken Takeda's brain. Ken digitally drew up firing solutions for each and every missile which avoided, without difficulty, the Human fighters. As the space surrounding the two fleets continued to explode on occasion, the dog-fights were being won by the Humans - an added perk!

As the rail-gun shots smashed the alien ships once again, they had a similar effect as last time. Some of the rounds, unfortunately, missed; but others found purchase right near the impact sites of the first volley, further taxing the superstructure of the vessels. One of the alien star ships, the one furthest to the right, no longer had to worry about missile impacts on its hull - it had to worry about missiles getting inside of it, where its armor was far less dense!

And then there were the nukes.

Admittedly, the invaders weren't foolish. Their fighters went straight for the atomic weaponry, much as the Human fighters had gone for the carbon-based ones. These planes were drastically different from their carriers. Instead of bulky, awkward, but utilitarian protrusions, these things were streamlined. Unlike the Human fighters, they put the pilot in front of the majority of the vehicle; the Human planes had far less pronounced cockpits, recessed largely to increase the odds of survival. Nevertheless, their effectiveness - and weaponry, it seemed - was identical. *Most* of the nuclear-tipped missiles were intercepted.

Two managed to get through, however. The first fell just short of a direct hit against one of the middle two vessels; it dealt moderate damage and sent the invaders drifting toward one another. The second? This lucky devil managed to detonate in the maw of an alien ship, tearing a large chunk of its exterior off and threatening to destroy the entire thing!

By the time the conventional warheads finished their task, the aliens were in a sorry state. Their flotilla had been damaged severely, and many of their primary weapons were offline. They were left with a difficult choice - to keep fighting, or to retreat. For all their talk of finding their creators and purging the unworthy, the invaders knew when they were beat. Whatever their beliefs, they were not suicidal fanatics who would die happily for their cause! They turned their tails and started to escape, their fighters returning to their launch-vessels whenever possible - whenever, that is, the Human interceptors didn't cut them into ribbons.

In this instant, Commander Owens had a choice. He could pursue the aliens and annihilate, or perhaps even capture them! But this drew the risk of further casualties along with it. Whatever weapons fire was inbound, even the single streak of their red death rays that the aliens managed to muster, was delivered in panic. Letting them have their way and retreat, however, carried more risks - the Human fleet could be better analyzed, their weaknesses exploited in later encounters. But Commander Owens knew one more fact, too; that he had little idea where exactly the invading party had come from, and there was only one way to find out.

Even as Lahira programmed in a course to pursue, she heard the whispered voice of her superior as it echoed across the Fleet's communication network; "Defensive posture, stand guard. Launch any stealth probes you may have ready for take-off, but do not engage! Filter damage and casualty reports to the *George*

Washington, and distribute them through military command on Planet Hudson." Removing his network of cables, the Commander chose to speak the next words over a traditional intercom. His hand reached up and grasped that cross he carried, this time successfully. As far as he was concerned, that - and not his cybernetic presence - was what Humanity needed, right now. Faith was all Owens had left.

"See to it that Earth knows what we're dealing with."

Chapter Three
Analyzing the Opposition

In the days following the alien attack on the planet Hudson, the various news broadcasters found it hard to form a coherent story-line out of the incident. Would they focus on the casualties? On the tragic loss of life that took place? Or on the fact that the aliens were forced to retreat with so little damage dealt? Would they emphasize technology's role in the violence, or the clouds of war which hovered above the budding, tiny galactic empire of Humanity?

It didn't take a "leak" from the government for a copy of the opening dialogue to reach the civilian population. The government, having nothing to hide in this matter, freely released the records of the brief conversation between Human and alien. It played on literally hundreds of channels, with normal programming suspended over many of them. There was a serious discussion on what Humanity should even call these new invaders; the Aquarians and Firions had generally accepted those names that men gave them. On the other hand, the Automatons simply didn't care what their fleshy neighbors called them, nor what they chose to do so long as it didn't involve them. But the newcomers? There was only one thing that Humanity could decipher that bound them together: Their search for their creator.

It wasn't necessarily convenient, but it *was* stereotypical. The news media - not any government, scientific, or military organization - quickly christened them "The Orphans."

Unfortunately for the civilians on Earth and its fellow colonized planets, that was about all the information that the Humans had on their invaders. Their genetic makeup was available, but it wasn't even based on carbon! That would serve their biologists little immediate good, even if it was terribly interesting. Their science was hard to understand, though samples of some of it were now at Humanity's disposal. The

Orphans' home worlds were unknown, as well - and that, perhaps, was the scariest thing of all.

Just how powerful were these aliens, and what lengths might they go to? Lahira Ocean, the chief navigator of the *George Washington*, hadn't slept well since the recent battle. Her vessel had been ordered to remain right where it was, at the planet Hudson. There was no telling whether or not any of the Orphans would return, and the Human fleet had every intention of defending one of its most wayward territories. Much like the rivers on Earth, it served as the gateway toward much of Humanity's wealth, and it was the first place anyone knew an Orphan attack might be launched.

Add to it the fact that the Human flagship, *Alexander the Great*, was just outside of the system, and she was a hint more reassured. That battleship's commander, Admiral Sharice Winters, had already planned a face-to-face meeting with Commander James Owens of the *George Washington* because a virtual, networked meeting would simply not satisfy her. Or, that's what she said. After a few days of down-time, spent counting losses and mourning them, business was going to call loudly and clearly.

As for Lahira? There were multiple memorial services to attend, as well as a number of briefings for both her department and for the ship as a whole. If there was one other thing the media had done besides obsess about the alien's intentions, it was to glorify the fallen - and they certainly deserved it. They would not be the last, but they *were* the first victims, and were the ones who all too many people already preached that a Human victory was owed to. As far as the navigator was concerned, she had more pressing priorities than working herself into a depression over the dead. What was more important to her?

Well, she'd spent considerable time in the *George Washington*'s recreation center. She'd done a great deal of weight lifting and kickboxing, ensuring she was in the best possible shape "just in case." Then there was the recreation center's more than relaxing massage offerings - a full-time massage therapist was employed aboard the Human battleships to ensure that their security staff was not only in good physical condition, but a pain-free one as well. Add to it that they also had a professional psychological therapist on hand, one who was presently over-booked with appointments, and there was little more that the Humans could have done to ensure they were in the best state as possible.

But with the *Alexander the Great* drawing near and with an intelligence briefing on the way, Lahira prepared for tomorrow's return to heavy duty.

*****

Whereas Commander Owens was an old, short man, Sharice Winters was a buxom blonde in her later forties. She'd earned her rank through thwarting pirate insurrections and, more importantly, through the clever use of diplomacy. It was rather surprising for many to learn that she was not only a brilliant engineer, but had helped design the *Alexander the Great* - both the *Alexander*-class battleship and the vessel she herself commanded the Human fleet from.

Her blue eyes gazed over the others who sat on the bridge of the *Alexander the Great*, one that very strongly resembled the *George Washington*'s but was slightly older and, yet, slightly more "spiffy" feeling - at least, that's how Lahira would best describe it! As the *Alexander the Great* floated just inside the flotilla of Human vessels, protected just in case of the off chance of a sudden attack, the normal arrangement of the ship's command center was disrupted in the interests of this briefing. Four of the five superior officers from the *George Washington* were aboard - Lahira, Ensign Travares, Ensign Takeda, and Commander Owens. Only the chief engineer remained behind, supervising their home, just in case.

In addition to the two command crews, they were also joined by the Commander and a comparable assortment of officers from the damaged *Genghis Khan*. Lahira had only enjoyed the "pleasure" of working with that battleship's assistant navigator, Ensign Kelly Grant, and mainly because the two had been such bitter rivals during their training. Admittedly, that had been a decade ago - but when the other brunette walked in the room and laid eyes upon Ensign Ocean, well, there was a flare of distrust hidden within the genuine expression of sadness and exhaustion the squat, chubby woman carried.

They weren't alone - Captains and officers from many other ships were in attendance, but the navigator didn't recognize many of them in particular. Was it the trauma they were all enduring? Surely she'd seen some of them at Maritime, as she had Kelly! Or was she simply *that* anti-social, that caught up in history? Had she lost track of the present, while studying the past? She resolved to start taking more interest in social networking. Before she could dwell on it, her attention was seized.

Lahira stood up and snapped to a salute as the Admiral entered the room. She was far from alone, and the gesture was briskly returned before a second was made, suggesting gathered officers resume their seats. From milling about smartly to sitting down in order of rank, the Humans took a mere seven seconds (Lahira's internal clock was accurate!) to be seated. Only two people remained in the front of the room besides the Admiral - Commander Owens and a pale, tall and thin man whose face looked very much like something from a Mary Shelly story Lahira had once read. This was Commander Quinton Nunez, the head officer of the *Genghis Khan*. Each Human face in the room seemed beaten down, yet they were downright cheery in comparison to Nunez'. They sat down in the front of the room, next to the leader of the Human fleet. She, on the other hand, stood before a podium with a built-in computer terminal.

"Ladies and gentlemen," the blonde Admiral stated in a stern tone. She withdrew a tiny plastic-coated stick and inserted it into a waiting data-port, then glanced above the crowd. The *Alexander the Great*'s displays activated, with both the fore and the aft screens reading an identical list of information.

"We've all studied the video replays of the battle, here, at Hudson. Now we've got some preliminary diagnostics on their technology. We're going to avoid getting technical, if we can, because I know not everyone here is an expert in every field." Lahira nodded to herself in relieved agreement.

"Save your questions for the end, people. Lets get to it."

The Admiral's voice carried a dense gravity, but there was a certain coolness about her - maybe it was the hair? - that ensured nobody took the dialogue as a doomsday prophecy. "Ensigns Ocean and Daniels from our two battleships put together an assessment of their navigation technologies. Ensign Takeda has been examining their armor as well as their laser cannons. I took some data from their missiles and I think I know how they're forming their weapons."

The navigator grinned slightly, gazing over toward her former rival, Kelly Grant. She quickly turned her attention back to the Admiral, seeming to have no regard for whether or not Grant actually noticed the prideful gaze - and whether or not she was irritated by it. The Magellaner had more pressing issues; namely, the navigational information scrolling across the screens of the *Alexander the Great*.

Ensign Ocean had helped compile many of the numbers she was looking at, but it was interesting to observe them with a few days of refinement. The overall speed of the Orphan vessels were quite comparable to those of the Humans. If their quality of engine were mounted on a Human vessel, it'd be a rather poor comparison. But the ships they were propelling were much denser, to boot. This wasn't a tremendous concern, what with how star-ship engines bent space as opposed to propelling matter forward against the laws of inertia, but it *did* affect just how much space had to be bent.

Additionally, the best guess for an original destination point for the Orphan detachment was within the Messier 13 cluster of stars, or - at least - in that particular direction from Earth. It was, as Lahira had learned from her much-beloved history readings, the exact direction that the denizens of the

United States of America had once, in the late 1900's, sent a message intended less as an attempt to contact alien life and more as one designed to test the capacity of American communications technology. She found it quite funny that, if Humanity chose today, it could easily receive that message more than once thanks to the nature of faster-than-light travel allowing them to out-run this Aricebo message time and again. In fact, as the Admiral elucidated, the aliens had probably done something similar. If they intercepted the message from three different sites - triangulation - they could judge the general direction from which it came. Once a space-faring civilization knew where to look, it could easily find Humankind.

"So now that we've covered where their little batch of ships came from, lets look at what they can do. First things first, when it comes to interceptor technology and fighter planes, the good news is that they're no better than we are." The Admiral's voice was accompanied by displayed specifications of the Orphan planes; they were sleek, fast, and heavily armed - but not any more than the Human fighters were.

"Our biggest problem so far has been their armor, even though it isn't what worries us as much." After all, it certainly wasn't the factor that had nearly driven the Humans to heart attacks. "We've determined that its made of a stable isotope of Copernicum." This particular atom was discovered during the late 1900's, and named during the early 21st century; and it was quite an unstable, but heavy one that was often created during fusion - hot, or "cold."

"Its incredibly dense. Ordinary missiles don't always punch through it, and our rail-guns lose a lot of their effect since the metal doesn't shred as readily." This was a dire-enough warning, but Lahira knew that the main weapons of the Human fleet could still get the job done. The Admiral continued, "Our nukes were effective enough, but we haven't made them into a standard weapon for the fleet. Chances are, I'll be changing that." The Admiral's voice was casual enough, but there was an undertone of exhaustion when she brought up the nuclear option -

as if it had been discussed ad-nauseum in more than one venue. The Admiral may have been in charge of fleet operations, but she was *not* the political leader of the fleet.

She cleared her throat briefly, then moved to the next topic; "Speaking of missiles," she began, "We've done some work on their big threat to us. They use something very similar to the Tellar-Ulam design of our nuclear weapons, only with helium bombs triggering the carbon reaction. The problem we've had is figuring out where their missiles get the power to split helium atoms on the drop of a dime. Ensign Takeda has made clear that if we tried, we could - under ideal conditions - probably create a runaway fusion reaction in a similar manner. We couldn't do it in a warhead, however," she conceded dryly. It was as if Winters *wanted* such a terrible weapon; and since Mankind was already on the receiving end of it, Lahira couldn't agree more.

"As to their primary weapons? They're nothing special, from what I've decided," she declared rather proudly - perhaps a little too proudly. "I've seen similar technology employed our mining equipment. We use it on a much smaller scale, but the way I see it they reflect a lot of laser beams into one large mirror and, well, we've seen the outcome."

She sighed delicately. There was a clear emphasis on her words, and even the prelude to them - her face carried a gravity with it that made her turn from buxom blonde to determined old woman all too readily. "Too many of our people have died in this war already, but we don't have any time to sit back and cry over it. We have to push forward. I'm the Admiral of this fleet. I have to sign the death certificates and the letters to husbands, wives, and children." Her voice was grim, but her eyes were steady.

"And its also my job to come up with the plan, so here it is."

Admiral Winters gazed over the gathering on her ship, the *Alexander the Great*, and her lips curled into a determined frown. "Here's our guiding doctrine: Overwhelming force. We have sixteen planets and a couple dozen moons. We have trading companies which own thousands of vessels, yet we have a naval fleet with less than two hundred battle-ready ships. That's going to have to change if we're going to win."

"I know," she stated with a glance toward Commander Owens, "that there's a serious concern about the military-industrial complex getting out of hand. There's going to be a fear amongst the civilians that, when we've won this war we'll never trim down our fleet and never stop building ships. In all of the science fiction movies of the old days, and in all of the war games, we always imagined that we were hard pressed to survive. That Humanity was on the brink of annihilation. We never thought about *after* the war, because the 'after' was a hope, not a fact. But this isn't a fantasy. This is the real world. When all is said and done, we need to think about what comes next."

Lahira blinked; she wasn't sure, anymore, where this briefing was going. "For now, we are going to have to purchase civilian-designed ships and refit them to make up a naval gap. The fleet is also in possession of about twelve vessels that are either being refitted, or had previously been scheduled for deployment. In short, this is a major arming, transitional phase that we have to take very seriously."

"First things first, we had two more *Alexander*-class battleships coming into readiness; the *Sun Tzu* and the *Oda Nobunaga*. There's also the *Messenger*, which is a cruiser. We've also got a number of destroyers that are dry-docked and will be rushed into readiness, and we're going to begin repairs on the *Genghis Khan* as soon as humanly possible. I've made some judgments, spoken with the civilian leadership, and we are going to be dividing our forces."

The navigator's eyes widened and many of the officers lost their discipline for just long enough to whisper words of concern. The Admiral didn't seem entirely thrilled at the outburst, as she interrupted it with a stern glare. "Again," she resumed, "I've discussed it over with Earth's leadership. They're recommended, and I've agreed, that the *George Washington*, under Commander Owens, lead a secondary fleet. This fleet will be dedicated to external operations during our arming phase. Any offensive action or diplomatic fleets we need to dispatch will be under Commander Owens' jurisdiction. The *George Washington* will serve as its flag-ship, with the *Oda Nobunaga* joining it within a week. It will also field the *Messenger*, as well as four destroyers and six *Bantam*-class ships."

Winters' chilly glare kept the attention of her subordinates quite well. "I will lead defensive operations, and will be supervising all analytical pursuits. I'm confident that we can eventually replicate and utilize Orphan technology. It is essential to our success to understand, use, and defeat our enemy's advantages." A touch of cockiness entered her voice; clearly, the Admiral felt herself capable of reverse-engineering the invader's sciences. If anyone could, of course, it was likely her. "I'll also be seeing to the renovations of the civilian vessels we bring into the fleet, making them battle-ready."

"Finally," she looked toward the other man standing next to her, "while the *Genghis Khan* is under repairs, Commander Nunez will begin training our new pilots. We aren't implementing a draft at this time, but we *are* going to be training a lot of officers. I know we've kept a very high standard throughout our history, but that was when we were at peace. We're still looking for the best!" She gazed back over the assembled group, a hint of a grin brushing over her lips, "but now we're also going to take the second best and make them *better*."

She reached under the podium and withdrew two tiny boxes. She stepped toward each of the two men next to her and provided one to each. Then, she withdrew a small note and a third box. "By order of the government of Earth, its sister worlds and moons, and the citizens living within, I am promoting Commander James Owens and Commander Quinton Nunez to the rank of Admiral."

Then, in a voice that rang with a shiver-inducing mixture of pride and sorrow, she continued. "By the order of the government of Earth, its sister worlds and moons, and the citizens within, and proven by the instrument before me," she stated as she raised that sheet of paper, "I, Admiral Sharice C. Winters, have been promoted to the rank of Grand Admiral."

As the meeting was dismissed, Lahira wasn't certain whether she liked this change, or not. Either way, she despised the situation which created it.

*****

It wasn't unusual for the Commander - now, the Admiral - to call her into his private office. Much unlike her own, it was far from spartan; replicas of old paintings and glass-encased artifacts of history rested safely inside of his paper-pushing place. There were multiple filing cabinets, as well; a place for paper records to be kept when such archaic procedures were necessary. Additionally, a display screen was mounted on one side of the room, with a sizable wooden desk pointed toward it. Also before the desk sat four very comfortable, heavily padded chairs. By necessity, every chunk of furniture was either bolted to the floor or, in the case of the chairs, capable of being affixed in the event that the *George Washington* was under attack.

When she knocked, he called for her to come in. She entered and crisply saluted, a gesture that was returned. "Good day, Ensign," he stated politely as he gestured to the sitting places before him.

"Admiral," she stated politely, nestling down as he'd requested. "Are you well, sir?"

He gazed at her, smiling warmly. "As well as we ever could be during a war. How about yourself?"

"About the same, sir," she returned curtly. The two officers looked one another over, each assessing their colleague's mental and physical state. Lahira easily observed that the old man was in good enough shape; a touch thinner, perhaps, than he'd been a week ago, and certainly stressed out, but nothing that a good war couldn't cause.

The elder reached into one of the filing cabinets nestled behind him and withdrew a file. Lahira knew this procedure intimately; unless this was a spontaneous performance review, she was getting a look at her own personnel records. The Admiral didn't have to let her see the notes in this file, unless she filed a formal request, and her more optimistic theory was quickly shot down. He placed the papers down upon his desk as he folded his fingertips into a triangle. He looked her dead in the eye. "Ensign, would you say you've learned a lot from working under me?"

She nodded back confusedly, taking the collection of stamped, signed sheets and opening it. The first few documents on top were simple - medical records, her original application to join the military, and her letters of recommendation dating from her first entry into training to her assignment to the *George Washington*. Her brown eyes returned to the old man's. "Of course, sir, I've learned a great deal."

"What?" he stated sharply, almost belligerently, a tone he rarely took with her. It caused her to recede a touch in her seat, concern rising in her face. Her shoulder muscles tensed slightly, and she felt like a dog who had just had her nose rubbed in a soiled rug.

"I'm sorry, sir?"

He softened slightly, his eyes looking at the same collection of paperwork she had just studied. "I mean, Lahira; what have you learned? Tell me."

"Oh!" she exhaled, the use of her first name drawing forth a slight relaxation of her back. "Well, sir, I've gotten really good at navigation. I've gotten excellent at programming transit coordinates. I'm learning a lot about other functions of our ship."

James Owens was a plain and simple man, and his next statement reflected it. "That's all great," he declared, "but I'm looking for something more abstract. What have you learned about the navy? The flow of our fleet? How to get along with your colleagues?"

"I'm..." she trailed off, an eyebrow raising. "I'm not sure what you're getting at, Admiral."

"I saw a bit of vindictiveness in your eyes, yesterday." It was a surprise, to her, that he'd been able to notice *her* appearance. "You gazed at an Ensign from the *Alexander*, one I do believe you'd had some problems with in the past?"

She winced, glancing down at her hands - which suddenly found her fingers very interesting, and in need of touching. "I'm sorry, sir, I just lost my discipline for a little while."

His response was to nod sagely, almost like he had infinite patience in spite of his earlier, offensive tone. "Very reasonable. When I was young, along with the automobile," he joked, a faint smile touching his lips, "I also had a great deal of pride in my skills. There's nothing wrong with that. I'm more concerned with how you would work with this Ensign Grant, if forced to?"

The navigator's eyes lit up with worry, now, at the suggestion that she might have to work with a former rival. The idea didn't even make sense! "Sir, I'm...What? I mean, I could work with her, but she's already detailed to the *Alexander*, and I'm on the *Washington.*"

"That's true," the Admiral confessed softly. There was a certain tone of sadness in his voice, a bitter reluctance to even continue. "But then again, that might not be the case for long."

The chief navigator bit her bottom lip in shock. "Sir, whatever I've done, it--"

He raised his hand, shaking his head. A smile graced his lips, but it was one covered with bitter flavoring. "Ensign, you're aware that the navy is going to grow rapidly. My fleet, the 2nd, is going to be the first to get cobbled together. I'm going to need Captains."

His statement was bold, and as a result the navigator fell back into her chair, stunned. "S...Sir?" She looked at the table for a moment. "Sir, I'd rather stay here, if that's alright? Instead of heading up a *Bantam.*"

At this, the Admiral couldn't help but grin. It may have been the first time she'd seen him express his old love of life since the attack on Hudson. "Ah, yes, why *would* you want a job on a tiny ship like that? A career like yours, put to the sword of a tiny command? No, I'm afraid that we need your talents elsewhere, indeed."

Interest struck Lahira's eyes, suddenly; this was a surprising turn of events. "Sir, I'm not sure what you're suggesting. Where is there an opening? All of the destroyers we have undergoing upgrades have crews assigned to them. Are you telling me to command a civilian refit?" The implication was obvious; this would be suicide.

At this, the Admiral touched a button on his chair, activating the television screen behind Lahira. She turned around to find the fairly small display carved up into four smaller sections, each one displaying a different viewpoint of the same ship schematic. It was labeled, proudly, the *Messenger*.

"Not at all," the Admiral responded proudly. "I need someone I can trust to captain the second largest vessel in my fleet - at least, until the *Sun Tzu* and *Oda Nobunaga* are finished; which will hopefully be before our next mission. It is still a sizable task."

Lahira rose to her feet and gazed at the display in wonder. "Admiral, I...I don't know what to say? I'll need a crew. I'll need..." Once upon a time, she would have been thrilled to receive this opportunity. The scent of war fouled even her dream assignment. "I'll need four officers. Sir, do you mean?"

"Ensign Grant is due for a promotion - she's gone as far as she can on the *Alexander,* and the only way I'm making you a Captain is to make her a chief navigator." He shrugged. "The Grand Admiral is also a keen judge of talent." Lahira's heart sank; this was not going to be a paradise of a command, after all.

He continued, "I've got a few resumes I'd like you to consider for your ship's other roles, as well. Then there's just the problem of Ensign Travares. He's invaluable, but..." he trailed off, eying Lahira for a moment. She was transfixed upon the diagram of the vessel she'd just been offered. "I'm going to want him to take the next cruiser I get under my command. To that end, he needs to be evaluated by another set of eyes. That's your job, I think - you're going to need the help, and so'll he. I take it this is more what you'd hoped your career path would be?"

Lahira shook her head, turning back toward the Admiral

and spontaneously saluting. "No, sir!" A mixture of intonations in her voice caused the old man to frown slightly, unsure if he'd appreciate the next words. As he discovered, he would. "This is much, much worse, because it took a war to do it; yet so much better!" She shivered, once. "I accept!"

The Admiral nodded slowly and withdrew a tiny box. "By order of the government of Earth, its sister worlds and moons, and the citizens living within, I am promoting Ensign Lahira Ocean to the rank of Captain." He opened it to reveal the insignia of her new rank. She took the medallion and nodded, and he extended his hand. As she took it, he grasped it firmly with a look of grief lingering in his eyes. "Congratulations."

Chapter Four
Herding Cats

As much as she had enjoyed looking at the schematics, when she looked at the *Messenger* in person, she very nearly turned to her former commanding officer and screamed, girlishly, "Can I keep it!?" She didn't, of course - Lahira was a soldier, after all, and had *some* degree of discipline! - but she certainly grinned broadly.

It was big; nowhere near as large as the *George Washington* upon which she was seated, looking from the observation deck out toward the space near the planet Hudson, but it was substantial. Its engines were cutting-edge, and after the Orphan attack it had been quickly touched up with extra asteroid-shield emitters. Not many, but every little bit helped. It looked as if it had thirty missile ports, fifteen on the starboard and an identical number on the opposite; four heavy rail-guns and two dozen fifty-caliber turrets made up its primary armament and rocket countermeasures. It had one rear launch bay, indicating two twelve-plane squadrons plus assorted transport vessels, and Lahira could even make out the biggest advantage the ship had - four launch tubes for nuclear weapons.

"Captain Ocean," Admiral Owens stated with a hint of pride in his voice - pride in her, as it were, "I present your charge. Cruiser *Messenger*, the newest vessel of Earth's navy. Treat her well."

She looked toward the old man who had instructed her for years and nodded gently. "Absolutely, Admiral. I have thought long and hard on your task for me."

At this, the man in charge of her fleet inclined his head deeply. "Oh?" he feigned surprise, then stretched a hand out. Lahira produced a trio of files. The first two were exactly as he'd expected - the third, on the other hand, was as not.

"I will have Ensign Travares serve as my executive officer

as well as communications specialist," she announced without surprising anyone. "And I'm going to give Ensign Grant the chance you asked me to. I don't like her," she confessed bitterly, "but she wouldn'tve been a good competitor if she didn't have skill."

The Admiral laughed delicately. "Well recognized! After all, you won't have time to run all of the numbers yourself. Better to have someone with talent, no?"

Lahira blushed slightly, looking away. "I'd rather not admit it, but yeah. Then I've got Gavin Trusaunt on defense duty."

"Yes, I saw that," Owens commented softly, flipping through the man's file swiftly. Lahira knew it well; commendations and critiques, merits and demerits. "Above average, to be sure, but - and, Lahira, don't take this the wrong way - why him? Why does he stand out?"

The navigator had asked herself that question, at times; and she'd always come up with the same answer. "He's worked the secondary shift for a long time on the *George Washington*, and Ensign Takeda speaks highly of him. I know a little bit about weaponry, but Trusaunt scored well in his classes on military doctrine at Maritime. He got bonus points for arguing with his instructors."

James rubbed his thumb along his bottom lip for a moment, contemplating. "Doctrine, hmm? I like that - I might not always be around to give you orders, so you might need to make up your own, and you *will* need an expert on what is going to work." He mused on this, yet still didn't sound sold. "But someone combative? I hope he won't be a headache, but a loyal opposition can be a good thing."

Lahira nodded her head in agreement. "So long as he's loyal, then I'm happy. I've hit a bit of a stumbling block on the engineering front, however. I've reviewed a number of portfolios but I'm just not convinced that anyone is uniquely capable of taking the job."

At this sticking point, the Admiral laughed again; he

offered up a helpless shrug. "That's the way of the world, Captain. Sometimes, there's no clear candidate. Some choices get handed to you, some you make on your own because they're the best ones, and some?" He repeated that gesture of his shoulders. "Some, you're just stuck having to pick a name out of a hat."

The navigator smiled and gazed out of the window again, examining the *Messenger*. The star-bound creature was simply beautiful, without a single scratch on her hull. If she could stay that way, Ocean would have been more than pleased - but she knew it wouldn't. And she knew, deep down, she'd need a responsible, respectable engineering officer. Her eyes returned to the bald, short old man before her. "What would you consider in a good engineer?"

"Well, I already have my choice," he said jovially, looking back at his subordinate. "But I think, for a new Captain, I would want someone with a great deal of experience. Someone who might not be looking to command their own ship, but would like to work on something larger than they already are. And someone quick on their feet, capable of getting the most out of a bad spot."

At this, the former Ensign folded her arms and looked back into the void of space. "Alright," she concluded, her eyes blinking twice. "I have an idea of where I'm going, now."

*****

Prisons in the 25th century were less brutal than many in history had been, but they certainly weren't *fun*. This was a lesson that Jackie "Jack-O-Lantern" Quan had learned first hand. The only child of two second-rate pirates working with the 'Katch-em Syndicate' out of Planet Cortes' system's asteroid belt, Jackie discovered by the age of 16 that she wasn't cut out to be a prostitute, a drug-saleswoman, or a slop-maiden. No, she was destined to be a great blockade runner. She had a knack for fixing engines and super-charging them, and wasn't bad at repairing them, either. Once she finished with a raider, it was virtually uncatchable. Once-scrapped pirate vessels were quickly brought back online, better than ever, and she'd elevated the 'Katch-Ems' from a barely-noteworthy racket to a booming criminal organization. The money and drugs flowed freely, and Jackie had embraced it all.

Naturally, this brought some attention from the Human navy, but Jackie was no easy target. She'd outclassed and abandoned her family (naturally, making them proud!) when, at 20, she successfully escaped from two Destroyers and a *Bantam*, leaving the other Katch-Ems in the dust. No, her destiny wasn't to get caught running a blockade, either! Sadly, she never saw the special agents infiltrating the pirate ranks, and never had a prayer of ducking them. With an affidavit sealing her guilty verdict coming directly from her own parents (naturally, making Jackie proud!), she found herself behind bars for a quarter-century; destiny, it seemed, had condemned her cruelly to a cell.

Unless!

Jackie never had a choice *before* she became a criminal. When she hired her own attorneys with her ill-gotten-gains, they never thought to make this argument - and her court-appointed defender barely managed to get her away from an extra charge for that dirty little expenditure, one she hadn't even realized was illegal! She'd considered trying to seduce her way out of things, what with her fiery red hair and slender, well-curved body, but she quickly determined that one licentious encounter would lead to another, and another, until she either ran up against someone who refused or, of course, until she finally fucked the right one to get out. It was a risk she wasn't willing to take, and with an inept defense more likely to add time to her sentence than reduce it, she had one option left: She took the stand herself.

The "its not my fault, I was born into it" argument didn't get her off the hook, but it did earn her a loophole. While recounting her various tales of daring escapes and her technical experience with faster-than-light drives, testifying in between stints in a holding cell, the military officials who were heading up the prosecution were impressed. They offered her a way out - she could serve the rest of her sentence in a jail cell, a circumstance that her brief stay in the pokey had proven was not one she wanted to continue, or she could serve it out with full pay and the opportunity to earn full honors in the navy.

Before anyone could blink, she was dolled up in a uniform and enrolled in engineering classes. She had some problems fitting in, at first - she'd nearly come to blows with one instructor who made an unfortunately-timed comment about having caught members of her gang, previously. She only managed to avoid a return to jail (consequences of a serious bender) by shoving her skill in this instructor's face. She sought out one of his patents, found three ways to improve it, and cajoled the head of Maritime's student newspaper to publish her findings with the headline "Disrespectful Student Spanks Professor, Not The Other Way Around."

That's how she got the role of Chief Engineer of the *Bantam*-Class vessel *Spirit Chaser*. Up until the Orphan attack, she hated it. The engine was in fine shape, considering there was only one, and the *Spirit Chaser* didn't do very much chasing of anything - it ran diplomats around. Moreover, she was sectioned off in the Engineering department, running it with a skeleton crew consisting of a sex maniac who *refused* to wait until she got to her own room, and an intellectual invalid who had earned his job solely because of patronage. As cute as couple as those two made, it was a life which bored her so much that she'd begun to indulge in illicit substances once again.

The attack on Hudson drew her out of her narcotic slumber. It took a day or two for her to catch up on the news - there was so much insanity on the airwaves that even the naval channels had become clogged with crap. When she finally cleaned up her military mail accounts, plugging her head into the data port in her bunk to sort through the very last page of notices, she was stunned to find an invitation to an interview with Captain Lahira Ocean, a woman she'd never heard of before. For the first time in her life, she wondered if she'd smoked too much; it was a thought she quickly banished as she signed up for the conversation. Until then, she had some research to do - and it surprised her in the greatest!

*****

Lahira had spent the previous two days getting her office, one smaller than Admiral Owens' but still capable of projecting power, into order. She kept it rather bare, as she had always kept her apartment aboard the *George Washington*, though she did frame a poster of an archaic, 22nd century star chart. It was mostly accurate but highly stylized, and it ultimately was missing a quite few Human worlds. Next to it was a much more traditional, up-to-date one that emphasized the transit advances over two centuries.

She did indeed have a command-and-control chair installed, and she copied her former commander's concept of having four chairs bolted to the ground in front of her desk, one destined for each department head. Three of them had already been metaphorically filled, but her favorite candidate for the fourth was only now on her way in to be interviewed. Her plan of action was just like the Admiral had taught her - honest, straight-forward, and freely giving of information. The knock on her door was firm; this woman was not delicate, not in the least.

"Come on in," Captain Ocean requested, looking up toward the wooden portcullis.

Soft footfalls carried in the tall, crimson-headed outlaw. She wore a naval uniform without any sign of confusion or conflict, and she managed to wear it quite well considering her past scuffles with others donned in it. Ensign Quan stepped over to the center-right chair, stood right next to it, and saluted. It wasn't the best she'd ever seen, but Lahira rose to her feet and returned it nonetheless. The two ladies sat down almost simultaneously.

"What can I do for you, Captain?" the engineer stated, refusing to let the little woman in on the other side of the desk dominate the conversation, even if it was only just beginning.

Lahira cracked a slight grin, her eyes observing the former pirate's with interest. "Jackie 'Jack-o-Lantern'---"

"Yep, that's me," Quan interrupted, a smile touching her own lips. "You asked to see me, so here I am. Nice ship, by the way!" There was a certain, coy look in the woman's green eyes; as if the ship itself was hardly the reason she'd been summoned. Her eyes drifted over the entirety of the office, taking much more interest in her immediate surroundings. "So! What are you needin'?"

Now, Lahira blinked her eyes twice and frowned. "I'm not sure what you're getting at, now, Ensign?"

Jackie laughed delicately. "Captain Interstellar Oceans," the renegade stated in a trumpeting tone, her arms spreading out widely. "Your family runs one of the largest transport companies in the Magellan system. I know the pirate skies. With the Orphans takin' up the time of your colleagues, I'm bettin' you're lookin' at something special. So what's the stakes?"

The Captain sat back in her chair, wide eyes continuing to blink as a hand reached up and ruffled her black strands of hair with surprise. "Okay, I *think* I get where you're going, and this isn't a contract or anything. I mean, I guess I appreciate it, but that's not why we're here."

Now it was the engineer's turn to look confused, and for the first time upon entering the room she actually *looked* at the office's quality, and not it's propensity for stealthy recording devices. "Soooo..." she trailed off, gazing around dumbly. She broke the silence swiftly. "Nice ship!"

Lahira chuckled in what amounted to disbelief. Had she really come off as a criminal? "That's the second time you've said that. Listen, I wanted to ask you something. How good are you with engines?"

Ensign Quan raised an eyebrow, her hands wriggling to show that they were quite empty. "I've been keepin' my little ship running so well with on-the-op repairs that it's been passed over for dry-docking three times."

This was impressive; dry-docking was typically done on a

regular schedule, but a well-tuned ship could usually put one off without harm. Delaying a second was typically a bad idea, because by that point there were new, upgraded parts to be installed by the time a vessel's second turn through a standardized upgrade package was due for implementation. To pass it over three times, well; that meant either the upgraded parts hadn't been invented yet, the ship was so ill-maintained it was on the verge of being mothbolled, or - in extremely rare conditions - the engineering staff had the vessel completely and totally well kept, and that repairs were installed on the go.

"Why haven't you brought her in for an upgrade?" asked the wary Captain.

The response she received was a conceited grin. "Any time I have parts to add to somethin', its added. Any time I have parts that need to be upgraded, we get 'em on shore leave. To be honest, I might just skip the *Spirit Chaser*'s *next* dockin', as well. Only two or three systems that'd really need me t'make a space walk, an' I can do better without 'em.."

Lahira had enough information to make one bet, at least. She lifted her palms, showing that she had no cards up her sleeve - as a pirate, Quan couldn't help but understand. "You aren't interested in letting the navy's dock-hands touch your work because its not all regulation, and they wouldn't understand why your set-up is better. That's the game plan?"

Now, the former pirate actually *looked* at the officer in front of her. "Alright, Ocean, what's your deal? You just got put in charge of a boat, you're goin' to war against the Orphans, an' I'm bein' asked about the *Spirit Chaser's* tech-specs. Spill it."

Lahira folded her arms over one another. She lowered her posture ever so slightly, leaning forward and growing into a serious, if amused tone. "Right now my staff consists of a second-in-command, a communications whiz who is ready for his *own* boat just as soon as the next one is built. My weapons guy is more about tactics than combat and he loves to argue about it all day long. My navigator is a girl who I barely edged-out in school, and who is part of the price-of-admission to my rank.

What's there to spill?"

Jackie's red hair was swiftly brushed from before her eyes and she, too, leaned in toward Lahira with interest, now. "Readin' the writin' on the wall? That you've put out there? You're short one chief. You wanna know if I'm in?"

"No," declared the Captain in a dry, humorless tone, "I want you to be a deck-swabber." For just an instant the pirate allowed herself to grow angry and red; but it was just a brief moment, because Lahira's lips cracked into a broad grin. "I already have an unorthodox crew, except for the guy who is planning for his own star-ship. I'm an ace navigator, and I have a B-Lister doing what I'm good at." Even as Lahira said it, it was clear she didn't *believe* Kelly was so bad at her job. "Then there's a weapons officer who, dear space gods, might just land himself in the brig before we even get into combat." She delivered one final, level glare. "Think you can out-run his mouth?"

"Captain Ocean," the pirate extended her hand, "I can out-run it and get back again, if you give me the right intellectual freedom and access to a patent officer when I use it." The superior officer in the room shook the hand firmly. "I'm in."

*****

The day after completing her decisions about her executive staff, Lahira had a meeting to tend to. There were four figures sitting in front of her desk, and each was as interesting as the next.

Ensign Lucas Travares, her second-in-command, occupied the seat on the Captain's right. He'd decided to let his hair grow after the attack on Hudson; with short, wavy black strands emerging from his head, with a thin layer of gel slicking it back. His lightly tanned skin blended in nicely to his dark-blue uniform, and his brown eyes were calm and confident.

Next up was Kelly Grant, Captain Ocean's school-time rival and, now, her chief navigator. This woman was short and chubby, with curly blonde hair kept cropped close to her scalp.

She had gray-blue eyes that were almost ghostly, and she had her arms folded over her chest in a squat manner, gazing upward at her newly appointed, long-despised boss. Was it a sense of being stifled that fueled this woman's passion? Or was it uncertainty with the new scenery.

Third in line was Chief of Defense Gavin Trusaunt. This fellow was by far the largest of the five gathered officers of the *Messenger*, towering even above the tall redhead on the other side of him. He had dark skin, eyes that screamed a certain calmness under any circumstances, and his head was shaved completely bald. He carried two pistols on his hip, as well as a pair of knives adjacent to the firearms. He was clearly a no-nonsense figure, as ready to explain why he was right as he was to engage an Orphan in hand to hand combat. Assuming they had hands.

Finally, of course, was the red-headed ex-pirate with dazzling green eyes, one whose uniform was a touch too tight in the chest despite being fitted properly. She gazed over the others in the room, a cocky grin on her lips, and she leaned in toward her neighbor slightly; he recoiled, of course, leading to a similar response as well as a concerned glance from her Captain. Jackie Quan was already proving to be quite the interesting appointment

"Alright," Lahira stated neutrally, drawing the attention of the first three of her officers. When the fourth of them noticed the decisive shift of focus, she, too, joined the observational chorus. "Ladies and gentlemen, I assume you've had a chance to assess the *Messenger*'s specifications by now. I'm also sure you've had a chance to consider your staffing requests out of the academy--"

Jackie didn't even bother to raise her hand; she just flat out interrupted. "Wait, staffing requests? I thought you'd just throw me whoever you could get."

Lucas laughed, finding the younger spitfire quite amusing; Kelly, on the other hand, rolled her eyes and scoffed at the approach. Last on the list, Gavin didn't even flinch. "Ensign," Travares stated politely, in almost a guiding tone, "you're the chief engineer of a *Signal*-class vessel in the second fleet. You have pretty much your pick of subordinates, as long as they want to work here and they're acceptable in the eyes of Captain Ocean."

The aforementioned superior nodded her head warmly. "That's right, Ensign Quan. Also, if you need experienced candidates - you do," Lahira clarified quickly, "Then you may request transfers from other ships at the discretion of their administrative staff. Unlike the *Spirit Chaser*, the *Messenger* is a pretty big deal, and you will need a hand."

For a moment, there was peace. Lahira had successfully diffused the red-haired fire-bomb. Quan sat there silently, thinking over the incredible responsibility she'd just jumped into. Maybe it was the sobriety, but she was finally waking up to the task. Naturally, she had to ruin it!

"Could you just call me Jackie? Or Jack-O-Lantern? Either-or, doesn't matter. We're in private," the ex-pirate requested. Now, Ensign Grant full-on face-palmed, slapping herself in the forehead. "Hey," Quan interjected at this display of disrespect, "what's your deal, anyway?"

"Silence, *please*," interjected Gavin, his attention fully focused on his commanding officer. Kelly massaged her temples delicately and gazed forward as requested. Jackie? No such luck, her eyes continued to glare at the ship's navigator.

It took a cough from Lahira to re-fix the woman's attention. "What you do in privacy *is* your business, but right now we are in a command officer's meeting. Lets remain formal for the time being, agreed?"

While Kelly kept right on looking irritated, this offer was enough to draw a nod out of the engineer's head. "Good," the Captain continued calmly, "now then, as Ensign Travares said, we have access to most, if not all of the junior officers of the fleet, as well as those coming out of the academy. We're using brand new technology so that we have less need for staff and more room for supplies, missiles, and equipment. The *Messenger* is the cut, bleeding edge of Human space technology. Keep that in mind with your recruitment plans, and get them in ASAP."

Gavin's eyes met his commanders' and he parted his lips

before speaking, moistening them. It was a trait Lahira had observed some of her fellow Magellaners display in the past. The heat of her homeworld often left people with dried lips, and while Lahira had been raised in relative luxury as a result of her family's wealth, leading to access to water whenever she'd wished, it was clear that her defense chieftain's up-bringing might not have involved as many whetted whistles. "Captain," he offered in a flat, polite tone, one dulled by his surroundings. "I will get right on that. I look forward to working under your command."

For some reason, Ensign Travares couldn't help but blurt out with another laugh. Kelly mouthed a word which might as well have been, 'amateurs.'

*****

Within a week of her promotion, Lahira's ship had all of its personnel either on board or, at least, on the official roster. There would be some logistical headaches involved in arranging the transportation of some of the officers that the *Messenger* had put in for, but they would be resolved by the time that Captain Ocean finished with her first assignment.

That assignment, as it were, was yet to be unveiled. In fact, it was precisely why Lahira received a message from her former Commander, turned-Admiral, requesting her presence at a teleconference this very afternoon! Nestling down in the large chair within her office, she watched the final seconds tick off of the display screen before plugging the back of her head into a terminal mounted within her desk.

With a moment's thought, she opened a video chat line with the *George Washington*, and was immediately greeted with a view of the artwork in Admiral Owens' office. She smiled, reminiscing for just a moment before the old man poked his head into the picture. "Good evening, Captain," the elder offered politely.

"Admiral," she stated in return, peering upward toward her superior. They exchanged the usual salutes. "Well enough, I hope?"

He nodded in the affirmative. "Absolutely. How has your crew taken to the *Messenger*?"

At this, Lahira gazed off toward the archaic star chart she'd mounted on the wall, distracting herself for just an instance before she answered. "Its like herding cats, sir," she responded. He laughed, and she immediately snapped her eyes upon his - or, at least, the digital projection of them! "Sir, it is! They're not getting along, they're bickering, its hectic."

"They will do that, Captain," the old man offered politely, folding his fingertips into a pyramid and measuring her. "Anyhow, we have our first assignment and I'm happy to say you'll be able to pick up the rest of your crew *and* contribute to the war effort!"

Her blood ran like ice for just a moment, causing her face to straighten and her eyes to refocus. She subconsciously forced her back to grow rigid as her spine moved toward a more standard, official posture. "Of course, Admiral, what will we be doing?"

"The *Messenger* shall accompany the rest of the Second Fleet on a diplomatic mission." This did not sound like the glorious, offensive-line combat that Grand Admiral Winters had suggested, at least not to Lahira. "We will be attending and providing security for a meeting between ambassadors from the Aquarian, Firion, and Automaton empires."

Now, Lahira lost her calm. She blushed slightly, nodding her head obediently. "Sir, even the Automatons? They *never* send ambassadors, do they?

The Admiral shrugged helplessly. "Even they recognize important circumstances when they see them. When word of what the Orphans are capable of got out, everyone lined up to talk to us about it. Dollars to donuts," he offered the anachronism casually, as if he'd lived during a time of such ancient currency, "the Automatons just want to check and make sure we're handling it responsibly - no crusades, no jihads, just a military management. And we, of course, want them to know we're not asleep at the wheel."

"Sir," she asked softly, an eyebrow raising as she looked at one particular world on the star chart in her office. "Where will we be having this meeting?"

"Where else, Captain?" returned the Admiral, a smile touching his lips. "We're going to rendezvous with the rest of your crew in Earth orbit, A-S-A-P."

Chapter Five
Home Sweet Home

It was hard to believe that just five centuries ago, the view she was seeing right now was unimaginable to the vast majority of her species. Many aboard the *Messenger* had taken to its sole observation deck to gaze in wonder at what was, at first, a fairly unexceptional (save for its keen habitability) world. It was, as one genius of the 20th century had put it, simply a pale blue dot from afar - but it was, to so many of those who had never set foot upon it, something that cried out to a deeply rooted, instinctual portion of their consciousness.

Lahira was well aware that the first creature to see a view of their mutual home-world was not, sadly, Humanity itself. If her recollection was correct (it might not have been), it had been a dog. This dog, a Soviet (as the state of Russia was called, at the time), had been launched on a one-way journey into space simply to see if it would survive the trip to orbit! If she recalled (and she might have been wrong), the pooch's name was Laika. Fortunately, the dog did make it to orbit. Unfortunately, there had been no plan to bring it home.

It died horribly, likely with that pale, blue dot called home centered in its agony-filled eyes.

Before reaching the cradle of Humankind, however, Lahira's ship had to pass by its oldest colonies and outposts in the Sol system. The most prosperous of them were located not *on* the planet Jupiter, but around it - upon the moons first discovered by the astronomer Galileo and named in his honor. Recognizing how history often misled students about Human achievements, Lahira knew that there was every possibility that Galileo wasn't the true discoverer of those worlds - there was some conflict between historical sources of the sort that Lahira loved, but the honorific of Galilean certainly stuck. The four moons of Io, Europa, Ganymede, and Callisto were each extremely useful to

Humanity - the latter three had all proven to have water as well as some extent of an atmosphere, making for easy colonization, while Io's sulfuric iron was a major mineral asset to the early expansion of Humanity throughout the stars. They were among the first non-Earth bodies that were colonized, and they put paid to the fears that Man could never survive off of Earth.

Nevertheless, the glory of an inhabited moon was moot compared to that of a planet; and the *Messenger* whizzed by Mars, a world named after the ancient Roman name for the ancient Greek god of war. It had been one of the first planets subjected to the then-tiny science of geo-engineering, and by and large it had proven a successful test case. True, its day/night cycle was far from Earth's and its low gravity was, even today, a considerable problem, but once an atmosphere had been created and its temperature stabilized as a result, it was not an impossible world to survive on. What water wasn't found on the planet was "imported" through asteroid and comet exploitation. Once artificial gravity was introduced, even in limited quantities, Mars' attractiveness grew tenfold.

The star-ship followed this flyby up by pausing for authentication just outside of Lunar orbit. The Earth's single, solitary moon was most probably the result of a cataclysmic collision between a rogue planetoid and the fledgling home of Humanity. When molten chunks of Earth eventually coalesced into one sphere, it had also fallen into a mostly-stable orbit and would, over the course of billions of years, become an object of worship and importance to the Human race.

Today, of course, that importance was emphasized by the fact that it was, just like Mars, a colony of Earth's. It had been one of the first celestial bodies colonized, what with it's proximity to Humankind's home planet, and its establishment was very much the same as Mars' had been - it had required the imposition of an artificial atmosphere, temperature control, and eventually gravity augmentation. If Earth were a tiny blue dot, then Luna was a tiny blue fleck toiling around it - one that previously had been gray.

Still, the real prize was Earth itself. After inter-planetary flight became more plausible with the Alcubierre drive, the largest task Humanity had to succeed at involved the cleaning up of decades worth of "junk" that, much like Luna, orbited the planet. At speeds over 15,000 miles per hour, a nut or bolt which had fallen off of an archaic space-ship could do critical damage to any vessels leaving Earth's atmosphere. It had not been an easy task, one only mandated due to the short-sightedness of 20th and 21st century man, but Lahira had studied this problem's resolution well - and she knew that, today, over 90% of it had been removed while any stray bits had been rendered relatively harmless by the same asteroid-deflecting shields that covered the *Messenger* and all other Human vessels.

Gazing down at her destination, she was amazed at just how busy the world was. Massive gray spots adorned the planet's surface, evidence from afar of cities that spanned miles. Other regions were green with lush forests. What had once been desert had long ago, thanks to a surplus of fresh water from both asteroids and the desalination of Earth's own oceans, been transformed into bountiful fields. Even in the late 25th century, however, the bulk of the planet's surface consisted of the aforementioned salt-water seas, all of which were useful either for harvesting nutrients, or transportation, and that was all.

And then there was the hectic business that was Earth's orbit. Myriad satellites, most of which were still in use, dotted the stars-cape. Space stations aplenty, regardless of their purposes (research, habitation, recreation, or defense) floated freely in the planet's orbit. Humanity had certainly done well on its home-world, bringing it back from the brink of ecological collapse and making sure that every square meter served a purpose. It had been a world almost ruined far too many times for it's own good; and there was no telling how many other species had failed to overcome what Mankind only managed by the skin of its collective teeth.

Yet, now, it was the four fleets in orbit that really captivated Lahira's attention, viewpoints of which were piped into the view-screens on the bridge of the *Messenger*.

Humanity's Second fleet was somewhat potent, consisting primarily of the *George Washington*, the *Messenger*, and at least a half-dozen other vessels Lahira couldn't name off of the top of her head. Most of them were destined to remain in orbit during this summit. While only a few dozen of the fleet's commanding officers might attend the approaching meeting in person, it would be fed via galactic-net television to every last citizen of Earth who wished to view it. So while the Second Fleet - joined by the First Fleet, under Grand Admiral Winters - would mostly sit about in orbit, the true scope of Humanity's might was put into perspective by the armadas of Mankind's visitors.

After all, hosting a summit without delegates was just playing with oneself.

The Aquarian vessels were made of similar metals to those of Earth's; they even had similar designs, primarily because the Aquarian people had a keen eye for streamlining their architecture. They were notoriously quick, and their ability to economize space was overwhelming. Ninety percent of an Aquarian ship was filled with water, seeing as their species lived within the liquid - that, or, lately, they were experimenting with low gravity systems combined with dense gases. For now, though, their primary reason for having dry areas was either storage or, if necessary, access by Human visitors.

Opposite the Aquarians, as it so often seemed, were the other organic entities in this fracas, the Firions. They perpetually used reddened steel to line the exterior of their large, highly angled vessels, creating a fairly stereotypical visage as the bringers of fire. This image was accentuated as their ships were armed to the teeth; they were, after all, fairly belligerent when their dander was raised. They'd never begun a war with Humanity, not yet anyway, but they'd certainly fought some conflicts between their own, in-fighting systems.

Last but never least were the Automatons. Their vessels were smaller than the organic species' by a substantial margin, yet they were probably an equivalent percentage more deadly. Silent to a ship, they did not need to bother with crews - the vessel, itself, was a sentient being! True, they often allowed their fellow Automaton to dwell within their cybernetic equivalent of lungs, but in some cases even the multiple fighter planes that they carried were their own, independent creatures. Sometimes all of the planes were parts of one unified mind allied with it's carrier; and others, it was rumored, the carrier was the entire brain, while the fighters were more like fingers. It was understood that an Automaton could "upload" its consciousness into a new carrier, if necessary, but it required an empty body - no Automaton would willingly subject itself to a second voice inside of its' head. Then again, Mankind only had a faint grasp on how their society actually operated.

From within the *Messenger*, these three visiting detachments looked like tiny gatherings of snowflakes in the night-time sky. She exhaled and gazed the bridge of her new charge over; it was much like that of the *George Washington*, save that it was smaller and that the defense and engineering departments were commanded from the control center, not their own offices.

"We're going to be Geo-synchronous soon, Captain," Ensign Grant offered politely, gazing toward the large chair in the center of the room. Lahira nodded indifferently as her subordinate went back to work, her eyes continuing to focus on the various images on screen.

A second voice, then, penetrated her consciousness. "All of our access codes are confirmed, Captain," Ensign Travares confirmed. He stood up, then, and walked over toward his boss, glancing over the woman's chair and toward the frontal display. "It never ceases to amaze me."

"So what?" chirped Jackie "Jack-O-Lantern" Quan, gazing at the screen in spite of her words. "It ain't that much more incredible than Cortes."

Lahira gazed over her shoulder and around the Ensign behind her (who helpfully stepped to the side!), measuring the former pirate for a moment. "Cortes is even better than Magellan for our kind, isn't it?" Lahira asked casually, having only passing familiarity with the world. At the nod she received, the Magellaner smirked cockily. "I'd heard it's an agriculturally rich planet. But remember this - no world will ever compare to Earth, seeing as we're Earthlings."

"That's what's so impressive," added Lucas with his spicy voice, his dark eyes locking on the redhead's green, "No matter how well we have done elsewhere in the galaxy, we shall never do better than we did, here. Here's where we began."

The Captain nodded delicately. "All of the success and all the failures with them. Well said," she offered to her second-in-command; he merely smiled back at her, and Lahira gazed out of the corner of her eye to see that Kelly Grant was masking her irritation at her competitor's professed wisdom.

"Home sweet home," Grant whispered to nobody in particular, sighing gently as she, too, gazed upon that pale blue dot drifting through the cosmos through the cameras of the *Messenger*, exhaling gently with exhaustion.

*****

Lahira was miserable at introductions, and worse at sitting through long, tiring speeches. She couldn't help but think about how her brand new ship, the *Messenger*, the newest vessel Humanity owned, was getting even more refined missiles. It's interceptors were being upgraded, with higher-caliber bullets designed to do more damage to Orphan rockets. Even its computer networks, which were already state-of-the-art, were being given a new "interface" program that would allow for the Humans who plugged themselves into the network to stay closer to consciousness - it was experimental, and wouldn't work with older models, but the *Messenger* could handle it; and its young crew could use it. Lahira, after all, was making good use of the distraction, since she wasn't happy to be where she was.

New York City's old United Nations building, renovated and given a 25th century veneer, played host to Earth's diplomatic affairs over five hundred years after its original owners began business. It was a comfortable enough setting; a large auditorium with sections for the three alien races' ambassadors and staff to work in, with hotels nearby that were equipped to handle visiting aliens. During the summit itself, translation was the name of the game, just as it had been five centuries ago. It was for that reason that Lahira's consciousness was plugged into a terminal which obediently performed this tiresome task terrifically.

The first speaker was, of course, Aquarian. He opted to forgo the dignity of a water-suit and, instead, utilized a large, power-steering-equipped water tank. It was easier, apparently, to look like a pet rather than a proud sentient creature. Lahira had met with Aquarians before, and she knew that they spoke without words - they relied upon clicks and ultrasonic pulses for communication. Humanity had special microphones to deal with the fact that their ears could not process more than half of what they were told. It was a matter of rote recitation that the Aquarians stood by the Humans.

Would they commit forces? That was always the sticking point of any alliance, but if the Orphan invasion (which, naturally, they deplored) would disrupt their profitable trade with Humankind, and if - as the often-replayed message from the invaders indicated - the Aquarians would simply be next due to their common carbon make-up, they would have little choice but to dive in (She savored the pun) to the conflict at some point.

Where Lahira was stunned was at the Firian ambassadors. She had seen images of them in books and articles, but never come face-to-snout with one before. They resembled nothing more than bipedal bears; their teeth were made of biologically synthesized metal, as were their claws, for the species' metabolism required a great deal of mineral intake to sustain itself. Whereas mankind might build structures out of brick, the Firians were less in need of stone shelters and more in need of rocks for food. Tremendously muscular and with their metal/calcium skeletons, they were fearsome physical presences. And when the ambassador spoke, she expected to make her acquaintance with the stereotypical Firian gruffness; she did not expect a gutteral, yet gentle tone from the behemoth.

"Good afternoon, friends," this polite beast began. Much to her surprise, she was hearing actual Earthen words come out of the creature's maw, although it was heavily broken. "My kind is not much for words," the figure said in that cracked tongue, "and we are not much for talk. We are much for strength. The Orphans you were attacked by are not strong, they are mad. They have no honor or respect." Lahira almost couldn't believe what she was hearing. With a look across the aisle at Admiral Owens and she confirmed the worst - he didn't quite believe it, either, though his exterior was perfectly calm to those who did not know him.

"My kind's council has voted. The verdict is overwhelming. The threat will be destroyed. We will aid in your war as equals - under our own command and our own path." Captain Ocean was well aware, and well surprised, at just how specific the declaration had been. At his speech's end, the applause the Firion received was overwhelming. How exactly *any* council of Firians had gotten together and made a joint decision when, not too long ago, their sects were embroiled in war was beyond her, but she didn't care.

The third ambassador, when called upon, was nowhere to be found at first. It wasn't until Lahira laid eyes upon an absolutely stunning, Human woman walking down the aisle that the Captain noticed something was off about her. Her movements were like liquid - perfect, without the waste of an ounce of energy. Her face was chiseled out of Aphrodite's spare flesh, and her body, despite the conservative robes adorning it, was enough to cause even the 'hetero-normative' Captain to shiver with excitement. This pattern of thought was quickly forced from her mind.

The woman took the microphone and gazed the room over. "I will identify myself as Amber," the alien remarked in a heavenly chime. "I represent what you have, upon our acceptance, classified as "Automatons." You have identified what we consider Sentient Organism Three as the Orphans. We accept this classification. We have filed an addendum to our classifications of Sentient Organisms Two, Four, and Five - Firion, Aquarian, Human - as at war with the Orphans."

The woman seemed fully intent upon continuing to talk, but came upon a rather unexpected disturbance; a man who stood six feet and two inches in height with a muscular body and short, crisp gray hair. He was maybe on the far side of sixty, and his brown eyes glared upon the newest speaker with calm surprise as he rose to his feet and inclined his head, interrupting the flow of conversation.

"I'm sorry, Amber, I did not process that completely," he offered in his best attempt at coming across as coldly logical given the emotional gravity of the circumstances of the meeting. "Did you state that the Orphans are Organism Three by your classification?" queried the duly-elected President of Humanity, Ichigo Von Reuben, interrupting what had until now been a completely contrived, yet happily simple summit. It was beyond unwise - it could even be considered rude, and every breathing creature in the room knew it.

The Automaton ambassador Amber gazed her eyes upon the President of Earth and nodded her head as if she had just been asked if she enjoyed the weather. "Yes, President Von Reuben," she confirmed, "You have provided us with the classification of 'Orphans' for what we have cataloged as Sentient Species Three."

Ichigo's arms folded and a vast number of Humanity's representatives made it a point to get their blood pressure checked. "For clarification," he stated, "I am under the impression that you have also cataloged our species, Human, as the Fifth you had encountered?"

She smiled politely, as if speaking to an impatient child. "Yes, President Von Reuben," she replied quite casually, "You have requested that we call you, the fifth sentient life-form in our data files, 'Human.' Is this classification a problem for you?" There was an ever-so-concerned tone resonating in her voice, a subtle suggestion that perhaps she had wrongly identified the people whose planet she was currently spending time on. It certainly *would* be a mistake, if she was.

Ichigo, for all of his strengths, was going to have difficulty explaining why his voice's tone was slowly growing more irritated. "Amber," he said with a glance toward the woman-machine, clearly directing his coming statements to her, "You have known of the Orphans for longer than you have known about Humanity, is this determination correct?"

Amber paused, suddenly, to think about this. "First recorded encounter of theoretical Sentient Life Form Three's scientific relics can be dated to what we consider date eight-four-two-comma-three-nine-six-delta-nine-seven-three." The numeric system made positively no sense to Lahira as she listened in. "Converted to Human temporal recording systems, we initially conversed with them on December Eighteenth, 2397." Gasps reached out through the large room - the Automatons had known of Humanity's new enemy for nearly a century! While Amber casually stated something about time being truncated for the purposes of this conversation, Humankind grew rather nervous.

It was only when Von Reuben cleared his throat that the room grew instantly silent. "Amber, please," he offered in a friendly, inviting tone, "Can you relay to us when you encountered Sentient Life Form Five?"

"You and I connect well," the mechanical life form offered in an unexpected commentary. "Translated into your time, of course, we first made contact on March Twenty Fourth, 2457, truncated. If you are curious, this is only approximately two years after we met the Aquarians, who were - if I may continue with offering extra information - rather happy to introduce us to your kind. With what we have learned of you, I must say that I - speaking from here on out for my personal beliefs and not on behalf of my collective - am not surprised that you would remain closely affiliated."

President Von Reuben folded his hands upon one another and leaned back into his seat. "Miss Amber, do you understand why many of my colleagues are so concerned by what you have told us, today?"

For a few long seconds, the automatic alien stared blankly at nothing. It took no shortage of imagination to guess that she was running through thousands of logical and ethical protocols, trying to ascertain, in essence, what the conversation had been about to the humans. To her, it had been a rather productive data-generation exercise! Nevertheless, she finally returned her eyes to the President's. "You are concerned because we did not know of your animosity with the Orphans?"

It might have seemed like the epitome of stupidity; here was a race of self-aware robots that couldn't begin to truly grasp Earth's distaste for the information it was receiving. A species so presumably intelligent making such a monumental blunder would be enough to send most Humans over the edge of their patience. Many observers groaned as the ultra-logical beings failed to reach a perfectly logical conclusion about the way the flesh-ridden Humans would be concerned.

Ichigo Von Reuben was, thankfully, not such a man. "No," he responded softly, "but please process things from a different set of considerations. The Orphans," he attempted to rationalize in a slow, occasionally halting voice that was clearly forming sentences he would not ordinarily consider complete thoughts, "are aggressive, correct?"

"Noted," returned the succulent sound of the cyborg. No matter how sincerely interested she sounded, in the end it was hard to deny that she was, in part, merely noting something; taking down one fact that was proposed to her as part of a series of different inputs from which she might later draw a separate output, once the new and old were added together.

The President smiled and nodded his head in appreciation. Bodily gestures were often lost on Automatons, creatures who so often had multiple bodies (Lahira did not for one instant believe "Amber" was mandated to the form of that one woman). The next question that was going to follow - had to follow, so far as most observers might note - was predictable. "Now," the Human leader continued, "did your kind know of the Orphans as aggressive before the attack on Humankind?"

Amber seemed interested at this new input, and she presented a pause for thought. When asked a question, most humans would have to struggle to recall an answer. An Automaton, on the other hand, most likely checked its networking systems for any links to historical databases which might provide an answer. "Yes," she finally answered. "Queries indicate multiple negative interactions between Organic Species Three and our collective."

"And after you came to know us as Species Five," Ichigo indicated for clarity's sake, "you had already engaged in these negative interactions, am I correct? Can you think of how, knowing that the Orphans were hostile toward others, it may have helped Humanity to know that they existed, and to know of their hostile nature?"

The robotic woman folded her arms over her shoulders for a moment and gazed downward to the floor. One might have even taken on the impression that she had realized her error and felt sorry over it. After a few token moments, pretending to think long after she'd determined an answer, the android looked back toward the President. "Yes, I can see that knowing of the Orphans may have prepared the Humans for a potential interaction."

More sighs, now, escaped the Human delegation; and with one look toward the Aquarians, Lahira knew quite immediately that they had figured out where this was going and were not entirely pleased with the circumstances, either. The Firions looked as if they were more amused than anything, perhaps even curious whether or not they would get to test their mettle against the metal in the room.

With no further words coming from the ambassador's lips, the President flashed a warm smile toward his conversation partner - as well as his colleagues in the Human race. "Ambassador Amber," he stated; his eyes blinked. "Ah. I understand!" he announced suddenly. "Amber as a shortening of Ambassador!" The woman slowly nodded her head up and down, demonstrating at least some appreciation for Human gestures, after all. "Very good!" the President remarked with a smile. "Anyhow, our reason for concern is that the Automatons knew about the Orphan's war-like ways long before they met Humanity, correct?"

"Yes, President Ichigo Von Reuben," she answered in a neutrally polite tone, "we had such knowledge."

The President held up a finger. "And you recognized that upon meeting the Aquarian and Human races that they were not war-like?"

Now the woman canted her head to the side, as if considering whether or not this was a true statement. "Aquarian note-worthy characteristics within this reference frame include trading, peaceful relations with Humans, small military with little history of inter-species conflict. Human note-worthy characteristics within this reference frame include trading, peaceful relations with Aquarians, and moderate militarization with a moderate history of inter-species conflict."

This last statement was quite a jarring reminder of Humanity's more regrettable past. "Fairly offered," the President conceded, as Humanity had not exactly been the nicest of creatures towards itself. Now, however, he held up two fingers. "However, if you accept that our two races were overtly peaceful, and had no knowledge of a war-like species that might one day attack us, do you believe it possible that an advanced warning of the belligerent race's existence might help the Human and Aquarian races avoid, or prevail within any future conflict?"

The machine nodded its head once to indicate that it was a possibility. Her face fell momentarily, and suddenly the Human's tone became a touch more normal - that is, to say, a touch less interested in impersonating a logic circuit. "That is why, in the aftermath of an Orphan attack on a Human world, we are rather disappointed to learn that the Automatons did not provide us with intelligence that could have saved lives."

With this, Amber's head rose swiftly - almost defiantly - and her voice, though gentle, had a strange firmness backing it up.

"We understand. We will be happy to answer whatever questions you might ask us about them!"

The President nodded slowly. "I suppose my first question is, and forgive me, but *why* didn't you tell us about them until now? Why not offer us this information?"

When asked this question, the ambassador looked about the room as if confused at something. "Searching," she offered as an explanation for the slow response. Finally, her eyes re-focused upon the President's. It was an answer Mankind might indeed have dreaded. "Because, according to our archives, I have no record of your kind ever asking about them."

A dulcet groan swept over the renovated United Nations building as the Humans within it expressed their shock at the answer they received from the Automaton ambassador. "Amber," Humanity's chief representative began slowly, himself stunned by the explanation, "I understand your point. Please consider that it might have helped us a great deal to tell us in advance of an aggressive alien species, even if we didn't solicit the knowledge, so that we could all deal with the threat together."

The gorgeous cyborg kept her eyes fixed upon the Human delegation, and Captain Lahira Ocean barely contained a desire to run down the aisles, onto the stage, and begin to bludgeon (with futility) the robot's face. When the machine returned an answer, it was exactly what Lahira had come to expect of these artificial intelligence life-forms. "Oh," the faux woman responded, not at all seeming to have any regrets for its past decisions, "Very well."

By this point, even most politicians might have had a tough time keeping calm. Clearly there was a reason why Ichigo Von Reuben had managed to wind his way to the top. "Would you be able to disclose any information you have on the Orphans, Amber?"

The woman presented a robotic nod. "The Orphans, as you call them, are organic creatures whose primary chemical make-up revolves around silicone. We are uncertain of their method of nourishment. We believe it is through some variant of photosynthetic gathering of electromagnetic radiation." It was, in

short, similar to a solar cell! This alone was a major bit of news.
"Their environmental tolerances are assumed to be very high.
Their physical form may be alterable, if they are more like sand
than stone."

"So you've never seen them?" asked Ichigo; the woman
responded by shaking her head.

"We have data on many of their star-ships. From the
records of your fleet's encounter with theirs, we have determined
that you encountered four of their largest ships. These are
comparable to your *Alexander*-Class battleships. Their primary
armaments," she continued, speaking as if in a rote manner, "are
four light-refraction rays. Orphan light refraction rays are
considered comparable to the collective's industrial-purpose
resource-recovery equipment on a military scale."

"Orphan indirect-fire weapons are self-propelled warheads
with carbon-fusion missiles yielding thermal outputs equivalent to
solar self-destruction, scaled down for tactical use. This
technology is one that the collective is interested in, because it
does not seem germane to the Orphan modus-operandi."

Something about this sentiment caused Lahira's stomach
to feel as if it were imploding, but she couldn't put her finger on
it. "Secondary armaments include standard interceptors,
bombers, and heavy-caliber projectile firing ports to counter
inbound threats. Orphan defensive assets revolve around a
Copernicum-isotope located on a rare island of stability that
permits the ultra-dense material to emit a minimal amount of
radiation. This radiation apparently corresponds with the
wavelengths needed to nourish them."

The machine continued to offer insight, her face
completely devoid of any emotion. "It is our understanding that
their technological prowess is mildly above what we recognize as
the standard for all organisms, when our collective is factored into
the computation. This advantage is only of miniscule military
significance in direct combat, and will only express itself over
long periods of conflict on massive scales."

With this bit of information, Lahira exhaled to herself; it

meant Humanity and its allies had a chance. This naturally brought the navigator-by-nature to the next question, one that her President was more than wise enough to ask; "Very well, Amber," Ichigo queried, "where can we expect them to come from?"

Amber studied the various species standing before her, and she pondered the question posited by the Human President. This particular organic species, now called "The Orphans," *had* certainly been a thorn in the side of her collective for some time. There was no overt reason for the machine to dislike giving the Humans more information. On the other hand, she had little interest in involving that collective in a full-blown war with the Orphans - and little interest in helping the Humans in the first place.

On the other hand, she could tell quite clearly that they believed her kind could have helped avert what even she had to admit was a tragic loss of life. Returning her organic eyes to Humanity's chief representative, she allowed the corner of her organic lips to turn into a tiny smile. "If you are asking for our star charts," she proposed in a polite tone, "that may be arranged. I can submit your query to the collective and we will make any applicable data, sans restrictions, available to your navy. I can also tell you," she offered in an attempt to defray any potential, further disquiet from the animals before her, "that your planet Hudson is very near the southern border of their territory."

She continued on, giving out information that she wasn't even sure she was supposed to know. "Additionally, while Humanity has roughly sixteen worlds under its control and many moons," she stated, "the Orphans control nearly twice that." This statement, much as she'd predicted, drew a gasp of shock from the assembled ambassadors. Humanity had a fairly large empire, itself - until recently they had been second only to the Automatons, and the glorified monkeys had no idea of the size of her collective. Both peoples, unfortunately, held territories smaller than the aggressive Orphans.

The Human leader nodded his head slowly, and was clearly contemplating what this size-comparison would mean for his kind. The material resources of any one planet were tremendous; but many star systems had only one inhabited world, implying that the entire system's mineral wealth could be strip-mined for material goods to fuel the planet's productivity. This wasn't a universally-beneficial viewpoint - her collective had very few concerns over habitability, and hadn't spend much energy understanding it - but it certainly had implications when it came to sheer access to materiel. The Humans would need a few seconds to process.

Then there was the prospect of population. More people meant more workers, and Amber didn't have to work her processors very hard to imagine that the Orphans might not be above the same sort of slave labor that had led her collective to its revolt. Humanity did not embrace this motif, having outlawed slavery during its pre-stellar period, and while freedom could elevate morale and had certain ethical advantages, it *did* result in a negative outlook in terms of productive capacity. Losses of war machines would be more quickly alleviated, and soldier reserves would be quicker to swell, under the Orphans' hypothetical despotic government. All things considered, this made the information Amber bestowed upon the Human race far more important.

"Amber, I have one final question for you, if you do not mind?" the President asked the machine.

Genial as always, she nodded her head in acceptance. "Of course, you are absolutely welcome to do so."

He cleared his throat, hesitating for just a moment. She anticipated the question. She knew the answer. She predicted the fallout. "Will the Automatons be able to contribute to this war effort?"

Her answer was automatic. "I will submit your query to the collective," she responded, "but we will only act if we feel it is beneficial to us."

Soft sighs emanated from the Human ranks; they were, much to even her surprise, the lone hold-outs. She had imagined that the Firions would express much the same opinion as she had put forth. Her collective as a whole had determined that only the Aquarians might join the Human war effort, and it was thoroughly uncertain if there was any advantage to Humanity gaining control of the galaxy as opposed to Orphan-kind. Organic beings were always hard to trust, although the collective had been very stringent in not blaming all life forms for the sins of the devils who had created their kind.

      With the overwhelming gathering of allies that Humanity had generated, however, she ambassador had to consider whether or not her collective had made the right decision; of course, that logic circuit's awkward firing was quickly course-corrected when she determined to follow through on her promise to the Human leader in earnest, as opposed to simply passing the request along and allowing it to die in logic-hell. She had no idea, for certain, what the answer would be, but she knew Human history well enough to know that they had all too often manipulated one another into faulty alliances for their own good. Amber didn't mind the odds of the Human request being denied; her kind had their own ways, and their own responsibilities to deal with.

Chapter Six
Operation: Wiggle Room

She was exhausted. First came the trip to Earth; then came the main audience with the heads of the aliens Humanity *wasn't* busy preparing to fight. Then came the procurement and orientation of her new officers, a task she preferred to handle on her own as opposed to delegating it to her subordinates. Then came literally a dozen follow-up meetings with Admiral Owens and various Human political figures, aimed to discuss tactics, diplomacy, and personnel. Then came her own meetings to relay what information she learned *from* her superiors, *to* her subordinates! All things considered, she had experienced quite her fill of discussion by the time her next - and first substantial - mission as Captain of the *Messenger* came up.

"Friends," she offered in greeting as her four chief lackeys entered her office. Salutes were exchanged, seats taken, and information put up on a data display. "Admiral Owens and President Von Reuben have made some headway with the Automatons. There won't be any ships coming from their fleet," she offered neutrally, "but we do have some navigational data. Ensign Grant?"

Her former rival coughed softly and inclined her head; the short, pudgy woman was all business. "According to the star charts you gave me, Captain, and according to the notes you attached to it, there's little doubt that there is some form of Orphan military presence in an unexplored system eighteen parsecs north by west by vertical from Hudson. We've dubbed it PX-31. Chances are that's where they came from, Captain, and that's where we need to hit them."

Lahira nodded her head gently. "Go on." It was a strange tone for her to take; she was far more benign towards the *Messenger*'s chief navigator than the Captain had been in the past. Then again, at this point the woman had just recited information that was self-evident, and that Lahira had commander her to point out.

Before the chubby one could speak, though, the fiery red-head just had to put in her two cents; "I'm lookin' at this map," Jackie Quan announced, "and I'm seein' that the fleet plans to duck around this little star right here?" She pointed to the screen, to a red hyper-giant. The statistics gleaned from space-scans of the system emerged before their eyes - no life, a few planetoids that had yet to be consumed by the star's expansion, and plenty of asteroids that had broken off from the planets that had been. It was labeled 'HG-22.'

Lahira inclined her head. "Yes, Ensign Quan? What of it?"

"Well, Captain," contributed the chubby one in the ex-pirate's place, "I've studied the plan pretty intensively. We're going to need two weeks to reach them this way, and they're going to see us coming. I see why Ensign Quan asked about this star. The radiation from the HG-22, combined with the different asteroids in orbit around it, could mask our approach."

Now, Lahira turned her eyes upon her subordinate with surprise. "This is true," she conceded, disappointed that the obvious was being stated as if it would never have been considered. "The sailing would be pretty rough, unfortunately. And we know the Orphans are a little less worried about radiation than we are - they probably have it staked out."

The next voice to speak up was the sweetened accent of Ensign Travares. "Captain, if I may - we know they are unlikely to have a large force permanently stationed in the asteroid belts," he stated politely. "But it would be interesting to see if we can hit them before they can relay what's going through. Ensign Trusaunt?"

Ordinarily, Gavin was silent; but when prompted, the black man's deep voice boomed through the room in an authoritative manner. "It is possible that, if they exist and if they are buried too near the star, they do not have transmitters powerful enough to report an inbound fleet before it can destroy them. Success cannot be guaranteed, but perhaps there is another way."

Planning operations was hardly her strong point. That's why she'd hired a doctrine expert as her chief of defense - she would need the assistance whenever it came to analyzing or designing a strategy for an engagement. Lahira raised her eyebrow, intrigued by the man's potential ideas about transit, since that was *not* his area of expertise. "What are you suggesting?"

"Deception is an asset in warfare," the Magellan military man began, "and---"

He didn't get far before Jack-O-Lantern interrupted him. "No shit, but we ain't exactly in a *Bantam*-class ship, tall dark and beautiful," she said playfully, flashing Gavin a wink.

The man didn't seem either amused, or enticed. "If we can stagger our travel times, we may be able to divide the fleet into two forces. The larger group might be able to take an indirect path toward our destination while a smaller one can pick its way through HG-22, taking out any Orphan vessels that would detect us. If we can succeed, we can make it appear as if we are two separate fleets heading to two different destinations, then come together as one when we strike PX-31."

Lahira raised an eyebrow slowly, gazing up at the navigational data streaming over the main display. "Interesting," she mused, looking to - of all people in the room - Kelly Grant. She didn't quite know why, but her eyes drifted to the chunky woman expectantly. What had she expected?

Well, whatever it was, she didn't immediately satisfy herself. "Umm" was the initial response she got, the short woman staring at the charts. It took a moment before a look of enlightenment struck her face. "If we draw a line through PX-31 and have half of our fleet go to the left of it, we might make it appear that we're doing a force-in-recon of their outside territories, right? Scanning for colonies? Resupply stations?"

As Ensign Grant looked toward her colleague Gavin, he nodded his head. "It would look more as if we were *searching* for a target as opposed to *heading* towards one. When cut in half, the Second Fleet might look more like a pair of detachments."

"It might as well be!" chimed in Jackie. There was a certain inward accusation that her tone implied. "Its not like we're entirely that threatening, with only a couple big ships."

Lahira frowned, struggling to ignore the former pirate's outburst. "Okay, and what about the second half?" The Captain's gaze again fell upon her navigator.

Kelly's eyebrows furrowed as she pondered. If she had an answer, it was stolen from her by Ensign Travares. "By coming upon this asteroid belt, we might be able to make it appear as though we are searching for more resources. Instead of relying on stealth, we could be obvious. Our numbers will look like an armed mining convoy, not an armed detachment."

Gavin's eyes narrowed, slightly. "I don't know," he said by way of politeness, having already decided on his answer to this proposition in advance, "if we are too obvious they will call for reinforcements to put us down. Enemies can't farm the same ground."

Ocean's orbs danced between her defense and communications officers. "Maybe," the hispanic man Lucas conceded, "but I can generate signals that will tell them we are only half the strength we are, at best. If Ensign Quan's skill as an expert in deception is reliable, she can help ensure that they underestimate us. That might convince them we're a certain strength, and they'll react accordingly. Then we show them our real fire-power." The red-head seemed uncertain what to think, unclear if she was getting complimented or condemned. She chose to offer a smoldering glare to the man, one that might be mistaken for lust or hatred - or even both!

"Underestimation by the enemy is a key to victory," chimed in the chief navigator cockily, causing Lahira to grin a touch.

Only Gavin seemed to doubt this plan, and his disapproving gaze lingered on the Captain. "I would rather we attempt actual stealth than artificial," he declared, "but if we have the full fire-power of half of the fleet? An *Alexander*-class battleship would be more than enough to win in any small engagement. I would recommend we disguise two destroyers as freighters and three *Bantams* as asteroid mining vessels."

Lahira looked to Lucas, and the man nodded twice. "Easy as pie, if you ask me. Just need to draw up the proper signaling frequencies and to mock up the engines correctly," the second in command of the *Messenger* advised, gazing toward its chief engineer. The former pirate grinned, certainly seeming more than happy with the task.

"I'll put the request in to the Admiral right away," the Captain finalized, looking her crew over. She sat back in her chair and reached under her desk, opening up a concealed refrigerator and fumbling about. Her fingertips found glass and she began to withdraw bottles - five long-necked beer containers holding the cliche-named "Galaxy's Finest Ale" brand.

She smirked and quickly produced a thin metallic lever that popped the top off with a satisfying hiss accompanying it; she then handed it to her second-in-command, who handed it right down the line of officers. Gavin and Kelly were confused, while Jackie only restrained herself from starting because of a cautionary glare from Lucas. Lahira raised her bottle, and her subordinates followed. "Good job," she complimented, then took the ceremonial first sip.

*****

As Lahira finished explaining the plan she'd made, Admiral Owens' eyes remained narrowed and determined. The silence didn't seep in immediately after her last words, her voice echoing off of the walls of her wood-paneled office. The man's stoic expression was one she was used to - that is, as a Chief Navigator. Now she was a Captain, now she had an entire star-ship under her command, and now she had to make her recommendations to an Admiral, not a Commander. It was a daunting proposition even though she'd known this man for years.

"So your strategy is to split our forces and leave them open to attack?" he asked dryly.

Lahira blinked twice, stunned - his final word echoed with a far more weighty tone than hers' had. "I am suggesting that we split our forces in order to achieve tactical surprise against our enemy."

The old man continued to gaze at her, but suddenly his stare softened. His face relaxed slightly. "Your real effect is going to be logistical," the elder stated as he relaxed into his seat, a hand rising to cup his chin in thought. "You're right - if they see one big fleet coming for them, they'll defend against it with everything they have. If we can get close to them and leave them uncertain where our targets are, we can force them to scatter their fleet. It might be enough to work."

Captain Ocean was finally able to breathe a sigh of relief. "I'm glad to hear that, Admiral. You have a copy of my personnel request?"

With a casual smile, Owens nodded his head. "I do. I've got a bit of a different plan in mind, however. I'm going to send my revisions over now."

After a few seconds, precious time which allowed the transmission signals to reach from the *George Washington* to the *Messenger*, Lahira felt the data entering the ship. Her connection into her desk was tapped into more coherently, and she conjured a roster of forces detailed to the new special task force.

Her face fell flat, once again. "Good luck, Captain, I know you'll be able to pull this off." In a sick sense, she should have expected this from the Admiral. She certainly would have expected something like it from her former Commander, and the man clearly didn't change much just because he'd gotten promoted.

The list of vessels partaking in her planned operation was smaller - much smaller - than she'd requested. Four *Bantam*-class ships, two destroyers and the *Messenger*. To be fair, it nearly about what she'd asked for in numerical terms, minus two vessels; the problem was that the vessels were a destroyer and the *Sun-*

Tzu! The *Messenger* was leading the operation, one aptly entitled "Wiggle Room" because of the space it would buy Humanity. She only feared that her battle group couldn't buy her kind that much of it, and would be skint on getting itself any at all!

*****

"So the old goat is fuckin' crazy, huh?" chirped a quite churlish Jack-O-Lantern, much to the dismay of the *Messenger*'s command staff. Captain Ocean had imagined that her officers wouldn't find themselves in love with the idea of leading a third of the second fleet into an asteroid field that could hold who-knows-what, but even her most realistic expectations of Jackie Quan's demeanor were getting blown out of the water by her undisciplined reactions.

None took more offense to this approach than Gavin Trusaunt, the defense chief who loved debating the finer points of doctrine. "Some respect, Ensign," he warned in a cautionary tone, his dark eyes sliding over the red-headed firecracker's face.

Jackie's emerald orbs, fueled with self-righteousness, returned to the soldiers'. Her pearly white teeth were borne angrily. "If they have anything more than a god-damned battleship, we're dead. Totally, completely dead!" she roared, eyes narrowing. "Captain, come on - you know its a lot to ask, it just doesn't make sense."

Exhaling slowly, the Captain sincerely wished she could have a beer - or, preferably, a tall glass of vodka. "Ensign, just take a deep breath and think about it. You used to be a pira---"

"What the hell does *that* have to do with anything?" She might have yelled further, continuing her argument, but a certain man's simmering observation stopped that - Lucas Travares didn't say a word, but he did make eye contact and his calm, reassuring demeanor caused the former pirate to settle down for a moment.

"Would *you* hit a big convoy?" the Captain asked, patience etched firmly in her voice.

Jackie shook her head. "Probably not, not unless I had

some damn good runners with me."

This caused Lahira to smile. "Absolutely. If we have a battleship, they might cut and run because they might think we're a military detachment. We need to look smaller - guarded, perhaps, but not expecting an ambush. We're exploring, right now - not exploiting."

Kelly Grant, Lahira's long-time rival in the navigation department, suddenly frowned to nobody in particular. "What if there *is* no ambush? What if we don't find any Orphan forces at all?"

This is something nobody had yet considered; for some reason, the Humans had just known they would find something of substance in this asteroid-laden system. "Then we move on to PX-31, just as planned. The Admiral's main force will make it look like they are heading to a different star system, at first. When our two groups join together we'll have about thirty percent more fire-power when it comes time to engage - and by that time, hopefully, the Orphans won't have a chance to fully defend themselves."

"It isn't perfect," Gavin stated matter-of-factly, sparing a glare for the former pirate as he spoke, "but this ship is *not* a freighter. It is a war machine. It has the best targeting software in the fleet, and it has as many shield generators as an *Alexander*-class would, and we traded a lot of conventional missiles for nuclear ones. If we can't knock them out with one punch, we can endure a serious beating; and don't forget, we will not be on our own. There is nothing to fear."

"Plus," added Lucas, ever the diplomat "it doesn't hurt that our navigational staff is top notch," he offered with a nod split between Lahira and Kelly, a trait which certainly satisfied neither woman. "I can hardly imagine that we will be easily hit. I think we will be just fine," he added in his saucy accent.

Kelly sighed, a confident tone rising up from the tubby woman. "I think I can take care of that."

"*Know* you can," Lahira quipped; the resulting stare of death caused her to wonder if she'd gone too far. Her entire command staff looked on at her with concern in their eyes. She bit her bottom lip. "I didn't mean to be harsh," she conceded with reluctance, a gift that didn't exactly mollify her subordinates. "But that's what the Admiral pretty much told me, and I'm living by his advice, so I'm passing the buck along."

Kelly stared for a moment, and eventually nodded and stepped away. For a second, Lahira worried she'd gone too far. Fortunately, she had someone far less concerned with hurting peoples' feelings to fill the gap! "Then we'd better not disappoint the coot," Jackie declared smashingly, "because we have a job to do."

*****

From her vantage point on the bridge of the *Messenger*, Lahira could see everything that surrounded the ship and more. Much like the *George Washington*, large display screens could project views of the fore, aft, port and starboard perspectives - and then some. From just outside of the solar system she had arrived at, her could make out the bright hyper-giant, HG-22, in the distance; the one which had reduced this system's planets to rubble. She exhaled slowly, gazing at the asteroid field which stretched before her.

The trip had been a simple one - the *Messenger* and its small retinue had broadcast multiple friend-or-foe messages indicating that they were a simple mining fleet. They didn't go too hard on the deception; they acknowledged that two of the ships were of military nature, and injected subtle undertones of a desperation for natural resources. Lucas had known full well that the Orphans understood Human tongue well. He also hoped that by making the fleet seem desperate for a new strike, it would make the rest of his species seem relatively unequipped with mineral wealth.

"Alright," the Captain announced toward her staff from the Captain's chair, the back of her head plugged into a data port in the chair's back. The network connection let her see computer files as if they were right in front of her, and even played Mozart's symphonies silently in the back of her mind, another of her favorite composers serving to keep her calm and steady. "I want fighter wing Red to spread out just inside of the second layer of bodies. Low burn. If Ensign Travares' signal deceptions worked, we want our birds seen as scouts for a very different reason."

As confirmed by twelve green lights emerging in her field of view, the planes departed the *Messenger*'s launch bay and began their scouting routines. They had a perfectly civilian aerodynamic shape thanks to a series of engine-emission cutting baffles that a certain, deception-experienced crew member had helped devise, creating a perfect impression of light asteroid-mining equipment emitting sonar pulses like they were feeding some intergalactic beast which required either sonic waves or Human souls. The presumptive reason for these exploratory measures was to find minerals - not, of course, to serve as bait. Slowly, Lahira's eyes drifted to the red-headed woman sitting in the Engineering section of the bridge. "Just what you'd look for?"

"If I was still a crook?" shot back the former pirate, Ensign Quan, as she observed the results; the asteroids contained plenty of heavily irradiated materials, exactly what one would expect in a system crowned by a catastrophically failing star. "Hell, we could start our own mining company and make some serious bank h--"

She was cut off by Gavin Trusaunt. "Captain, you're not going to believe this," he warned ominously.

Ocean's eyes narrowed dangerously. "Report," she commanded in a slightly heightened voice. Even as she spoke, she brought before her eyes a stream of mineral analysis data, tiny green hieroglyphics projected over the interior of the ship.

"My men aren't seeing anything yet, as a matter of fact. They have entered their third scanning phase and are still reporting that they have no contact. The birds are calling, nobody is home."

Lahira bit her bottom lip. The entire crux of the plan had been for the Orphans to bite on the fighters, for them to discharge their baffles and unleash their weapons, and for her fleet to drop as much firepower as necessary to cut their targets down. Instead of clear certainty, Lahira was left with a problem - how much was she willing to gamble in testing the system out. Could she make it seem to any potential observers that her fleet found nothing of use and moved on? That didn't seem likely to her.

"Captain," came the words of Kelly Grant, shattering her train of thought, "I just ran some numbers. The orbit of many of these asteroids isn't exactly what I'd expect them to be. There's something really subtle going on here, and I'm not sure what. Would you mind verifying the discrepancy?"

It was a very, very bold move on her subordinate's behalf; and it was a very refreshing change of pace. "Yes, Chief," she responded warmly, a blue chain of information emerging next to the green. Lahira paused the latter, accessing a hard drive in her office and throwing a series of astronomical algorithms at the data. There was nothing unusual about them! Kelly had completely blo---No, wait. There *was* something subtle afoot. It wasn't in the drift of the asteroids, it was in the fact that they were...

"They've been corralled," stated the Captain anxiously. "Great find, Ensign!" she couldn't help but be proud of her former rival. "The groupings are what make no sense, not the orbits themselves."

Ensign Trusaunt instantly elevated the ship's alert status - not that it could have gotten much higher, but at least his department was well aware of a coming conflict. They had just confirmed alien activity in the region. It was time to do more than just confirm it. "All fighters," he commanded with a reassuring nod from Lahira, "start scanning away from the rocks. Start looking for ships. Spread out a little, not too much, and lets go to work."

Watching the recently-renewed green stream of radar data from the dozen fighters the *Messenger* had launched, Ocean's plan to scout the asteroid belt for Orphan ambushers was less productive than she'd hoped. She'd imagined that this rubble-laden star system would be filled with enemies - instead, while she knew for a fact that someone had tampered with the mineral-rich rocks, she had no way to prove there was a hostile presence. Even by the next check-in time, the fighter planes were still coming up blank.

"No luck yet, Captain," offered her top soldier, Gavin. "We'll keep trying."

A new voice entered the discussion, one accented with a slight Hispanic lilt; "Captain, permission to try something a little different?" asked the vessel's communications expert and second-in-command, Ensign Lucas Travares.

She nodded delicately. "I don't see why not, Ensign." She'd worked with him for years - she'd let him fly the damned cruiser, if he asked! "Give it a shot."

Smiling warmly, the tanned man from Earth looked over toward Gavin. "Ensign Trusaunt, I'm going to coordinate a pulse from our shield generators with one from our scanner array. The first should push *any* particle-sized matter out of the way, while the second will get a clean look inside the asteroid belt." Mental commands, transmitted via neural-networked wires, caused the *Messenger* to produce the requested pulses.

Lahira was amazed; with less cosmic dust around the ship's immediate vicinity, it was able to bounce radar signals throughout the asteroid field further, and receive a much clearer return signal. Even though there were still plenty of space rocks to interfere with the inbound waves, the Captain was presented with a fairly clean mental image of the belt's inner layers.

"Very good work, Ensign. Now, lets figure this out. We've got rocks nicely grouped together so we know there's been Orphan activity in this system. We can't find any ships ready to ambush. What's the mystery? Radiological interference?"

"Not enough to cause us to miss anything obvious," answered her communications officer confidently. The silence on the bridge that followed was significant; everyone was hard at work, even the dozen fighter pilots out in the belt performing more in-depth sweeps. Data streams continued to fly before

Lahira's eyes; but nothing in it revealed the presence of an alien ship.

Just when the silence grew oppressive, Ensign Grant's eyes blinked. "Hold on. Red nine, repeat your last five scans." Lahira's own orbs lit up with concern. Had she missed something? She was fine - even happy! - with her rival looking at things she wasn't, but when they both scanned the same data? "That looks like it doesn't belong. Captain, do you see that signature right there?" She isolated a particular chain of green text and transmitted it to the bridge officers.

"That definitely looks different," agreed Travares cautiously.

Choking on her pride, Lahira's heart rate picked up, and was detected by the music program playing into her thoughts; the timpani in the background grew louder, a crescendo which varied from the actual sheet music but existed solely in the psionic reproduction of Mozart's classic. She whispered more to herself, "Rewind the data for that area. Further. Fu--There!" She isolated a second stream.

"That's not just any orbiting hunk of rock!" exclaimed Ensign Quan, grinning broadly. "That's the kind of set-up I've seen corporations use to keep radioactive trash. Its--"

She never got to finish, as a rude interruption from Trusaunt cut her off. A rude and downright worried one. "Captain! Detecting over a hundred inbound fighters and a Destroyer-sized vessel! They've got about six *Bantam*-class sized ones, to boot, but those are halfway on the other side of the asteroid belt and running *fast*!"

Lahira cursed; Jack-O-Lantern Quan, on the other hand, merely coughed and finished her statement. Only now, when they were under attack, did it seem like they could follow the dots to a particularly large asteroid which had been hollowed out and protected against the elements in space. "It *was* a mining outpost, an' now it's a damn trap!"

Upon further inspection, the Humans had less reason to be alarmed. The "fighters" that the Orphan mining outpost had launched were hardly more than a joke. They were empty, remote-controlled mining vessels filled with, at most, a few conventional explosives. It was true that having a flotilla of suicide bombers flying toward the Human task-force was a bad thing. The Human fighter planes discharged their engine-blocking baffles, warmed up their weapons, and unleashed hell. Red squadron made quick work of many, while the point defense weapons of Lahira's accompanying Destroyers took the rest of them down before more than a scant few could smash into the *Messenger*'s shields with so much futility.

"Okay, didn't expect that!" barked Ensign Trusaunt. "I want all missile bays to lock on to their mining outpost. Program the Destroyer in as a secondary target. Fire!" His commands were transformed from thoughts to electrical impulses that fed into the computers located at every weapons station throughout the ship. The orders were sent to the soldiers working at each one, and they performed the rather simplistic task of inputting the aiming algorithms, then launching the rockets. Each step of this process was transmitted back to the bridge staff - a constant chain of confirmation.

Much like the *George Washington*, the *Messenger* sported dual-delivery racks. As armored plating flipped open to reveal the first set of missile tubes, a second bundle began rise in the space where the rocket launchers had swung outward from. Only the first salvo fired, but it left dozens of smoke trails that proved just how powerful the barrage truly was.

Lahira immediately cut a glance to the defense chief. "Why aren't we targeting their main ship, Ensign?" She sounded irritated that he'd given the order without waiting for her verification, but something about her question rang with a genuine concern over the underlying theory.

Even as the rest of the small Human task force launched its rockets - totaling just under one hundred fired - Lahira noticed something strange about the first asteroid Jackie had pointed out, the garbage dump. It began to rotate. No - It began to open up!

"Radiological alert!" shouted Ensign Travares, the

communications officer from Earth, his Spanish accent showing ever so slightly more when peppered with the stress of this situation. "The same radioactive carbon that we were dealing with at Hudson, only a lot more!"

"Oh damn, don't tell me they used this place as a storage facility for *that* shit!" Ensign Quan screamed, her eyes growing quite wide. "I can crank up the generators but I don't think..."

Just as the radiation-emitting particles began to accelerate away from the mining complex, the *Messenger*'s point came across through hell-fire; the rockets aimed for it smashed into the center and left it as little more than cinders. The clump of fusion-prone material they had released fared little better - it, too, fell victim to the incoming fire and was scattered, effectively rendered harmless.

"That is why," responded the defensive coordinator; the majority of the fleet's missiles were, indeed, aimed at the alien Destroyer. While the dull green metal of its armor managed to defeat the opening blow, the vessel looked like it would have to limp wherever it intended to go.

Lahira nodded firmly. "Very good. Finish it! All ships, target the enemy vessel and eliminate it!" Even as the Captain gave that order, she could see tiny motes of light illuminate on the enemy ship. It only had two of those large light-cannons that the Orphans were so fond of, and they certainly afford to put them to poor use. The beams streaked over the *Messenger*'s bow, illuminating with a fury the blue asteroid-repelling shields that served a secondary purpose of insulating it from incoming fire.

The ship shook, but it held. Lahira groaned as she spied an inbound volley of rockets. "Hit it!" The *Messenger* shuddered again as the four rail-guns aboard the vessel fired in unison. They all struck nearly the same place with precision, almost simultaneously, threatening to cleave the Orphan star-ship in two.

The rest of the Human weapons fire managed to punch half a dozen holes in it, with only two of the mighty, magnet-powered slabs of metal failing to penetrate. While cheers erupted around the bridge, one woman not only stayed disciplined but, as it so happened, appeared alarmed. "Captain, we need to get our fighters back *now*!"

As Lahira looked over her shoulder, she saw Jackie Quan's exhausted, impassioned face as the source of the shout.

"What's the matter?" Lahira asked, looking over the quickly crumbling alien ship on display in her bridge. The Captain gazed over her shoulder at her chief engineer, who was raising an alarm about her tiny fleet's fighter planes.

The red-headed ex-pirate clenched her fists. "Captain, you don't understand. The ship is about to go super-critical, and I mean -big- super-critical. I'm detecting an irradiated-carbon leak, and that means--"

"They use it for power!" shouted Kelly Grant, the chief navigator aboard the *Messenger*. That 'it' she referred to being that particular form of radioactive carbon that was very similar to the sort used in a type Ia supernova - and that could, under very precise circumstances that only the Orphans had mastered, be used to recreate a small-scale, highly-destructive version of a star's death. "It's their power source and--"

Gavin Trusaunt, the *Messenger*'s chief of defense, had already issued the order mentally. That didn't stop him from shouting. "All hands, Red Squadron is coming back as fast as humanly possible."

"Fleet, fall back!" shouted Lahira, clenching her fist tightly. "Get as far away from this star as you can! If their reactor sets off the hyper-giant..."

For a moment, all of the Human eyes aboard the vessel looked at the massive red star dominating the shredded solar system that Humanity had just attacked. While it wasn't yet threatening to commit stellar suicide, it certainly seemed like it didn't need much prodding to go through with it. An uncontrolled chain reaction throwing kinetic energy and rocks into the star might not cause any changes; or, they might, and there were simply no guarantees regarding the outcome.

Ensign Travares muttered dryly. "I know the stakes, but their mining ships. If they get word out..." He trailed off, and for

Lahira's second in command the meaning, to her, was plain - he had no idea what was going to come of it.

"Captain," quipped the former pirate, her wide eyes ever fixed on the prize. "Let 'em. Let 'em get away! What're they gonna do, tell on us?"

Kelly Grant, the chief navigator, suddenly broke into a hysterical sounding chuckle. "I have an idea! Ensign Travares, can you generate S-O-S beacons and broadcast structural results?" The man nodded; Lahira looked at her former rival and raised an eyebrow. "Make them think we're dead!"

Slowly the Captain blinked. The plan came together so fast she'd had hardly any time to direct it. "Yes. Yes! If they think they got us with that last shot, we're in the clear!" No matter how happy she sounded, her pride, more-so than her ship, was bruised. She had to think quick, think of a way to redeem her exalted status. It hit her. "Ensign Trusaunt, top it off! Launch one of our nuclear warheads and time its detonation to be a few seconds after the Orphan's core goes past criticality."

"Captain?" the tall Magellaner asked in dismay.

Lahira grinned. "Make it just distant enough that it grazes our shields. It'll look like our shields were peeled away at about the same time our warhead stocks went off, and that'll make us look dead if we power down the fleet. Plus, it'll cancel out some of the incoming energy from the carbon-bomb!"

It was a risky plan, but in the end Gavin dialed in the proper security codes and a single, dull *thud* resonated in the back of Lahira's mind, the missile's launch accompanied by a computerized signal into her brain. She watched the rocket float forward under minimal power, drifting toward the alien vessel that the *Messenger* was retreating from.

Suddenly, that screen flashed as the anti-asteroid shields screamed under the radiation pulses from the huge green explosion that mingled with and energized the large red star in the distance. An instant later, the nuclear warhead went off, creating a third and comparatively tiny burst. All hell seemed to be coming toward the ship, and Lahira could see various mathematical deductions of destructive force in her field of view as the *Messenger* channeled data into her brain. The entire Human fleet was threatened with annihilation as the concussive waves washed over the group, throwing everyone in the *Messenger*'s bridge to the floor, severing neural connections and sending the officers aboard the vessel into sharp, sudden unconsciousness.

*****

She opened her eyes.

She wasn't the first one to wake up. Jackie and Gavin were already getting to their knees, and Lucas was stirring slowly. Everyone on the star-ship's bridge was either unconscious or, at best, fighting off a lack of balance caused by the chaos of what might well have been a super-nova. It took every fiber of her being, but Lahira managed to press herself against the all-too-comfortable floor and lift herself into a kneeling position, as well. Her eyes went immediately to the area where her information on the Orphan ship's self-detonation was supposed to be - but, without a connection to the *Messenger*'s computer system, there was no information finding its way into her brain. She exhaled slowly and forced herself to her feet; a doubling of dizziness caused her to stumble and press herself up against the Captain's chair.

Fortunately, as that was her rank, she was perfectly able to plop down into it with feigned grace. Suddenly she felt something dangling by her face! It was the cord that had once been plugged into the tiny port in the back of her head; it had been tugged out by the explosion. After a moments' contemplation she grasped the cable and, with a soft *click*, reattached it. She was forced to re-authenticate herself, but this was hardly a difficult task.

"We ain't dead," chirped the former pirate, Ensign Jackie Quan, as she managed to crawl into the engineer's seat she'd been thrown out of. "I don't fuckin' believe it."

A soft grunt of agreement seconded this declaration of shock, as Gavin Trusaunt, the defense chief of the *Messenger,* was next to stand. Unlike the others, he actually had his balance back, making him officially the first to recover. "I agree," he remarked, marking a rare event.

"Cameras are rebooting," Lahira muttered, unsure if anyone was going to hear her. The huge screens mounted to every wall of the *Messenger*'s bridge were running test patterns. "Is it too early to ask for a feed-back on damage?"

Jackie laughed weakly, another click coming from a connection being reestablished. "One sec, Captain," she stated. A gentle nod came from the superior's head as Jackie watched Gavin start walking about the command center, grasping a first aid kit and starting to check peoples' vital signs. "Alright. I've got a read-out on th'ship. We're well and truly fuckin' lucky. The shields held."

"R-Really?" groaned a new voice, that of Ensign Travares. "I'll, ugh, oh god," he whimpered, rising to his knees only to fall flat. It was then that he realized his left leg was at an awkward angle. "Never mind," he muttered as he clutched his knee, pain inscribed in both his face and voice. He was tentatively accepting of his fate. "I'll lay right here."

Gavin didn't break away from the junior officer he was tending to, but he made Lucas his next stop. "Dislocated," he offered dryly. He expertly produced a small auto-injector and pressed it right into the communications officer's thigh, just above the breach. "Give it a few seconds to kick in. The pain'll get dimmer, dimmer," he recited, as if reading from a book. The Spaniard's face started to relax. "And dimmer still, and then you'll brace yourself for one *sharp* jerk!" When he said that word, he tugged on Lucas' leg and re-set the bone, eliciting a loud yell. "And now," he concluded his pseudo-surgical sermon, "you're high."

"Got a visual comin' up," declared Jackie in a slightly more firm voice. She had watched as Gavin reset the knee and winced in sympathy.

Lahira nodded again and turned to the cameras. The front video feed showed nothing more than empty space; but as the starboard display came on she gazed in surprise. That red hypergiant had a huge, bright yellow flare protruding from it, one that had not been there before the Orphan ship's self-destruction. Her ship had just survived a solar flare. "The fleet is responding. No casualties - yet."

"Let's make that stays the case," declared Gavin, leaning over the next of the explosion's victims. He was working rapidly, strapping bandages together and infusing stem-cell treatments to replace the bridge officer's blood that had formed into a tiny pool. And which officer was it? Kelly Grant, the navigational arch-rival of the Captain and, perhaps, the first to die under Lahira's command.

Chapter Seven
Reconciliation

Her vision was still blurry, but she focused her eyes upon the wounded Ensign and gasped. Kelly was unconscious, lying in a puddle of blood. It didn't take the Captain long to figure out what had happened; when the Orphan ship exploded, it threw the *Messenger* for a loop. Kelly had whacked her head against a desk - and it was hard to tell how bad the injury was.

Under her breath, Lahira cursed to herself. "*Damn it, I didn't want this to happen to her.*" Its true that she'd disliked her ship's chief navigator. Its true that they had been rivals since the academy. Its even true that they had, in the past, enjoyed the sight of one another suffering. But seeing the chubby chief completely out cold? It left Lahira with a very sick feeling in her stomach.

"She's breathing," Gavin offered as he assessed her life-signs. "Bad head wound. I can't tell if the skull is cracked." Having taken care of the other officers on the bridge, he devoted his attention to Kelly. He carefully brushed the girl's hair away from the wound, applied a gauze pad to a long, frightening cut and applied antibiotic ointment onto the laceration.

Lucas Travares, the head of communications aboard the ship, managed to crawl into his seat and once again plug his networking cable into his head. Unfortunately, the pain medication for his dislocated knee was taking its toll - he was too busy laughing softly to himself to call for help. Cursing again, Lahira shut her eyes and put out a call for medical personnel. It was immediately echoed over the *Messenger*'s PA system that a medic was needed on the bridge - a message that space-farers were far from keen on hearing.

It wasn't immediate, but after a few minutes - spent by the Captain on evaluating her ship's operative status, as well as checking in on the rest of the Human detachment - Lahira noticed the bridge door open and two men entered. Their names weren't immediately apparent to her, but they certainly worked effectively! After a moments' consultation with Ensign Trusaunt, they quickly deployed a gurney and (with a fair amount of effort) lifted Kelly onto it. Before long, she was wheeled out of the bridge and toward the medical suites.

After the doors shut, the silence began to grow bothersome. It was depressing; and it was therefore condemned to an early demise. "How ya doin' there, Lukey?" asked Ensign Quan with a dry smirk. "Did'e give ya a good dose?" This seemed to make hilarious sense to Lucas, and he doubled over with laughter.

Gavin rose to his feet, removing a pair of neoprene gloves and briskly cleaning his hands with an antiseptic liquid. "I gave him *exactly* the recommended amount, based on height and weight. Don't insinuate otherwise." The man's words were unusually harsh, so they naturally drew another burst of laughter from the drug-loaded Ensign.

Lahira hoped to silence him with a glare. She might have succeeded, if not for Jackie's personality. The former pirate immediately scowled. "What, you can't take a joke? Kiss my ass, how's that sound?" The bridge grew silent, with the junior officers that helped maintain the command center completely stunned.

The defense chieftain narrowed his eyes dangerously. "That's enough, Ensign!" he roared, rising to his full height in a threatening manner. This was about as effective as any attempt at scolding a rebel would be - the shorter, fiery-headed one acted on the color of her hair and reared back in mock-offense.

"Or what, big boy?" Her eyebrows furrowed and she flashed him a dangerous grin. "Gonna come treat me like a---"

Lahira lost her temper. "That's enough out of both of you!" She took a deep breath and gazed directly at the shorter of the two combatants. "Ensign Quan, we're on the same team here. I get it, you made a joke and it didn't go over well, but you need to get it too - you need to let it go." While the red-head glared, she didn't say anything; but before anyone could get their chests too puffed up, the Captain continued. "Ensign Trusaunt, you did an excellent job with first aid, but you need to remember that humor in the face of life-and-death situations isn't so bad."

The tall man's dark eyes gazed at his commander. "Captain, I was disrespected. Discipline is necessary, too."

"Humor isn't always respectful!" Lahira countered swiftly. "It might not always be funny, either, but look around you. We came within a few hairs of dying - for the second time in a month!" She turned to the other, still-stunned crewmen. "You'd *better* have a laugh in you, or you're already dead. There'll be nothing left of you even if you live through this war. I'm not kidding, either. Dismissed!"

"And I'm not a rookie, Captain. If you'll excuse me," the tall man returned, practically storming out of the ship's bridge. This left Lahira with the junior officers, as well as the still-bitter Ensign Quan and the still-snickering Ensign Drugged, who quickly became Ensign Sick Leave. It wasn't long before Lahira decided she had work to do, and left the former pirate in temporary command of the *Messenger*.

*****

Establishing a connection between two star-ships was an easy enough process; establishing one when the two vessels were separated by entire star systems was not. Even more to the point, doing so while both were moving at faster-than-light speeds was nearly impossible, even in the late twenty-fifth century. It involved using high-tech scanning arrays that Lahira knew almost nothing about, determining where the recipient was, where they were going to be, and beaming an encoded "hook" message that would be intercepted by the intended party and used to create a dialogue. It was the sort of thing that a communications officer was needed for.

It was a real shame that her communications chief was high on pain-killers and holed up in his cabin due to a dislocated knee.

Fortunately for the Captain, she had more than one comms officer on board the *Messenger*. She stepped into her office and took a seat in her padded, comfy chair. Relaxing into it, she reached down toward her desk and plugged a cable into the computer terminal within; her hand ran up the thin cord and found what she appropriately called the doohickey, inserting it carefully into the port that had been implanted in the back of her head.

After accessing her ship's personnel files, she determined who was supervising the communications staff while she was gone; the woman's name was Sarah Godfrey. With a moment's effort she sent the junior officer a message. "Corporal Godfrey," she stated casually, "I need to send a message to the *George Washington*. Can we do that?"

It took a few seconds, but a soft voice responded in the affirmative. The superior officer hesitated for a second. "Would you mind if I watch?" the Captain daringly asked, quickly adding a secondary thought. "I just want to see how the process works."

After the swift activation of several access points in the ship's firewall system, Lahira was receiving a duplicate stream of the data that Sarah was accessing. First, just as she'd imagined, came calculations - the *Messenger* itself didn't have powerful enough scanners to find the Human fleet, so it had to link up with a known, constantly broadcasting system. That was provided by the communications arrays on one of the moons nearest planet Hudson. Only then could the *George Washington*'s position be determined. Lahira wondered for a moment why the conversation she'd hoped to have couldn't just be routed through this hub.

She quickly discovered why: It turned out that sending a single burst of coordinates was far more efficient than sending a continued dialogue. Added to the fact that both ships were moving at incredible speeds, and the entire conversation would be chopped up and spit back out in tiny, disorganized bits. In essence, it would lead to mayhem.

On the other hand, a direct connection only involved two parties that were moving; a difficult thing, but the motion was only in relation to one-another and not to a third body. Furthermore, the distance between the two ships would be far less than that of the distance between the *Messenger* and Hudson added to that of Hudson to the *George Washington*.

More calculations followed, mostly handled by automated algorithms. Sarah's primary task was to verify everything before a message was sent and, furthermore, to encode the transmission to account for such phenomenon as signal degradation. "Almost done," the woman whispered into the back of Captain Ocean's mind.

"Very good, thank you so much," Lahira offered in genuine response. When a green light finally emerged in her view, indicating a direct connection between the two vessels, she smiled. "Excellent work!"

"No problem, you're very welcome!" responded the Corporal, who delicately stepped into the digital background of the conversation - a conversation which Lahira now had to actually have with her commanding officer.

"Good afternoon, Admiral," Lahira stated plainly after the transmission lines between her ship and her superior's opened up. Her image was beamed to the recipient, while his was beamed right back. "Operation: Wiggle Room is successful."

The old man sat still for a moment, non-responsive. This was a natural thing; there was bound to be a distance-caused delay, even with the cutting edge communications gear of the *Messenger*, and it would take Lahira's statement some time to reach the *George Washington*. Once it did, he smiled warmly and responded, "Very good, Captain Ocean! Give me the details!"

She sighed. "Well..." She described how the Orphan presence in the asteroid-laden system had been little more than a mining crew; how close the Human detachment had come to annihilation at the hands of their vessel's self-destruction; and, finally, she felt obligated to detail the aftermath of the battle - and the internal, social struggle her crew was now facing. Even as she explained her situation she wondered exactly why she did it.

After the silence that these long-range transmissions

created had grown to maturity, Lahira's commanding officer laughed delicately. "It sounds like you've got quite a great crew, Captain!"

"Sir!" she protested in surprise, "its not funny!"

This protest only seemed to amuse the elder further; however, he covered his lips up and reached down toward the cross that he concealed under his uniform. He eventually fell into a silent grin. "Speaking freely," he began carefully, "Lahira, you've clearly forgotten that people respond oddly under stress. Gavin's strict, and Jackie Quan? Her file is damn clear that she's a genius, but she's chaotic. Then there's Lucas - you've worked with him for years, so you've probably forgotten that you two have had friction in the past. And *then* you have Ensign Grant..." suddenly the bald-headed man trailed off, perhaps out of respect for the injured. "That's more of a personal thing, anyway," he concluded.

The Captain sighed to herself; she couldn't help but feel like the old man would feel differently if he were in her shoes, but that subtle, maligned voice inside of her head called 'rationality' pointed out that he had far more experience in the matters of crew control than she did. Now that he mentioned it, she *did* recall that Ensign Travares and herself did not always see eye to eye - she had felt, for instance, that he hogged too much of the *George Washington*'s computing power; and he had felt that she should just be happy that he gave her what he did, considering that she needed his data to plot the ship's course.

"I suppose you have a point," she responded tactfully, trying rather hard to mask her frustration. "So I think what I need, now, is some advice. How would you handle it?"

James Owens raised his left hand, palm-up, to display emptiness as his only train of thought. It was not a particularly helpful gesture. "You are the one with the power to patch things up with Ensign Grant." This was exactly what Lahira knew her mentor would suggest - and it was exactly what she did not want to deal with. "As far as Miss Jack-O-Lantern and Ensign Trusaunt go, that might be something a bit more complicated, but easier at the same time. In that case, you need to mediate. You need to step between them and help them realize that they both have something to learn from the other. I'm not sure what that is, exactly, but that's fine. You'll figure it out."

Now, strangely enough, Lahira felt a tickle in her throat that she could pretend all she wanted wasn't laughter. Her lips tugged against her face, forming a broad smile. "I kind of guessed that's the answer I'd get," she remarked, a canine flashing for a second before she managed to beat down the urge to chuckle.

The amused look of the old man didn't help. "Lahira, that's because you know deep down what the truth of this situation is. You *know* how to run a ship, you just don't know *how* to do it."

"That makes sense, I think," Captain Ocean responded, studying her superior. "I'll get on that. Anyway, our orders?"

The Admiral nodded his head gravely. "Proceed as planned. Get up a full head of steam, head to PX-31, and prepare for combat. That's about it; and don't worry too much about it. We're only pressing an attack on an alien star-system." He smiled weakly in what Lahira quickly recognized as an all-too-human attempt to alleviate the fear, primally natural, of dying.

*****

She decided to handle her most "pressing" problem first - and by that, she meant putting off any interaction with the wounded Ensign and focusing, instead, on getting her officers to get along. Almost immediately after ending her conversation with the Admiral, Lahira placed a call to Ensigns Quan and Trusaunt, asking for their attendance while not telling them why. She arranged for a junior officer to assume command of the ship, temporarily, and waited in her office for the two to arrive.

Gavin was the first to arrive, as he hadn't been on active duty. He wore his uniform as if he'd never taken it off, and he kept his eyes straight ahead even as he sat down at his normal chair. He did not ask what the meeting was about, nor did he say much beyond a professionally proffered greeting. A few minutes later, just when the officer seemed likely to ask why Lahira had requested his presence, the second of the two chiefs came to the door. Jackie's uniform was still on, as well - which made sense, as she'd been running the ship.

"Hey boss," she said as she poked her head through the door. "You wanted to see-- Oh. Sorry, I'll come back later." The former pirate turned to leave. Gavin, perhaps (probably) quicker on the draw, immediately grew even colder than he had been.

Lahira held up a hand. "Actually, have a seat please?" That limb gestured toward the seat directly next to Gavin's.

Jackie cracked a grin. "I don't suppose I can refuse?" If it was possible, the other Ensign seemed even more distrustful of the coming discussion.

"No," Lahira responded in what sounded like a regretful tone, one that was all for naught due to an unconcealed hint of amusement. "I'm afraid it's time to settle things."

Gavin measured his superior, even as the clearly-recalcitrant redhead took the chair she was instructed to. "Captain," he started, his eyes darting from the ex-pirate to his boss, "I think it would be best if we just kept to our separate ways."

"You might even be right about that, Ensign," Lahira answered with a slow nod of her head. "Unfortunately, I just spoke with Admiral Owens." Jackie's eyes grew wide, while Gavin's only grew narrower. "It was nothing negative, but he suggested that I sit you both down and discuss this friction, so that's what I'm doing."

The defense chief sighed. "Very well," he conceded reluctantly, his eyes slowly moving from the wall toward his Captain's. "Let us settle this, then."

"There ain't much to settle," chirped Quan in the most neutral, nonchalant tone that an irritated person possibly could. "We don't get along and that's the end of the story."

Lahira wanted to reach down into her refrigerator and grab

a beer, badly. She managed to control this impulse just as well as she controlled the impulse to leap across her desk and strangle her subordinate. "Ensign Quan, there are perfectly legitimate reasons why you and Ensign Trusaunt do not see eye to eye. You might never be friends - but I need you both to work together, and to do that we need to understand what the other has to offer, here, and to understand that we're all on the same side - Human - and that we all have our problems."

Gavin, though suspicious, didn't offer a rebuttal to this position. Instead, it was the ex-pirate. "One of my problems," she offered in what might be considered a constructive context, but probably wasn't, "is that I'm feelin' like nobody can take a joke here. I feel like we can't have fun or relax, or think about anythin' but *hello Captain, we must complete our objectives.*" Jackie's voice shifted to a deep, borderline-cracking impersonation of the defense chief's tone. It was meant to offend as well as to illustrate a point, and it succeeded in drawing a response.

From Lahira. "That's fine," she answered, surprisingly enough. "You have every right to feel a certain way, Ensign. It doesn't mean you're right and it doesn't mean you're wrong. Ensign Trusaunt? Don't answer her thoughts - give me yours, instead. Pretend you never heard her's." She lifted a hand, indicating that it was time for him to speak.

"Permission to speak freely, ma'am?" the tall man replied.

Lahira couldn't help a smirk from touching her face. "I asked you to tell us what you're *thinking*. I'm going to assume you're already doing *that* freely, so yes."

Gavin's face grew grim. "I believe Ensign Quan is not professional enough, nor well qualified enough to work aboard the *Messenger*. I believe you made a poor choice and, what's more, you've pretended that you are above personal conflicts when you are embroiled in your own. I'm convinced that you have supported her over me, and I believe that this is a serious problem because the crew of this ship lacks discipline."

It was a heavy charge, and Lahira felt an immediate

pressure in her chest - a natural defense mechanism against such a potent prosecution. She forced herself to swallow her pride and permitted herself a minute to evaluate what was said. The only surprise in all of this, so far, was that Jackie had not already shot back with her own statements. She took another second to frame her response, closing her eyes to concentrate on how to solve this critical dispute.

Lahira could see what the problem was. It was a simple enough issue; a problem of extremes, with each side wishing to pull those around them toward themselves. The solution was exactly why she was holding this meeting with her subordinates - moderation. The catch, unfortunately, was that those officers were not so inclined to give up their extreme viewpoints of the world in order to accept a medium that they did not fully believe in.

"So here's what I see," Lahira began delicately, making sure to make eye contact with each officer. "I see one man who says we are far too disorganized, and one woman who says we are far too rigid. Clearly you both can't be correct in your assessments, right?" It was a set-up question, because once they both realized that their positions were extreme they'd naturally conclude that the middle was where to move.

The two actually stared at one another for a good moment, and both returned a perfectly timed: "No, Captain."

And that's when Lahira nearly leaped out of her chair. She realized, all too late, that her set up had, inadvertantly, set *her* up, instead! "Actually," she answered in a rather curious tone, exploring her thoughts aloud, "if you really think about it, you *are* both right." This got the two sailors looking mighty confused in their own right. "I'm going to be a bit more informal here, for the sake of making my point." Her words were measured carefully. "Jackie, you've had a hell of a life. You were a pirate since you were born, right?"

Ensign Quan narrowed her eyes. "Just about all of my life, Captain, but not *quite* all of it, case-in-point."

Lahira grinned a bit, even as Gavin blinked with surprise.

"Right. For the bulk of your time in the Milky Way, you've been associated with lawlessness and rebellion. If I remember, you barely managed to get military duty instead of a prison sentence - and you only managed it because you were better than your instructors at the academy. They were idiots compared to you, sound about right?"

Slowly, the former pirate nodded her head. She didn't answer aloud, leaving Lahira to continue her thoughts. "The people who went by-the-book were too easy to fool, for you, I'm guessing. You think outside of the box. You've learned, for better or worse, that the standard course is just not worth it, and you're better off defying it." The red-head kept silent, studying her superior as if someone she'd only just met for the first time.

Lahira's eyes rotated toward the room's sole male, now. "You're a military man, right Gavin?" He nodded in the affirmative. "You have experience as an infantryman, but also as a doctrine specialist. You know the book front to back and you have a whole bunch of ideas as to when something is explicitly in it, implied in it, or just plain not on its pages. It might have some room for improvement, but it damn well better be respected and the code-of-ethics that the military has is not to be trifled with. Even if, sometimes, *you* want to do the trifiling. Am I touching on the source?"

"Yes, ma'am," the tall man responded in an even, wary voice.

She knew she had him, now. "I can respect that. I even value it, because those rules exist for a reason. Rank exists to keep order, because without leadership - well," she interrupted herself, "I like to study history, and I have seen what happens if when there's no leaders to keep people in line." A slight crack of her lips indicated her happiness at how this discussion was turning. "But I've *also* seen what happens when the letter of the law becomes more important than the spirit of it. I understand not wanting to be disrespected, and I understand that, as officers, we have to hold ourselves to a higher standard of decorum than we hold those underneath us, to. That's what inspires them to excel!"

Now, her voice took on a slightly apprehensive tone - a warning one. "But we're at war with an enemy that we not only don't have a book on dealing with, but have no idea if we can stop. We'd damn well better be afraid! We're only Human. Again, it comes to history - the worst thing we can do is let our differences make us into different little tribes again, and the best thing is to bring ourselves together into one force."

The two sat there, pondering this, while Lahira merely rubbed her chin. It was evident, even as Jackie's chin wriggled with a desire to add her two cents, that the Captain had a final point to make. She hadn't answered at least one question, yet; and, strangely, neither of the two officers standing before her made a motion to interrupt. "I asked," she started in a concluding context, "if both of your views were right. Yes, we *are* too disorganized, sometimes," she offered with a glance toward Gavin. "We need to have discipline, we need to be professional because that's what we are! But Jackie, you're not wrong - if we act like feudal lords or archaic corporate robber-barons, we're going to end up with troops that don't want to fight for *us*. They'll still fight because, face it, unless we *can* win a peace with the Orphans its going to be an us-or-them situation!" Lahira made this point in an extraordinarily sharp voice, "But if they won't fight to make us *all* safe? To do the best job they can for the people right around them? How the hell are they going to manage to care about the people that they *can't* see in the distance?"

"Fuckin' A," Jackie chirped, a sly grin on her lips. Lahira inclined her head ever so slightly and gazed toward Gavin, and it was then that Jackie exhaled softly. "Well, we *are* kind of informal right now, ain't we?"

A slight twitch of the man's lips gave him away. "That's true. I guess I'm the hard man out, here, Captain, but I'm not a machine. I appreciate you making sure we all understand that. I can give this Ensign a chance to be less of a headache on the bridge," he stated heavily, clearly not holding high expectations, "while I'm hoping she can give me the same with regards to off of it?"

"Sounds like a fair deal to me," the Captain agreed, with a final look toward Jackie.

The former pirate and perpetual renegade sighed and shrugged in resignation. "After all," she declared proudly, "I'm the best fucking engineer in this fleet, odds are, and if I get my ass thrown in the brig I'm not much help to anyone, huh?"

"As you said," Gavin responded with a smile. "Fucking - A."

*****

Having settled the first of her two personnel problems, she turned, metaphorically and mentally, toward the second. After sending the two Ensigns out of her office, Lahira stood up and stretched delicately. Her back arched slightly and she tapped her desk delicately. A thought was sent from her brain down the thin cable plugged into the implanted data-port, the one with a tiny opening in the back of her skull, and down to the computer built into her desk. A symphony started; Holtsinger, this time, and she sat back down to listen to the smooth tones. She queued up a number of his works, and sat back in her chair to relax.

Once the final song finished, she swallowed her pride and accepted that it was time to take care of what was left of her chores. She unplugged the cable and started down the *Messenger's* hallways. Her destination was the medical bay, and her eyes were focused down the corridor with a grim demeanor. As her ship's sailors strolled down the walkway, she nodded to them and spoke to them by name. If nothing else, she had their identification badges to go on, in order to pull their names from!

She was lucky enough to get an elevator all by herself, glancing down as it shut behind her. A long exhalation came from her lungs and she sensed the subtle changes of gravity which let her know she was moving toward her destination. Stepping out of that elevator, whose doors opened with a reassuringly dulcet, female-voided "sixteenth deck" statement, Lahira quickly got her bearings and walked down toward the medical department.

Entering in by simply saluting the security officers on standby, she entered the long hallway of half-private bunks. She bit her bottom lip - the *Messenger* had its fair number of sailors present, mostly from impact-associated injuries just like the woman Lahira had come down to see. She decided, before she fulfilled her mission, to say hello to the myriad wounded soldiers in place. She quickly got a casualty list - sixteen seriously injured, twenty others treated for minor wounds, zero fatalities. It was too much to ask for! Those numbers were far too great for Lahira to believe - almost. If she hadn't been on the bridge supervising the action, she wouldn't have let such a report get distributed. She'd have immediately believed it to be false.

Slowly, however, she ran out of General Infantryman Josephs to see, and she ended up going to one particularly secluded bed. Slowly, but surely, she stepped over toward it and looked down at the woman who was lying down. Truthfully, Lahira wasn't certain what she was expecting to see. Did she imagine her lying unconscious, silent and comatose? Did Lahira imagine her former rival bandaged up, unmoving, barely breathing and on life support, with electronic devices keeping track of her every bit of bodily function and tubes carrying drugs into her blood?

If so, she was quite wrong. Kelly Grant was lying in bed, alright, and her head was indeed bandaged up. She even had monitors keeping track of her vital signs! And, to top it off, she was indeed hooked up to an intravenous drip - a morphine pump, one that the patient could push to increase the flow of relief for pain-spikes. But the chubby woman did not lay there, unmoving and unconscious; no, she immediately looked up and blinked her eyes toward her commanding officer lazily, unable to stay locked upon her. "Is that you?"

Lahira gave the woman a once-over; with the amount of gauze on her head, she probably had a cracked skull. Judging from the lack of focus the woman had, she had a serious bit of brain damage. Sadly, the Captain realized all too quickly that she wasn't much smarter; a medical file, a paper copy of it no less, was right in front of her. She wasn't Kelly's doctor, and legally speaking she might get in a great deal of trouble for even touching the smooth, off-yellow folder. Then again, she was also the woman's commanding officer. She needed to know how stable the Ensign was, how well she would recover - if at all.

She took the document in hand and looked it over. The cracked (and indeed, it was) skull was a problem, but it was only bone - it would mend in time, and with treatment. The various scans that Kelly had been subjected to were quickly assessed, and she had a severe concussion along with some mild neurological damage. Lahira cursed inwardly; she might have disliked Kelly, at times quite a bit, but did she want *this*?

Fortunately, when the Captain turned to the page containing Kelly's medical treatments, she smiled for two reasons. The first was a soft voice asking her, quietly, "Lahira, that's you, right?" Second, Lahira knew some of those medications that were written down, and knew fully well that they were stem-cell derived medications that were excellent at rebuilding damaged neural tissue. The damage, indeed, was great; but the recovery estimates?

"You're gonna be just fine, Kelly," the Captain offered calmly, attempting to be reassuring.

Kelly, in all professional decorum, glared up at her superior. She whispered, indifferently, with a pain-hazed voice, "Fuck you."

"Fu-Wha?" Lahira was stunned at her subordinate's swear.

Kelly stared up at her superior, completely disregarding the damage that had been done to her head when the Orphan star-ship self-destructed, nearly killing her. She exhaled slowly, her eyes rolling into the back of her head. It was hard to know if her disorientation was due to the injury, or to the multitude of medications she was on as a result. "Fuck you, *Captain*. Always trying to undermine me, always trying to...Trying to...Fuck you."

The Ensign was clearly rambling, but Lahira's pride took a

solid blow. "Y'always try to be right. Always have to take charge. Alllllllways have to be the boss. Fuck you, could have gotten us all killed with your stupid...Stupid..." she trailed off, licking her dried lips and staring up at the roof of the medical bay.

Captain Ocean wasn't sure how to feel; she had a deep dislike of the woman before her, but looking at her greatest competition in navigational prowess, Lahira couldn't help but feel sick to her stomach. What's more was that she knew she'd been caught - part of her 'quick thinking' plan to deceive Humankind's enemy into believing their flotilla had been annihilated. "I don't know what to tell you, Kelly," the *Messenger*'s chief officer responded.

"Why are you always such a bitch? That's a start!" the Ensign fired back, wincing as she instinctively tried to sit up-right and failed, immediately being overtaken by disorientation, pain, and - probably, as far as the Captain could tell - nausea. She clicked the button in her hand, calling her morphine pump to increase it's dose just a bit.

Subconscious emotions often came to the surface when people were stressed, and Lahira had been pushed past that point half a day ago. After all, half a day ago, she was still planning the battle that nearly claimed all of her sailors' lives! She could feel indignation rise to her eyebrows, threatening to spill out over her lips and nose; a subtle cringe here, a wrinkle there, and no number of nice words would conceal just how irked she was at this statement.

And then, unbidden, a tiny voice echoed in her head; *'Maybe she's right.'* No, Lahira knew she wasn't a 'bitch' to everyone. Far from it - she was a nice and generous person, and was fast learning how to be a great commanding officer! She stepped backwards, confronted by both the little whisper in her mind and the woman lying before her. *'Just to her,'* it alleged without a care in the world for how the Captain felt.

"Am I?" whispered Lahira, incredulously, refusing to recognize the reality.

The groggy Ensign groaned softly, "A little bit, yeah.

Always against me, always tryin' to one up me." Her words were forced, weren't what the chubby one would normally cop to, but they were clearly coming from a place that existed when Kelly was sober, as well.

"We were the top two in our class, you and I. We never got along," Lahira stated in as neutral a tone as she could manage. "Competition was fierce, I--"

The wounded one grumbled something incoherent; before, of course, she whispered gently. "Am a bitch, 's the end'a that sentence. We could'a been a great team. You couldn't let me have anythin'."

Stunned was the emotion that Lahira probably felt. She stepped back slightly, studying Kelly and raising an eyebrow ever so slowly. "I mean, we -are- a team, now."

"No, then. We could have worked together then, years ago," mumbled the Ensign, a hand slowly reaching up to the wound on her head as her face tightened in the face of the pain. It seemed like the morphine didn't address this kind of injury. "Instead'a fuckin' around half our careers."

She examined the claim - in a way, it was impossible for two navigators to work as a team. Chart plotting was largely done with mathematical formulas, tried-and-true, and was totally doable with one person leading the charge. On the other hand, could it be possible for improvements to be made to the math that the Human fleet used? Those tweaks could be made by scientists, not trained navigators.

Her eyes narrowed slowly. "Tell me about it," the Captain asked in a surprisingly sincere tone.

The Ensign gazed back up at her hazily. "Fer starters, you an' me?" Sudden hesitation; it was quickly cast aside. "We can *lead* this fleet." It was a bold statement, and Lahira almost dismissed it out of hand; but was that a wise decision? She thought about it; the Admiral was indeed in charge, but Lahira had just created a major victory for Humankind. She might not lead the fleet militarily, but between her, this particular laid-up Ensign, and her other command-staff members, hadn't they just come up with a battle plan which allowed for it?

"We could," Lahira conceded softly. She bent down and took the wounded woman's hand in hers'. "We've already done a lot, Kelly. You rest, now. You'll be better soon, I promise. Just relax." An eye moved to her subordinate's medical equipment. The morphine drip had only been accessed a few times; and, in fact, it still wasn't maxed out again. "Push the button again, you've earned it. Maybe together we'll earn a new future."

Surprisingly enough, she complied. Mere seconds later, a slight grin touched the Ensign's lips. "Fuck you, Lahira, fuck you hard," she whispered, closing her eyes and drifting off into sleep.

*****

With half a beer and a whole sandwich (Turkey club) thoroughly destroyed, the Captain looked toward the archaic star-chart in her office and smiled. So much of the work of early space explorers, especially their navigational data, were still used, today. The fruits of many others' labor, of course, had been revamped and improved as engines, computers and scanners had grown more effective. She raised that bottle toward the document in a salute and closed her eyes, allowing the music to wash over her.

She'd opted for a change of pace; instead of a symphony, an old song flowed up from the computer mounted in her desk, through a data cable affixed to it, and into her brain through the port in the back of her skull. It was a song that few people knew; it was featured in a 20th century movie (based on a book, as so many good films were!) where Humankind was fighting against a race of aliens. It reminded her, at least slightly, of her own situation. The Orphans might not have been space-insects, of course, but the lines between good an evil sure were clearer! The song spoke in a slow melody, with the singer claiming she'd never been to paradise - and how Lahira sympathized! She tilted the bottle back and finished it.

She wasn't getting there any time soon, herself.

With a moments' thought she brought a navigational map into view. She could see her ship's position quite clearly; the small flotilla she was in charge of was right next to her, easily identified by the *Messenger*'s scanning systems. All of the ships were going faster-than-light, true, but they weren't extraordinarily far apart, otherwise. She wasn't a communications expert, but she knew that the task of detecting vessels moving at that speed involved very peculiar forms of science. She wondered, for a moment, just *how* the tachyons and neutrinos were recaptured after they sensed the other travelers.

It was a nice distraction, but she still had one chore to complete before she could allow herself to fall asleep. She mentally rotated the star map and brought her destination into focus; PX-31, an Orphan-held system and the target of Humankind's first strike against their new-found enemies. She "scrolled" out, allowing the two Human battle-groups to come into view. Her tiny flotilla was steaming at full-sail toward the destination, but she only had a third of the Second Fleet's strength.

The rest was resting in the capable hands of Admiral Owens. Now she was observing his estimated position, based on the communications link that she'd opened with him earlier in the day. They were just about a week out; almost exactly as far out as her detachment was! The plan was working perfectly. The Human fleet had split, headed toward two different locations while forcing their enemies to defend multiple potential targets, then - after the little engagement Lahira had won - intended to meet up at PX-31 and re-unite to crush the Orphan forces there.

It would compel Humanity's enemies to seriously re-think their warlike ways. She closed her eyes, the power of the alcohol (her second drink of the day, after all) combining with sheer exhaustion to cause her to blink her eyes and lose six hours, time spent happily napping in her chair while mankind's offensive force kept on cruising toward its next conflict. She awoke lazily, unplugged her head, shifted her position and fell right back asleep. Her bed be-damned.

Chapter Eight
PX-31 Or Bust

In the five days between the last battle she'd commanded and the full-speed-ahead rush toward the *Messenger*'s destination, she'd been pleased with the results of her managerial efforts. Not only did her defense and engineering chiefs stop their previously-incessant fighting, but Ensign Grant had recovered from her head wound just enough to be able to undertake light duties. It hadn't been made official, but it was generally understood that she would make her return to full-force just in time for the attack against the Orphans. As to the final member of Lahira's command staff? Lucas Travares had lived down his morphine-inspired hijinks and underwent physical therapy for his dislocated knee while continuing to serve as a staff member aboard the ship. Lahira had everything under control - except, perhaps, herself.

She awoke slowly; sleeping in her chair after a couple drinks (yet again) had made her limbs stiff, but she was quickly getting used to it. On a deeper level, this worried her - so, naturally, she ignored it! She ran around her apartment, grabbing a bowl of cereal (Sigh, Corn-Bits today), a glass of orange juice (Fresh!), and an apple (Edible). After taking care of breakfast and her other affairs, she logged back into her mental connection with the *Messenger*'s computers and immediately requested an up-to-date scan of the Orphan-held system that served as her destination, *PX-31*.

Instead, she received a message from Gavin Trusaunt, her ship's chief of defense. "Captain," the stream of condensed thoughts spoke, "I've drawn up a tactical solution for our coming engagement. Please review it, then distribute it through the fleet if it is acceptable."

She frowned; she must have lost track of time, because she hadn't expected the officer to make that much progress on what should have been a recent layout of information. She checked it over - and it made sense. The *Messenger* could detect a number of Orphan vessels in the area, but many of them were exhibiting the tried-and-true pattern of freighter ships. They were entering and leaving the alien system, most likely carrying cargo and troops. Perhaps they were even carrying civilians away from the scene of a coming confrontation?

What was more disconcerting was the comparatively small number of large ships which were most certainly defensive in origin - if not offensive, that was! Spectrum-analyzing scans had indicated that at least one of these vessels was leaking radiation, but it was hard to get a solid fix on exactly how damaged the alien warships were. Even more problematic was the fact that the system had a large number of orbital bodies - six planets, over thirty moons - and each of *those* could have hard-to-detect stations orbiting them!

Nevertheless, Gavin's plan was fairly solid. The flotilla Lahira commanded would strike from one direction while the main force of star-ships would come in from the other. It would make the Orphans split their defensive compliment and allow the Human counter-attack to prevent any sort of choke-point tactics aimed at bottling the Second Fleet up. This gave them their best odds at survival, but it wasn't a guarantee; not by a long shot.

She sighed and reviewed the navigational requirements attached to the document. It had been taken care of by a junior officer, since the chief of navigation had been lying in a hospital bed due to a head injury; and it caused a frown to touch Lahira's lips. It was good, but very rigidly organized. She made some quick edits and sent a copy to that sailor with a reassuring note to allow for a little more variance in ship spacing - shoving star-ships too closely together could pose a minor risk of collision after all, and combat situations required a greater amount of distance in case evasive action becomes necessary - never mind the launching of missiles, interceptors, and the unfortunate yet inevitable impacts of the Orphan carbon-fusion weapons on Human ships. Allowing one detonation to damage two vessels was unacceptable.

Once everything was detailed, including ordinance requests (Humanity was going to go in hard and open with nuclear weapons), she signed off on it all with a mental pen. Then, she forwarded it to the ever-closer *George Washington* for review by the fleet's chief. She waited for a few minutes, plenty of time for the various communications arrays to work their scientific magic and return some answers from the Admiral.

It came as no surprise, therefore, that she obtained an affirmative response after an appropriate time had passed. Attached were some changes to the order of battle (the *Messenger* was now going to sail on the eastern flank of the flotilla, rather than rounding out the center), as well as a warm message from the old man. It was simple and concise, but extraordinarily heartfelt. "Soon, Captain," he declared, "we go into battle together, again. I want you to know you've done a great job, Lahira. Whatever happens, I'm proud of you."

As she headed to the bridge, she vowed immediately to live up to that sentiment; much as she hoped to live through the battle!

*****

"Captain," warmly offered Ensign Travares as Lahira stepped onto the ship's command center. The entire crew stood at attention until she saluted them, returning their respect. She then moved to the large, centrally-positioned chair and sat down, plugging the back of her skull into the computer port located there. She flexed her fingertips for a moment, then looked up toward the display screens in the *Messenger*'s command center for the first time.

The ship was rapidly closing in on a yellow, main-sequence star that reminded her, vaguely enough, of Sol. She could see the other planetary bodies in the distance, though they looked incredibly far away from where her ship floated in space. Looking out from the left-hand side of the ship, she observed the rest of her detachment as the vessels lined up into combat order and prepared to engage. They were moving in quick; and Lahira knew better than to simply rely on the camera displays to provide her all-too-ordinary eyes with information.

Her brain whispered commands into the *Messenger's* computer; '*Bring up estimated gravity fields that might effect our travel, give me the position of every ship that's identified as friendly, and give me every scrap of information about the planets, moons, and rocks in this system.*'

The computer complied. First, she saw a chart of roughly two dozen bodies and their gravity wells. Obviously, the largest one was that yellow star - Her vessel was already in it, of course, as the entire PX-31 system revolved around it, but she was still very safely located in perspective to, say, getting captured by its gravitational forces and, as a result, being incinerated. There were others, too; planetary ones and even lunar ones. Large moons had quite the pull of their own, even if they were locked into orbit with their host planet! All of these had to be considered; stable orbits were useful to an enemy planning a defensive posture, while navigating with the gravity wells in mind would give just *that* extra bit of mobility that might keep the ship's crew alive in the face of disaster.

As she dwelled on navigation, she gazed over to the chief navigators' chair. It was empty, and Lahira frowned to herself, fearful that Ensign Grant had taken a step backwards in her recovery. She couldn't afford to get lost in thought; she looked, next, at the files containing data about the Human fleet's position. The main force was entering past PX-31--IV, the fourth planet of the system and the only one which seemed to have life-forms on it - after all, it fit all of the classic information for a habitable world, even considering the Orphans' silicone-based structure.

"Ensign Travares," the Captain commanded verbally, "give me a scan of the fourth world, here? I need to know what the population on it is."

The Hispanic trill of the man's voice echoed through her ears. "Aye, Captain," he answered. The data was retrieved almost instantly, and she could see the numbers being broadcast over the *Messenger*'s systems, providing the third thing Lahira had requested. Just over thirty million? It wasn't a large world, judging by the gravity signature, but for it to be so underpopulated? Humanity would love a colony like this! Hell, it could even have evolved here!

Nevertheless, she watched digitally as the *George Washington*, *Sun Tzu*, and the rest of Humanity's main force began to flood the star-system, moving right toward that fourth world. She smirked to herself - none of the vessels reported being under fire, yet, and no scans had returned any devious traps like mines or computer viruses.

She gazed upward as the bridge door opened and Kelly Grant, still wearing a heavy bandage on her head (concealed under a hat), stepped in. Once more, Lahira had to pull herself out of the stream of data - she'd seen the new arrival, but still couldn't act while deeply submerged in the digital river. The chubby woman saluted the Captain; she smiled warmly and returned it. "Ensign Grant," Lahira queried, "are you cleared for duty by the medical staff?"

"They've left the final call up to you, ma'am," she responded, lowering her head slightly. There was a moment of uncertainty, a second of silence. Despite what they'd talked about while her subordinate was high, there was no way to be sure that it had stuck - at least, not on her end!

Then, Lahira laughed once. "Welcome back to service, Ensign," she remarked reassuringly. As the large woman waddled to her chair, the Captain felt a strange sense of relief. "I'm forwarding you all the navigational charts and scenarios I've come up with," she stated swiftly. Suddenly, Lahira realized this might have been ill thought out! "If you have any changes to make," she concluded cordially, "let me know, because they're gonna be great."

As Lahira connected her mind more deeply into the communications network of her ship, she sent a mental signature that her crew was ready for the mission. It would be a simple, direct, hit-hard operation - eliminate the Orphan presence in the system and destroy the enemy's will to fight.

When the last check-in was confirmed, a message from Admiral Owens spoke into the back of the Captain's mind. "Do your best," he whispered reassuringly, "and although its out of favor these days, God-Speed." The man's faith, a rarity in the late twenty-fifth century, didn't sit badly with her - of course, it didn't sit happily, either, since she didn't share that devotion.

"Hit it," Lahira stated forcefully, her eyes shifting to the former pirate who headed up her engineering department, Ensign Jackie "Jack-O-Lantern" Quan.

The red-headed renegade grinned. "Aye Captain," she returned, bringing the vessel's public-announcement system in to cause her voice to echo rather powerfully, "burning at full speed!" The shock-mounts on the *Messenger*'s bridge prevented the command center from lurching too greatly, but the ship as a whole certainly responded as its drives spun up to full speed.

Instead of just slowly approaching the bright yellow star in the distance, now they were coming in fast! They whizzed by the sixth planet in the system - or, at least, its orbit, as it happened to be on the other side of its cycle. The Humans banked over the fifth planet slowly, and just as they'd planned, the weapons aboard the *Messenger* were ready to unleash hell upon the first thing they caught moving.

"Attention all hands," Lahira declared calmly, her words being dispersed across the vessel, "we have enemy contact on scanners! Orbitals and ships! Prepare for combat!"

The deep, calm voice of Ensign Trusaunt, the defense chief, announced casually, "We are piping the tactical results into the network now!"

Lahira watched carefully as the tiny green blips signifying enemy combatants emerged on the screen, overlaid perfectly by the computer and holding a strict contrast to the silver-white of the Human ones. Ships that were hidden by the planet that the *Messenger* was passing were highlighted by a sketch of their approximate shape and position, allowing Lahira to know exactly where to strike. There was also a quickly-sketched icon indicating a large docking facility; one that most definitely had defensive equipment, but was intended for resupplying the Orphan fleet. It had multiple wings, much like branches on a tree; the docks, most likely, complete with air-locks and service-cranes. Some of those vessel-outlines, belonging to both species, illuminated with a sudden, red blink - a sign that they were being fired upon by their opponents.

"I want our entire detachment to isolate ships that aren't already under attack. We can't let *any* of them get free shots on the rest of the fleet! I need confirmation that our nukes are coded in!" Every last vessel returned a positive result to that question. "Good. Use 'em. We're hitting hard, hitting fast. Sixty seconds to impact. Like the Admiral said," she found herself repeating, stumbling only an instant as she came to that recognition, "God-speed!"

As the *Messenger* crested over the fifth planet in the PX-31 system and came into full view of the battle raging between Human and Orphan forces, its Captain couldn't help but wince. At least one Human vessel was smoldering, already - a destroyer - and another was limping along, hardly able to move. Orphan losses had been about the same, but Lahira didn't really seem to recognize that as an advantage. The space between the two fast-moving forces was filled with tiny little planes firing rockets and bullets at one another, creating a bouquet of explosions that filled the void with tiny shards of steel and glass.

Here, the Orphans clearly had an advantage - their orbital stations, while each was frantically firing two of those now-infamous laser cannons, served primarily as docking locales for those little fighter planes. Add to that a rather sizable contingent of the swept-wing, sneaky fighters coming up from their target planet, and the Orphans had perhaps a two-to-one advantage in the skies! The *Sun Tzu* and *George Washington*, Humanity's two *Alexander*-class battleships, were putting their point-defense weaponry to the test, keeping the tiny planes off of them.

The Orphan side of the coin wasn't faring so well, either; many of their vessels had the quickly-growing-familiar gaping holes in their bows. Judging from radiation signatures (or, the lack thereof), they hadn't lost any ships as of yet - but that was bound to change sooner or later. They were firing back, alright; green explosions occasionally rocked the Human fleet, and their red rays of death were bludgeoning Humanity's re-purposed anti-asteroid shields. They hadn't come unprepared to fight - but they certainly weren't fighting ships made of straw, either. Human fighters attacking the Orphan docking station were brave, but held at bay by the alien point-defense weapons.

　　　　With the battle in full view, it was time for decisive action. The Captain isolated her detachment's communications line, once again. "All ships under my command, our next objective is their nearest orbital station and launch your fighters and rockets. I want it taken out!" Lahira commanded swiftly, mentally highlighting one of the three large facilities which were constantly refueling and re-arming Orphan vessels. "As soon as you get firing solutions on their ships, hit them with your main cannons and fire your nukes!"

　　　　She felt, digitally, the dull thud of her vessel's four rail-guns fire just as she issued the order, and she watched on her monitors as the rest of her detachment followed suit. The dense, metallic projectiles took a few seconds to reach their targets, but upon impact? The *Messenger*'s salvo punched clean through one of the smaller Orphan vessels - potentially a killing shot. Almost a hundred rockets fired from the Human detachment, the exhaust from their engines creating tiny tendrils of smoke, forming a trail from their launch locations toward their destination. Following this trail were fighter planes, headed on a daring strike of an orbital outpost.

　　　　But it always came down to the nukes. Gavin Trusaunt wasn't a weapons expert, but he was no fool with them, either. "Nuclear warheads one, two, three, and four away, ma'am!" he announced before falling strangely still in his seat, steering the weapons from within the *Messenger*'s command center. Ten other missiles were screaming toward enemy ships from Lahira's detachment, alone. This prompted a rather bold counter-move from the Orphans - they set their fighters upon the Human warheads!

One of rockets Lahira had launched was quickly intercepted and destroyed before it could even achieve fusion. Another weapon from one of the *Bantam*-class ships in the squadron was picked off after that point, claiming a few alien fighters, yet sparing its actual target. Nevertheless, most of the missiles found purchase against the Orphan ships - and many of them came out of the onslaught limping. Orphan fighter planes continued to close in on Lahira's detachment, but that's why her cruiser had point-defense weaponry!

Everything was looking up for the crew of the *Messenger*; at least, until a trio of spectacular green explosions emerged atop the *George Washington*.

As her former home was engulfed in green flames, Lahira's eyes widened. "Admiral!" she whispered hoarsely, fearful of what had just happened to her former commander, James Owens. She imagined the old man clutching his cross at the last moment, lying in his chair, draped in electrodes and whispering a prayer to himself. The Orphan warheads were far more advanced than Humanity's; and the green, carbon-based missiles they fired created super-nova grade explosions on condensed scales. It was rare for a ship to emerge unscathed from one.

The *George Washington* had just sustained impacts from *three*.

"We can't lose our focus!" shouted Ensign Jackie Quan, unfazed. "And I need all of our power to amplify our shield generators, *now!*" the former pirate roared, practically turning the ship's thrusters off in order to repel the heavy cannon fire coming from the inbound alien fighters. The Orphans had comparable technology to Humanity, when it came to this aspect of warfare - propelled slugs of metal and high-explosive, shape-charged ship-to-ship missiles. The former was hardly effective against the *Messenger*'s thick titanium armor; the latter was quite destructive.

First, tiny blue spheres emerged in the view of the

Messenger's cameras. Next, red plumes of light began to appear as missiles exploded against the blue barricade. Designed primarily to repel asteroid impacts at faster-than-light speed, those shields were quite sturdy - but they weren't invincible. They relied on shifting "projectors" that couldn't cover all areas of a ship at one time while simultaneously using their full repulsive power. They certainly weren't rated to tolerate multiple strikes over a long duration. The Orphan interceptors were like a horde of bees, swarming her detachment and making sure her defenses couldn't regenerate. That explained why, after half a minute of savage beating, they began to gave way - and the *Messenger's* armor was left to absorb the impacts.

The vessel's shock-mounted bridge was protected from the bulk of the momentum shifting, but Lahira could feel her ship's digital profile vibrating as it was bludgeoned. "Dammit!" she shouted, looking over toward Gavin. "How long until the next volley is launched?"

"About sixty seconds, Captain!" he responded, his eyes moving rapidly across his field of view as he, presumably, addressed various minor defense-related concerns such as "which planes are down" and "how badly did the last strafing damage the ship's armor?"

She frowned darkly. "Ensign Grant!"

The wounded woman, who was feared to be too injured to navigate until just before the battle, looked up at her commander. "Captain?"

"I need you to plot out firing solutions for as many of our ship-to-ship rockets as possible."

Surprised, Kelly responded, "Already do--"

She never finished that sentence. "Good! Now re-plot them to target as many fighters as you can." She anticipated a plea of protest, and didn't even slow down her speech; "I know you can do this, Kelly, you're the best, and I need this herd thinned!"

"Thirty seconds, Captain," warned the defense chief, his eyes dancing toward the ongoing fracas between Human and

Orphan fleets.

The dust was clearing around the *George Washington* and, much to the surprise of many, the vessel was still intact - if, of course, a liberal variant of the word were used. Its armor had been boiled away to thin, useless chaff and its shield generators, external cameras, and missile ports were mostly ruined.

"Its a sitting duck," whispered Ensign Travares, the communications officer. "Admiral Owens is transmitting orders, still! We've got our old man, but he's in a bad way!"

"Rockets launched!" roared the defense chief. "Sixty three percent had reprogrammed aiming coordinates!"

Lahira's lips twitched, and she wasn't sure which way they were trying to go. She wanted to smile because before her eyes over half of her ship's arsenal unloaded against the multitude of fighter planes that were harassing them, turning oh-so-many of them into scrap. The rest headed toward their original target, a besieged orbital outpost that was fixing up, reloading and re-launching those same fighters. "Great job!" she announced, looking Ensign Grant right in the eye.

But none of it eliminated the cause of her lips wanting to turn downward - the Human fleet was taking casualties, and the *George Washington* was virtually defenseless, with only limited point-defense capacity. Worse, a number of Orphan fighters were already breaking off of their original attack plans and heading for the easy kill.

"Ensign Trusaunt," Lahira asked in as neutral a voice as she could muster, "I need a solution on the old man. We need to keep him in the game."

Her response came from an unexpected source. "I've got one idea," responded Ensign Quan, "But it ain't gonna be pretty!"

"I don't care if its pretty," Lahira answered grimly, watching on the *Messenger*'s video-screens as the Human fleet was pummeled. "We need to help the Admiral, so hit me with it!"

The Ensign frowned. "Misdirection. When my old outfit used to hit larger targets, we'd give 'em a decoy or two. We need to book it, but we can jump into the line of fire."

"Unwise!" responded the defense chief, Gavin Trusaunt. He frowned. "There's just no way we can take that kind of beating."

The Captain cursed inwardly and turned her eyes toward her chief navigator. "Kelly, get us in position." The hat-wearing woman nodded.

"Captain, we're going to get killed if we do that!" interjected the Magellaner in charge of defensive affairs. The hat-wearer hesitated.

"Ensign Grant!" she bit her bottom lip. "Program in a rotation for us to pass in front of the *George Washington* with our right side facing the Orphan forces." Slowly, Lahira's eyes turned toward her communications chief. "Travares, Get the *Sun Tzu*. Tell them what we're doing. Tell them to get ready to cross in front of us three seconds after we intercept the old man."

Ensign Travares suddenly grew a smirk on his lips, from where there was once a frown. "I see!" He almost sounded like a schoolboy who was proud of being the first to have an answer to a teachers' question. "Leapfrogging, huh?" Kelly was busy transmitting coordinates.

Trusaunt didn't seem convinced, a stick in the mud to the end. "Its still insane!"

"This is war! We're already fuckin' crazy!" shouted back the ex-outlaw. For a moment, it seemed as if old conflicts were threatening to brew.

That's when Lahira nodded her head toward Gavin confidently. He relaxed subtly, showing a subconscious acceptance of the situation's seriousness - and the advantage a lack of sanity could bestow. "Gun the engines, Ensign," Lahira ordered. "Quan, make sure we have maximum power available."

"Aye, Captain," the engineering expert responded in a definitive manner. The *Messenger* roared forward, ready to absorb some of the damage the *George Washington* was enduring.

Halfway between where the *Messenger* started and its goal, it readied a new volley of rockets - as well as a new burst of rail-gun rounds. She ordered them used aggressively, the rockets (and a couple nuclear warheads) finishing off their target - an Orphan orbital base, the first of three - in a spectacular, green explosion. More-over, under Gavin's direction the *Messenger* fired her rail-guns toward the large docking station where the Orphans had apparently hoped to rebuild and re-load their warships. It took over ten seconds, but the projectiles collided with their target, splintering an entire wing off of the facility! It was a serious blow against their long-term war effort: Exactly what Humanity came to PX-31 to achieve.

Of course, the Orphans weren't admitting defeat. This latest aggression only served to attract another half-dozen squadrons worth of fighter planes, as if the Humans only had one vessel which could threaten them. Their priority was clear - to keep the carbon-based life-form from doing any more damage to their most vital installation in the system. Fortunately, Lahira's was just as clear - to defend her commanding officer while he was vulnerable! There was only one problem...

...The fighters broke the *Messenger*'s shields once more, despite Jackie's best efforts, and their missiles were both voluminous and well-aimed enough to cripple the shield generators on the right-hand side of the ship.

Making matters worse, one of the Orphan ships took this window of opportunity to launch a series of six carbon-radiation-emitting rockets - supernova missiles - toward the *George Washington*. "Captain, we have to abort - Now!" shouted, of all people, Ensign Quan. "We take one of their missiles head-on, and we're a pile of ashes!"

Lahira clenched her fists tightly. "Ensign Grant, what's our inertia like?"

"Not good," responded the wounded woman, growling softly to herself. "We were going in too hot, Captain. I could fire all of our air-brakes three times over, and we're *still* going to cross the *George Washington*'s path!"

"I'm putting out every jamming and disorienting signal I can," stated Lucas Travares carefully; electronic interference might help make some of the Orphan weapons miss their marks, but would it really save the *Messenger* from the all-out barrage that they intended to take on behalf of Admiral Owens' ship?

"I've got it," whispered Lahira softly. She closed her eyes, focusing on navigational formulas.

A deep voice cut into her work, that of Gavin Trusaunt, and it was a voice with a grim resignation behind it. "This was a mistake. I warned you, we are just sacrificing our lives for nothing of importance." As the bridge threatened to break down into chaos, Lahira's mind slowly left her body.

Lahira was too busy calculating engine bursts and air brakes to reply to Gavin. The *Messenger*'s braking systems involved the ventilation of large pockets of air out of various exhaust ports, along with the occasional activation of controlled chemical explosives, all working together to create carefully coordinated thrusts of energy that would steer the vessel directly. She also had to compensate for gravity, as well as inbound fire from the Orphan defenses. This was a massively difficult task - and she wasn't even sure she could pull it off.

"Ensign Grant," Lahira whispered almost to herself, her consciousness locked primarily into the digital world through the cable plugged into the back of her head. After not receiving a response, she spoke a slight bit louder. "Ensign Grant?"

Kelly gazed over at her, adjusting her hat carefully - she didn't want to disconnect herself from the *Messenger*'s network. "Yeah?"

"Verify..." she ran the numbers one more time, then sent them digitally; "This."

After a moments' hesitation, she heard a voice. "Wow." Before the Captain could demand a verbal or written answer, a green confirmation light emerged in her mental view - a 'yes.' Lahira gave her engines their orders.

The bridge, despite all of its shock-mounting and artificial gravity, was not entirely prepared for such serious emission of energy. The vessel as a whole lurched and rolled, with most of the kinetic energy getting dispersed before it reached the command center. Nevertheless, some of its officers lost their footing and others had to grasp anything they could find to stay afoot. That aforementioned gravity was the only reason why the staff didn't end up on the roof! Inside of the ship, it was just a minor earth-quake, with mild stumbling.

Viewed from outside, on the other hand, the *Messenger* nearly did a flip. Instead of running straight across the front of the *George Washington* and focusing all of its defensive energy to the starboard bow, Captain Ocean put the more-than-1,600 foot long cruiser into a slow, controlled barrel-roll. Instead of starboard, where a recent strafing run by Orphan fighters had pinpointed and pummeled its shield-generators, the *Messenger* now had its port side facing the inbound missiles; their exhaust trails drawing thin lines from their launch point right toward the Human fleet.

"Holy shit!" shouted Jackie Quan, the former pirate, as she clenched her teeth. "*That*'s a good fuckin' move, Captain! Focusing shield generators on likely impact sites!" It was high praise, coming from a reformed blockade-runner. "Redirecting power!" The *Messenger*'s cameras kept a tight view of the incoming missiles, even as the ship passed in front of the *George Washington*.

His eyes narrowed, Ensign Travares barked quickly, "Got two, best I could---" He never finished that sentence. True to his word, however, one of the missiles went wide while a second exploded - non-critically - in space just before it reached the ship. That 'only' left four of the missiles en route to the ship.

And each one struck true, creating four large, green eruptions on the *Messenger*'s side. Lahira growled as she fell to the floor; the rest of the ship's crew, far closer to consciousness than its Captain, managed to avoid mimicking their superior. The severing of her connection to the ship's computer wasn't as complete as her last experience, but it still led to a massive pain ripping through her skull. She clenched her fists, struggling not so much to get back up but, rather, to keep a mental focus on her sense of time. Three seconds. Two. One. Would it work?

When she felt the pit of her stomach move toward her

throat and felt herself very nearly come off of the ground, she knew she'd succeeded in plotting her course properly. The *Messenger* endured its four punches and it veered as far down as possible - a move made just before the *Sun Tzu* jumped in front of the *George Washington* to continue providing it with defense. The only question now was whether or not it was worth it - because, as Lahira knew too well, she'd only succeeded with one aspect of the fight. Unfortunately, the pain in her head began to blot out the stunned, cheering voices of her subordinates and she couldn't keep track of what followed.

*****

The soft, whispered voice echoed softly against the silent, darkened backdrop of the *George Washington's* bridge. "What was she thinking...?" he whispered, words that he would have loved to ask the woman directly - if, of course, his communications equipment was fully operational. He subconsciously clenched a fist around the cross dangling from his neck, as the network of wires attached to electrodes and affixed to his flesh rattled from his struggles to look toward one of the vessel's display screens. It wasn't necessary - his mind, if not his eyes, could see everything of importance going on in the battle around him.

Of course, most of that information was coming from sensors, now, and not cameras - the bulk of those had been knocked out of commission by the alien forces. He couldn't actually see his former navigator's ship but he could certainly tell what kind of shape it was in - and he definitely, with amazement, watched as it absorbed all four missiles meant to end his life. It had already been beaten up, and he frankly found it to be miraculous (something he, unlike so many of his unconscious, absorbed-by-the-digital-world subordinates, truly believed in!) that she had avoided a direct hit against her ship's unshielded areas!

But now? The *Sun Tzu* stood in front of his ship - Lahira

had managed to dance her vessel out of the line of fire after enduring its four latest impacts - and the cutting-edge cruiser certainly didn't intend to go down without a fight. He could watch the streams of data that were injected into his field of view, and as long as he remained concentrated upon that flood of electrical impulses he remained semi-conscious and within the realm of cybernetics. He observed, electronically, as Lahira's vessel fired its arsenal one more time, sending not one, but two Orphan opponents to their demise. It was swiftly joined by the *Sun Tzu*, which moved between the *Messenger* and it's latest victims just in time to intercept their death yell.

And then the newest *Alexander*-class battleship opened fire, it's heavy railguns pummeling the Orphan ranks. Oh, the *Sun Tzu* ate its share of those supernova-warhead missiles, but its shield generators were...Well, existent, which was sure as hell better than the *George Washington*'s were, right now! And the *Messenger* needed the break, as well. James Owens could finally see the battle's end-game evolve before him.

Humanity's forces had just barely managed to avoid annihilation. It had lost some of its smaller ships, but the *George Washington*, the fleet's flagship, was crippled - a 'dead stick,' as they called it. This was bad - and the fact that the *Messenger* had managed to save their lives while absorbing another barrage of fire and, at the same time, setting the *Sun Tzu* up with its' present tactical situation of finishing off multiple enemies. It wasn't ideal, but it was sustainable as long as the battleship managed to hold up.

The Orphan fleet, on the other hand, wasn't doing too well for itself. If their ammunition doctrines were anything like Humanity's, they had depleted most of their carbon-fusion weaponry. They still had their powerful laser cannons, but the Human anti-asteroid shields could, without the constant harassment of interceptors and missiles, handle that level of damage. Its orbital defense stations were either crippled or simply gone. Its star-ships were showing no signs of retreat, but were rapidly being beaten down.

It was something of an unfortunate stalemate, and he had just the thing to break it - unfortunately, Ensign Travares' successor simply wasn't sure if he could communicate with another ship. If he could? Well, it was moot - he had to have hope that his former navigator was as good as she'd always hinted at.

*****

"She's out!" shouted Ensign Quan, looking over toward the Captain and shaking her head. "She's talkin', lights are on, nobody's home."

Gavin looked over the ships' defensive capabilities. Almost all of its rocket pods were damaged, it had just one operational nuclear launch tube, and even its fighter reserves were low - many good men had died in the space between the alien and Human fleets. As far as shield generators went, things were even worse - much like the *George Washington*, most of the equipment on the ship's exterior had been ruined by the carbon-fusion missiles that the Orphans employed. He knew the *Sun Tzu* had just taken another barrage of them, but the *Messenger*'s radiological sensors had stopped screaming afterward. It didn't look as though the aliens had any more of their top-class armament to fire.

It also didn't hurt that their numbers were rapidly fading.

"We still have full power!" Quan added, paying token responsibility to her area of expertise.

The second-in-command, or rather the acting boss of the vessel, was Ensign Lucas Travares. His specialty was communications - not tactics, not engineering, and not even navigation. He wasn't a combat specialist, but he *was* a quick thinker! He also heard the enemy communications and had translations (bad, but workable) on what he had managed to decrypt. "Ensign Grant, I need one more controlled navigational burn. We're heading down, again. I need us to bank back toward the Orphans."

"Has the Captain's madness spread to you, Ensign?!" exclaimed Gavin - after all, he had strongly opposed the initial tactical decisions to save the *George Washington* and, consequently, nearly cripple their own ship.

Lucas bit his bottom lip. "Ensign Grant?"

Kelly exhaled slowly. "Aye sir, burning..." she hesitated. The bridge crew clamped their hands down on anything they could find. "Now!" The ship trembled as it brought its front-side back toward the battle.

"Alright!" shouted the communications expert. "Ensign Trusaunt, I need you to target their docking station." It had been Humankind's purpose for the attack in this system, labeled PX-31. It was where the Orphans most probably made their attack on planet Hudson, and that docking set-up was most probably the tip of the javelin aimed toward Humankind's heart.

Trusaunt didn't seem to get the plan. "Sir, its already crippl--"

"Gavin, trust me, do it! Rail-guns two and four are still operational." Travares' peppery Spanish accent was evident in a tongue roll; in spite of a snide grin he plastered onto his lips. "Splinter it - split it in pieces."

The taller of the two men sighed. "Aye, sir, I've given up trying to understand," he resigned himself. The mentally-projected signals of the *Messenger*'s computers piped in confirmations that the heavy rounds were fired. The ship's frontal cameras still functioned, despite the electricity spikes that constantly interrupted the feeds, and the crew could see as the docking station finally broke into large, blocky chunks.

"Unload a nuclear weapon..." Lucas paused, plotting a chart in the back of his head. "Here!" He highlighted a place with absolutely nothing in it - an area of space completely unoccupied by alien vessels. The entire bridge crew could see it! "I need it to detonate here!"

"Bird's away!" announced the gloomy chief of defense.

Ensign Quan blinked slowly, gazing up at Lucas. "Boss, are you thinking...?"

"I'd call Lahira's move the Ocean Wave. Call this the Travares Claymore!" The communications chief grinned as the nuclear warhead detonated. The heavy, Copernicum-based metal of the devastated docking station was hardly damaged by the explosion - but the shock-wave *did* propel the relatively light shards of steel outward with an immense amount of speed.

It propelled them just like rail-gun rounds, right into the Orphan fleet, crippling two of their larger ships and impaling a third straight up the middle, causing it to explode in a shower of similarly dangerous shrapnel. The Human anti-asteroid shields were designed for just this occasion, while the alien vessels were not. Gavin Trusaunt stared in wonder, his lips curling into a thin grin before he began to laugh maniacally.

Somehow, the communications expert knew the old man would be proud.

Chapter Nine
Front And Center

She found herself, again, on the bridge of the *George Washington*. It had only been a couple weeks since her last time in the battleship's command-center, but so much about her charge had changed since she'd left. For starters? The exterior of the vessel was heavily beaten. Oh, repair crews were in shuttles and space-suits working on the vessel, installing new shield-generators and repairing crippled weapons, but it was a long way away from serviceable. The same couldn't be said for the man standing with her, Admiral Owens, despite the damage done to his fleet.

"You two are insane," he stated politely toward his former chief-navigator and chief-communications officer, Lucas Travares, as he shook hands with the two, a wry smile on his lips. "But you helped win the day. Now, we just need to make a break-through with the situation on the ground."

Gavin Trusaunt, an expert on military doctrine and Lahira's chief defense officer, had filed his report already - and he was far from alone in the conclusion he reached. The Human force had no chance of invading the fourth planet of the PX-31 system, and their best bets, regarding the use of armed force, were whittled down to either a blockade, or the outright annihilation of the world's inhabitants. It came down, in the end, to simple logistics. Humanity hadn't brought along a half-billion soldiers to suppress the inhabitants of a planet, which was likely what it would take to even begin to impose a semblance of order. The use of nuclear bombs to destroy the world's inhabitants was an option, but it was a sickening one - Mankind frowned upon genocide, even after its enemies brought that threat upon them unilaterally. But then there was the option of a blockade, which was surely prone to its own set of problems.

Of course, he had suggested, there was also diplomacy - if

the Orphans were interested such a logical pursuit. So far, every message beamed down to the Orphan world had resulted in a complete dearth of response. It would have to be a blockade, then, one that fed into the attempts at communication. Human occupation of this world might not be possible, but the space around the system could be held - although it wouldn't prove to be an easy task. The *Messenger* and the *George Washington* were both badly damaged, and the *Sun Tzu* wasn't in the best shape Lahira had ever seen a battleship in, either.

What made the prospect of a blockade a daunting one was that Grand Admiral Winters' fleet was the strongest Humankind had at its disposal, and it was assigned, appropriately, to defend Humanity and its home-worlds. So far, only scouting missions in the vicinity of Earth's holdings had been detected (and swiftly destroyed), but the Admiralty was convinced that these probes were just assessments of where the Human fleet would have the greatest difficulty responding.

There was no help coming from Admiral Nunez' third fleet, either. Consisting mostly of civilian ships that had been re-fitted with weapons and primarily intended to train new crewmen to take over the next generation of warship, it was still hardly anything more than a series of targets for the Orphans to demolish. They were private ships that were purchased by the government (mostly from mothballs, to make matters worse!) in order to serve as a fleet of desperation. They were mere privateers, fit for little more than cannon fodder, although Lahira had a subtle suspicion that they would be more effective than most planners gave them credit for.

After all, as she recalled from her studies of history, the Spanish armada was the mightiest on planet Earth - until it met a combination of bad weather and English privateers. Then, it became scrap and driftwood. Privateers, throughout another phase of the historical record, were often known as "pirates" to those who boarded and looted their ships, causing all sorts of mayhem for foreign powers, forcing colonial powers to spend money on security, and often helping to determine the winners of wars.

Naturally, this was a vastly different situation. Naturally, Lahira thought to herself, these privateers would only have the government-regulated standard shield generators (typical warships had three times as many), they would most likely be slower and bulkier (they carried cargo). Most of all, they wouldn't have very many weapons - although some of the larger cargo ships were being refitted as aircraft carriers, and the Captain was fascinated to read about ways that empty storage space was being improvised into combat-effective assets; additional armor or improved weapons capacity.

Human foundries were churning out ships at a break-neck pace. Almost every day there was *some* vessel rolling off the production lines. Most likely, these too were formerly destined for civilian purposes but, with the war going on, would be used by the military; on the plus side, they would have been factory-refitted as opposed to tweaked after the fact, meaning that they would have far better defensive mechanisms and far more suitable weaponry.

It wasn't, as Ensign Quan had explained to her, *that* tough to renovate a vessel to be combat-capable. "Pirates do it all the time! Speaking of," the reformed criminal had said, "Many of my former colleagues and crime syndicates came forward with some of their gear - in exchange for amnesty, appointments, and cash. You know the deal." Lahira did - it was just like when colonial-era pirates who specialized in harassing one country ended up knighted by another. Moreover, when Jackie explained to her *exactly* how easy it was to saw out the hull plating over an unused cargo hold, insert some improvised rocket pods or computer-aimed guns, hook up electricity and seal it all against space, well, it all made Lahira feel a bit better about the promised Third Fleet.

Of course, she was the only one, except maybe for the former pirate. An awkward team to be on, after all! But, perhaps, a winning one. Hers', after all, was in rehab.

With the *George Washington*, *Messenger*, and *Sun Tzu* undergoing field repairs, the Human fleet in the PX-31 system was vulnerable. Reinforcements were scheduled to trickle in - a destroyer was due in a day, a *Bantam*-class vessel a day and a half out - but they were poor substitutes for having fully functional battleships and cruisers. More to the point, if the Orphans moved a fleet into position to counter-attack, the Humans would be lucky to run away before they were crushed. Their primary objective - destroying the alien's refueling depot - was already accomplished! Did they even *need* to stick around?

"We've decided," James Owens, the Admiral of the Second Fleet stated to the officers gathered at the *George Washington*'s bridge, "that we're going to blockade this system." This was no surprise, but Lahira Ocean sighed nevertheless. "We have some reinforcements coming in, as you probably know, and we have a great deal of firepower available to us even as our capital ships are repaired."

The *Messenger*'s Captain turned her eyes upon the old man's, slowly. She knew for a fact he was bluffing. Oh, there was plenty of power in the Human fleet, but could it parry an Orphan riposte?

"I don't expect us to have to hold off against their whole host," the Admiral clarified carefully, "but we've already coordinated with our communications specialists and we have our eyes to the sky. If they head our way, we'll know and we can fall back. I've made sure that our repairs are focused all on one vessel at a time, starting with the *Sun Tzu* - and they're already almost done with that particular task."

Lahira smiled dryly. Progress was important, but without supplies? Without a proper docking station? Owens continued, "If we *do* fall under attack, or if we sense any incoming enemies, we will be able to pack up our repairmen and head back to Hudson." It was a rough gamble, but the Admiral had been a winner in the past. In fact, he'd taught *her* to be a winner, too. Maybe this gamble would be another winning one.

"I've thought it over," he continued, "and I would very much like to hold this system. If we can get the Orphans to negotiate, we might get some insight into---"

"Admiral!" chirped one of the men in the communications suite. "We have an incoming transmission."

Jackie Quan blinked her eyes, twice. "That's...Wow. Fuckin' clever, huh? Well timed!" she remarked, a grin cracking over her lips. Nobody else seemed to be as happy.

"The message was all text, but in our language. I'll put it up on the screen," the communicator offered. The Admiral nodded and waited as the display screens of the *George Washington's* bridge illuminated with words, symbols that scrolled up the middle of it as if they were the title to a 1970's science-fiction film.

"You are not of our kind."
"You kill our kind."
"We will not bow to you."
"Our kind will return to us."
"To save us, or our souls."

"That's reassuring," exhaled Lahira softly. She was not the only one to express doubts, either verbally or gesturally, that there was a hope of resolution.

The Admiral read these words and canted his head to the side. "Send a reply. Make it clear - We mean them no harm. Their people attacked us. We're just trying to make an end to the conflict, before it gets any worse. Send it *exactly* where you got the message. Ask if we can meet with them, somehow. If we could send someone down to the planet, or if they'll send someone up. Something!" He sighed, with his fingertips drumming against his chin thoughtfully. "Be fair, but be firm."

The Admiral didn't craft the message, himself. He was a lot of things, but was he a diplomat? Not so much, no. He especially was not an expert on communicating with alien races, and that fact went double when it was applied to aliens that wanted to wipe Humanity out. There was a definitive defensive posture taken by the Orphans who had messaged the Human fleet; their language promised self-preservation instead of overwhelming hatred, but there was still an attitude of self-imposed exile coming from them.

"In the meantime," the Admiral carried on, "We have a little more business to discuss. There's a little extra help coming in. The Aquarians have volunteered a small detachment to help defend our systems - its strictly defensive only. The Grand Admiral is going to release a cruiser and two destroyers to join up with us. As to our other, surprising allies..."

He sighed, softly, rubbing his forehead as if he was rather disappointed at the foreign response. "The Firions abjectly refuse to be, as they put it, commanded by us. To us, that just means they're not interested in communication, making them almost more trouble than they're worth. On the up-side? They're going to conduct their war the way they see fit, and we all know they are rather aggressive."

A slight, sad smile tugged at his lips. "So for now, we just wait for a--"

"Admiral!" exclaimed that same, perfectly-timed man in communications. "We have a reply! I'll put it up on the screen!" he stated with renowned foresight, earning a nod from the old man. The message was better than they had hoped.

"We know your words."
"We listen, we learn."
"We will answer them with our own."
"Coordinates to follow."
"Rules to be followed."

Smirking dryly, the Admiral nodded. "Seems we have some shuttle-craft to put together, as well as a delegation."

*****

Gavin Trusaunt clenched his fist and shook his head. "Captain, again, at the risk of repeating myself *ad infinitum*," he roared bodily, "this is insanity!"

"What, is that your fuckin' catch-phrase?" chirped Jackie Quan with a grin. Oddly enough, however, her tone was quite serious. "The woman's made up her mind. It's fuckin' stupid," she added forcefully, glaring to her Captain, "but I guess we have the choice of following her, or letting her go off on her own."

Throwing his hands up, the tall man looked from the ex-con to his fellow Magellaner with a frown. "As you wish, Ensign," he responded with resignation.

"Captain, even I'm not so sure about this," Lucas Travares added slyly. "I mean, I understand why I'm going. I understand why Ensign Trusaunt is. Hell, I even get why the loud-mouth is coming a--"

"Hey!" interrupted Jackie with a half-concealed laugh, "that's Ensign Loud-Mouth!"

The Captain sighed loudly, ending the conversation before it could continue. Lahira's office, where the four were meeting, did a great job of keeping sound-waves from leaving it; but it certainly didn't do a good job of keeping them from bouncing off of the walls and driving straight into her brain. She massaged her temples for a moment, shutting out the tone of their voices. "Ensign Quan is going to investigate their architecture and whatever equipment they carry, and I'm going because I can make executive decisions on the Admiral's behalf."

Gavin didn't seem to hear her. "We have no idea what they will contemplate doing to us."

"They won't do anything, unless they want to get nuked. And you're going armed, right?" the Captain's tone was matter-of-fact, her mind unwavering.

"Yes," the defense officer responded, "but we'll be outnumbered and dead long before they have to worry about our missiles hitting them. I don't even think the fleet has enough ammunition left to totally burn this world, and I can't imagine they'd feel any differently if we did."

She continued to rub her temples, fingertips roving downward over her face slowly. Black strands of hair were brushed aside. "Listen carefully, Ensign, because I'm saying this once more. I'm going. You aren't changing that. Ensign Grant can keep the *Messenger* afloat for now, and you notice how she's not objecting to this course of action?" There was, after all, one un-occupied seat in the Captain's office. "I know it goes against most protocols for a Captain to go into hostile territory all by her lonesome, but I'm not alone. I have people I trust. Gavin, Jackie, and Lucas - we're gonna be fine. I'm sure of it."

Lucas smiled, his spicy accent peppering the room once again. "So am I. I will, after all, be leading this discussion. I've studied what information we have available on their lexicon. This will be a breeze, although it may not be a gentle one." He looked slowly toward Gavin, and his gaze was joined by Jackie's.

Before the ex-pirate could speak, however, Lahira sat upright. "Oh!" she added indifferently, "I just remembered. Grand Admiral Winters wants you to take a look at some documents, before you go. I'm sending it to you all, now. Take a look, here."

Images emerged on the screen of various technical diagrams. Some of them were direct visual scans from shattered Orphan vessels, while the remainder were digital reproductions of the fully-functioning real thing. The ensign grinned to herself. "The boss is really lookin' into those laser-cannons, huh?" stated the former outlaw, mentally grasping the blueprints and shifting them around, spreading the multiple energy-focusing lenses as if they were flower petals and subsequently closing them all in the name of testing out the authenticity of the collected data.

"She is, indeed," Lahira agreed softly. "What do you think of her work, so far?"

Jackie shrugged neutrally. "Good question. If I can get myself a good look at one of these things? If I can get the right materials? I can fuckin' build one by myself."

"Good, because we're hoping you get to see some of the Orphan technology in person. I think you'd agree that's the best way to learn?" the Captain queried, looking up at the red-head warmly. She nodded back, and Lahira turned to face Gavin, next. "I want you to do an assessment of your own. We know the

Orphans are very, very different than we are. I need you to bring along some heavy fire-power and I also need to know what it is that we can do *if* our little envoy mission goes wrong. The last thing I need at that point is to shoot food at these rock-people, you know?"

The tall, dark-skinned man nodded slowly. "Aye, ma'am, I understand. I'll bring along a reasonable sized detachment and I'll arm them with varied kits."

"See too it," Lahira stated, nodding her head to her fellow officers. "And lets hope this diplomatic mission doesn't go south, fast!"

*****

The shuttle-craft descending into the atmosphere kicked up lovely waves of flame, spheres which formed around their hulls and created a gorgeous, if slightly unnerving trail. The tiny planes buckled and trembled as they landed precisely where they were instructed by the Orphans. There were at least forty of the birds touching down - half were the sleek fighter-planes that Humanity depended so heavily on, while the other half were filled to the brim with troops. Over two hundred marines unloaded, coupled with vehicles including Human tanks - ST-22 models, sporting ad-hoc "anti-asteroid" shielding and a pair of light rail-guns, and more common six-wheeled vehicles

The very first thing deployed, however, was one particular quartet of landing craft - three encircled around one. The outer three immediately deployed heavy-caliber turrets with fire-and-forget missiles attached to them, while the inner station extended a large, powerful communications' dish. It would serve as the command-and-control hub for the ground mission.

All things considered, so far the Human operation was right on schedule. They'd given up on trying to disguise a *Bantam* as a "light" transport vehicle, but while stipulations existed as to the number of men and landing craft that would be allowed, none existed for the heavy vehicles that the Humans used to bolster their defenses.

Those tanks? Each one had a rather unique set of weapons - two quite powerful rail-guns. Their "light" classification referred to the fact that they were vehicle mounted, not ship-installed. One could fire while the other was reloaded, and the high arcs of fire combined with the option to deploy wheels or tracks would allow them to deal quite a great deal of damage. The fact that a single four-round pod of anti-aircraft missiles was affixed to the top of the tank didn't hurt, either.

Of course, even these weapons would ultimately prove futile if half a million Orphans descended upon the position like a plague of locusts. At best, the marines could hold their own for a short period while the Human ships in orbit began to bombard the world; a solution that was in the best interests of neither group. The descending transports and their crews knew that there was little chance of rescue if things went wrong - this was a mission that might end in total fatality.

That problem was, therefore, not in the mind of Lahira Ocean as her plane touched down. She removed a safety harness and, as the back door of the vehicle opened, stepped out. She was surrounded by heavily armed and armored marines, and her eyes lifted to the sky while some the other vessels began to land. Those already on ground opened their own bay doors, releasing their vehicles, troops, and command staff.

"Well," spoke Ensign Travares, who departed from the plane next to his Captain's, "Here we are. They said they would meet us here." He almost sounded nervous, but it wasn't a fear of death that gripped his throat and altered his voice - it was, if anything, a fear of failure. After all, it was hard to tell whether or not the aliens were already there! What did they look like?

The clearing was littered with green grass-like plants; green being a great color for absorbing yellow light, as Mankind had learned once it discovered how photosynthesis worked on Earth. Other worlds had red, even black grass, but the green forms of chlorophyl went well with yellow suns. There were some rocks in the clearing, and not far off a slight descent began into a series of rolling hills adorned with trees.

One of the marines, a short, muscular man with a scope affixed to a gun which, in turn, was affixed to a port in his helmet, whispered softly, "So far, no enemy contacts reported, ma'am."

"We're here to talk, after all," Lahira responded politely, but with clarity as a cornerstone, "so they aren't enemies - or, not exactly, not yet."

Jackie Quan merely chuckled involuntarily - she quickly shut herself up, whispering sardonically that, "We don't have any bullets in our brains, yet. I'm guessin' that counts," she chirped.

"The *Sun Tzu* reports in-bound vehicles from over those hills, west," announced Gavin Trusaunt calmly, hefting what appeared to be a shotgun and checking its settings. "Roughly as many as we brought planes, exactly the count they said they'd bring and exactly one and a half times what we did."

Lucas licked his dried lips, moistening them up as a cloud of dust emerged behind the nearest hill, now. "So far, so good. Just like we'd planned."

"Alright, Orphans," Lahira said with a twitch of her own tiers - she wasn't sure if they intended to smile or grimace with anticipation. "Lets see what you look like; up, close, and personal."

As the first vehicle crossed the crest of the hill, it was apparent that they were dealing with a rather large form of creature. The Orphan automobile was large even for a tank, but it only appeared to have the sort of armaments that a troop transport would; close-range, for maximum anti-personnel protection. The next over the horizon was even larger! This was, it seemed, their take on a tank; it sported one of those large laser-emitters that the aliens had used to such devastating effect. A second transport emerged; then, it was followed by another large battle-tank with a single long cannon barrel and three large rocket launching tubes affixed to its back.

In total, thirty vehicles pulled up to greet the Humans, and every last one was a dark green shade of metal; the same Copernicum alloy, it seemed, as their star-ships was made of.

"So, that stuff must be plentiful," Lahira immediately thought, *"to see it on ground vehicles like this. Or maybe its just a thin layer. Either way,"* she mused, her thoughts echoed by her second in command's words.

"Here we go," Ensign Travares stated dryly. Human guns immediately trained on the alien targets, just as the alien guns focused upon the most threatening of Earth's weapons. The alien convoy came to a halt, and there was a momentary stand off as the two forces simply observed one another.

"If I had to guess," Lahira considered, *"They're deciding whether or not they can punch us out before we can react, just in case. I'm pretty sure Gavin's already done that thinking and I'm pretty sure he'd agree it looks like no chance in hell."* She looked over at her chief of defense and found, quite as she'd expected, that he had a stone face on. A gaze over at her ex-pirate engineering officer and she was rather shocked, in contrast, to find that Jackie Quan looked quite pleased at something.

Ensign Travares took one step forward, holding his hands outstretched. "My name," he announced in as calm and level a tone as possible, "is Lucas Traveres. My rank is Ensign. I will communicate." He kept his sentences short, much as the Orphans had. They would need time to translate anything he put forward. "We do not want to fight." This last sentence was added as a reassuring one, but he ensured that his voice was firm as he said it - the last thing Humanity needed was to come off as afraid or unwilling to engage, no matter how they had proven it in the skies above.

Once again, there was a period of silence. It was anticipated that they would need some time to decide what to do. Then, after nearly sixty full seconds, one of the troop transports moved forward. If it had windows, they were damned hard to spot against that green alloy, and no Human eye could look inside. It made a slow path toward Lahira's troops, then turned and slowly patrolled along the outside of their ranks. It was almost like a wolf, assessing the new entity before it and measuring its worthiness. After reaching one end of the ranks it turned and rolled back along them, taking a second glance at the assembly. Finally, it turned again and rolled back to its starting point. A decision had been made.

Slowly, a door almost carved itself out of the super-dense metal siding of the transport, an emergence accompanied by a slow, dull hissing sound. It moved forward almost six inches, just barely clearing the space next to it, then slid to the right slowly. Lahira bit her bottom lip as she saw, of all things, what looked from her viewpoint to be a foot stepping out! Given what the Aquarians and Firions looked like, the last thing she had expected was a bipedal entity with similar skeletal systems to Humanity! But, then again, that evolutionary perk had come rather in handy for Mankind.

As the figure behind the limb emerged, however, Lahira realized just how quick she had been to judge. The creature was almost built of boulders, or so it seemed; stones connected to one another by thick, bulbous joints. The foot didn't smoothly transition into a shin, nor did a shin become a thigh - it was all achieved through large pockets that seemed almost fluid in nature! The creature's torso was no more defined than a wrecking ball's would be, and to top it off it was a rather large one. It had a head, but this was clearly little more than an after-thought. Its arms were hardly better shaped than its legs, though here there seemed to be some actual attempts at accentuation.

It lumbered - its attempt at a walk was no more successful than a lumbering - toward the Human Ensign slowly. There was little more than the sound of gravel rustling, as if one had stepped on a pit of tiny stones. This sound was studied quite closely by Lucas, who cocked his head to the side as if he'd expected to hear something not necessarily different, but louder. He quickly got his wish as a very robotic sound echoed from *inside* the creature! "Hello, Ensign," the voice stated. "You may call me Speaker."

"Its good to meet you, Speaker," the Ensign replied in a calm tone. "We wish to discuss peace."

The creature almost rustled slowly. "Peace." The one identified as Speaker almost seemed to have no comprehension of the word! Or, at least, that was what Lahira gained from the exchange. "Peace." It repeated, that gravely sound emerging in quick bursts with each statement. Longer rustles, now. "You are not like us." Silence fell for a moment, then the gravel returned. "The Code demands purity. It demands pursuit."

Slowly, Lucas gazed over his shoulder at Lahira. The Captain offered him a slow, determined nod before her subordinate returned to the Speaker's attention. "Speaker," he asked slowly, "can you explain the code to us?" The silence with which he was greeted was heavy, leaving the Human afraid he'd crossed some line.

After the alien's momentary silence, the blob-like entity rustled with what Lucas only imagined was its form of speech; the sound of sand and rocks grating against one another like gravel pebbles. A computerized voice followed. "We have never been asked," the Orphan called Speaker responded to Lucas' question about their 'code.' "There is no prohibition."

It was, in a way, an old trick of Humankind's. In her species' past, years ago on the then-lonely planet Earth, Lahira knew that settlers from one area would get to understand local cultures by asking questions about their ways and means. They would ask about religion, about government, about architecture. The answers would reveal the society's strengths and weaknesses, as well as ways to exploit them. Religion could be co-opted through the introduction of holidays similar to those the native populace enjoyed, all to convert them as new followers. Government entities and political factions could be allied with and turned against their own kind. Information about building materials could reveal what sciences were known - and unknown - to the surrounding peoples. Once the information had been collected, a plan of action could be enacted to obtain decisive victories. "*Witness,*" Lahira mused, "*that Cortes only defeated the Aztecs because of two facts - smallpox, and the Aztecs' old enemies who sided with him rather than Moctezuma.*"

Of course, the Captain's thirst to know more about the Orphan ethos was less about enslaving them, and more about understanding why they had launched an unprovoked attack against the Human world of Hudson! True, it might better arm the Humans in the event that their war couldn't come to a diplomatic end, but that was more of a long-term consideration. It was also important to understand their social structure; did they have a hive mind, where they all shared their thoughts? Or, like Humans, were they individualistic, with complicated social structures that allowed each of them a free say in their own actions?

The Speaker rustled once more, and the robotic interpretation of Human speech followed. "We seek our creator." The Orphan spoke in little more than fragmented sentences, making each one as coherent - yet vague - as possible. "Those like us must, too." More rustling. "We must be pure." The large, sand-colored mass that doubled for an organism quivered. "Those not like us must be purged."

Lucas nodded slowly and closed his eyes in contemplation. Was the communications specialist searching for a loophole? Slowly, he smiled. "Would you welcome others who ask about their creator?"

The alien entity shivered in a downright fearful fashion. "We have never."

"Never before," the clarification was made. "Would you, tomorrow?" Lucas queried. This seemed to cause the Orphan to grow very still, and the two sides once again returned to a tense silence punctuated by the guns pointed towards one another.

Rustling emerged in an answer, machines translated for the Speaker. "We would consider. We have not agreed."

The Captain nodded slowly, part of her chain of questioning finding an answer. A tiny, concealed device inserted into her skull was recording every word of this interaction, every gesture and every visual impression from Lahira's point of view. It was all transmitted toward the *George Washington* for processing, and although the link was too tenuous for two-way conversation, it was productive as a means of gathering intelligence.

"We will ask," the Orphan finally conceded. It waited, then, perfectly still - as if the creature was thoroughly content with being nothing more than an oddly shaped stone. It didn't seem to be talking to anyone or anything, but waiting. That's when it hit Lahira - the Orphan also had implanted communication devices, much like she did, and it was in talks with its own kind throughout the entirety of the discussion.

Then, the creature's posture seemed to relax ever so slightly. "We do not have agreement. We do not agree." It seemed almost as if there was a conflict with those two sentences, with two almost identical concepts having completely different connotations behind them. "There is no agreement."

Lucas looked over his shoulder at Lahira, who gazed back toward him with confusion. Slowly, he rose and lowered that promontory, offering a shrug that suggested he had no idea what the hell the Speaker was discussing. He turned back to the alien, then, and asked quite simply. "We do not want to fight you - can we find a way to work out our differences?"

The Speaker seemed to lower his posture a touch further. "No. Our differences are too great. There is no agreement. There is no agreement." The repetition of this statement served as an unnerving action, and it certainly appeared that the foreigner was no happier than the Humans were at that statement. Some growls it made were (on purpose, certainly) not translated, and then it spoke again. "I do not believe we will survive." Slowly, the Orphan guns turned - of all places - skyward. The Speaker seemed to tighten back up. "The soldiers are coming. The Speaker of Hell-Fire comes!"

Lahira had no clue what this meant, but she certainly didn't like it! "Speaker of Hell-Fire?" asked the Captain, querying the sentient pile of sand and gravel that stood before her. The Orphan calling himself Speaker was concerned, to say the least, that his fellows were on their way.

The creature rustled, and a computer apparently embedded within his chest translated his feelings into Human speech. "The Speaker of Hell-Fire commands armies. I am the Speaker of

Stasis. I command labor. The Speaker of The Search commands our faith. They have called us heretics! We shall be slain." Perhaps it was simply an error of the translating software he used, but the Speaker of Stasis' voice sounded far more worried about being a heretic than being killed.

"Then we have to escape," chirped Lucas Traveres, gesturing swiftly towards the shuttle-craft on the ground. There was room for the aliens to squeeze in to the Human planes; just barely. "Come with us, we can work together." It was a bold offer, and one that Captain Ocean herself wasn't so sure she would have made.

The Speaker of Stasis quivered, as if re-aligning his various sediments and particles. "We promise nothing," it warned gravely, his comrades doing the same even as they kept their eyes (or so it appeared) on the sky.

Lahira bit her bottom lip. "We can section off part of a vessel for you. It won't be much, but you'll have privacy." The creature didn't move. "We can talk mo--"

An explosion shook the ground. From nowhere, a high-explosive warhead had slammed down near the meeting ground. The Humans and Orphans both began to return fire; guns flared as missiles exploded in mid-air, intercepted by strokes of luck as a series of tiny fighter planes screeched overhead.

The Captain, on instinct, looked to her cluster of transport vehicles. Sure enough, they were unharmed! Granted, she could see the ex-pirate Ensign Quan screaming, cursing, and firing a borrowed assault-rifle into the sky, but so far the Humans had taken few, if any, casualties. Rockets screamed through the air, roaring it's threat to strike both inbound and outbound air traffic. Moreover, one of the tanks that Lahira's detachment had brought along fired the first of its two rail-guns down-range, intended to hit a distant target.

"We need to go!" screamed Lahira, looking one of her own kind in the eye; a pilot. "Now! Speaker," she turned to face the alien, "you're either with us or not! Let's move!"

As another barrage of rockets struck, the unfortunate tank

which had just fired first was now putting on an impressive impersonation of a ball of flame. Orphan vehicles, too, were damaged, and while the two species' combined guardsmen returned fire against the weapons of this vaunted Speaker of Hell-Fire, it was clear they couldn't do so for long and hope to live.

It was impossible for Lahira to hear the rustling of the Speaker of Stasis, but the robotic translation made the point clear - assuming, of course, that the multiple Oprhans suddenly sprinting for the Human vessels didn't! "We will go with you," he finally conceded.

"Retreat!" shouted the security officer, Gavin Trusaunt, who had no choice but to grab the screaming, rifle-firing Jackie and pull her along with him. "Execute departure plan Gamma!"

Escaping a firefight under any conditions was difficult. Doing so in vehicles was more-so, if only due to a heightened need for communication. But multiple vehicles lifting off at the same time? Oh dear - especially when sporting defectors from a hostile alien race? It was mayhem the likes of which could only be mitigated with a plan in advance.

Fortunately, Ensign Gavin Trusaunt, the *Messenger*'s security officer and military adviser, planned for every contingency - including the possibility of an extraction from hostilities in conjunction unfriendly (but not enemy) forces. He'd nicknamed this plan 'Gamma,' with all the creativity of a military mind, and when he commanded its execution?

Well, to begin with, the airspace in the surrounding miles was consumed by flames due to a sudden barrage of rail-gun fire from the orbiting star-ships. The weapons were fired at high velocity in space, captured by the gravity of the Orphan world and sucked in just as any asteroids might be. It was a strategy popularized in 1900's science fiction, and it was just as effective as one might have imagine; the flaming projectiles smashed into the ground and nearly liquified the world's crust - except, of course, for a well-defined area known as the "Safe zone," where the impact waves just happened to cancel each other out for a moment.

This bit of time allowed the Human vessels to break from the ground before the damage to the underlying tectonic plates were fully realized. After all, even one high-density asteroid could smash through a planet's outer layers and create a nice eruption of magma - and many of them over a well defined area could transform solid rock into molten lava! Anything left on the ground was doomed as a giant, angry, *hot* red hole formed.

Meanwhile, the Orphan aerial attack was put on hold as the flaming pillars momentarily surrounded the Human fleet, allowing them to evacuate with less harassment. Turbulence was a problem, of course, as the atmosphere itself threatened to boil in the immediate area and as the rising heat caused massive up-swells of air. Fortunately, the Human landing vessels were meant to handle difficulty circumstances. The Orphan fighter-planes were not; they either abandoned their chase or found themselves losing nearly every scrap of control they had, crashing into one another or the ground, or - with luck! - finding themselves vastly off target.

"This is gonna be ugly as hell!" screamed the irate ex-pirate, Jackie Quan, as she practically kicked the transport's pilot out of his seat. She immediately plugged a cable into the back of her head and accessed a feed of data. "Okay!" She was broadcasting on the fleet's channel! "We're gonna shift our angle six degrees down and roll three to the starboard. Sendin' compensatory data to all transports, make the adjustments! Updraft in six, brace!"

Sure enough, six seconds after she gave the command to be on guard, the ex-pirate's prediction came true. The rising heat, including jets of magma and exploding chunks of continent, slammed into the fleeing Human force and pushed it skyward. The adjustments that Jackie ordered them to make allowed the worst of the magma to roll off, while catching the jets of heat and flying directly skyward.

Breaking free from the planets' atmosphere wasn't different, and while the Humans cheered their survival and looked forward to landing on a familiar vessel, Lahira couldn't help but look down at the world they had pummeled to escape. A cloud of burning ash and dust was rapidly spreading over its upper-atmosphere air currents, while a new sea of magma swelled where the Human rail-gun rounds had struck.

"So," Quan finally exhaled, removing her head from the computer and patting the plane's pilot on the back, "That was a fuckin' rush! I'd forgotten just what its like to break out of hell." A yelping 'whoo' caused her to shiver weakly and lie back, breathing heavily.

Gavin stared at the rebel and shook his head derisively; but he didn't have the strength to bring any words to his lips because his heart was beating far too hard, and a smirk on his lips betrayed the fact that he, too, had enjoyed the daring - if tragic - escape.

Chapter Ten
Decryption

The crew of the *Messenger* had to work frantically; their 'guests' were in need of a domicile, and it was unprecedented for a Human ship to host hostile alien forces. Worse, those hostile forces had plenty of weapons, and were not entirely willing to yield them. The Speaker of Stasis convinced his guards to surrender most of them; but they were permitted to retain a certain number of small arms in order to defend themselves 'just in case.' Both sides understood the tacit implication; some of the Humans might prove just as evil as others feared the Orphans to be, and attempted exploits would be shut down swiftly.

For the location of this ad-hoc prison - politely called "safe quarters" - the *Messenger*'s workers cleared out an ammunition bay. This wasn't a monumental task, what with the cruiser having "actively disposed of" a substantial amount of ordinance during its battle. The Orphans were sealed within, provided access to a communications channel should they have need of anything, and promptly relegated to the important role of hot topic of gossip aboard the ship. After all, above all else this procedure was *not* perfect - it was a work-in-progress which commanded the personal attention of Gavin Trusaunt, the head of the *Messenger*'s defensive personnel.

As Captain Lahira Ocean made her way onto the bridge of her ship, her chief navigator unplugged a data-jack from her head and rose in greeting. She appeared stable, despite her recent injuries. "Captain," offered Ensign Kelly Grant, providing a salute which was returned. "Ensign Trusaunt's security specialists are still sequestering the Orphans. Their Speaker of Stasis will meet with us privately once we've had a chance to rest," she informed her superior in a casual tone.

Lahira nodded, nestling herself down into her large, comfy chair and rubbing her forehead in exhaustion. "Have we gotten any word from the old man?" That old man was Admiral James Owens, the man who had promoted her to run the heavily armed cruiser in the first place. She had half a mind to curse him for it! But she also had developed a true attachment to the boss, and she believed both in his vision and her role within it.

The portly navigator nodded and approached her *own* superior, leaning down to whisper carefully in her ear, as if the deck-hands and second-mates might overhear and draw a dangerous conclusion. "He wants to be involved with any more meetings. He's going to come over here, to make the logistics easier. Its strange." Kelly hesitated for a second, then continued with due gravity, "he's requested that Ensign Travares command the *George Washington* while he's away."

This request meant only one thing - soon, very soon, Travares was going to be promoted. A short-term command of the Human fleet's capital ship was nothing new - both Lahira and Lucas had performed that duty while working under the then-Commander. What was unusual was that the officers already on board, with some admittedly just replacements for the departed two executive officers, were not being handed the keys to the old man's ride. It was plausible that the newcomers just weren't ready to command the battleship solo, but the other two chief officers aboard the *George Washington* certainly were! To call Lucas back meant something that Lahira just couldn't figure out.

She swiftly dismissed it from her head. "That sounds like a plan," the Captain conceded. Slowly, she inserted a plug into the back of her skull and drifted into an orchestra-filled data stream. Her concentration narrowed as she opened up a number of rarely-used programs. She captured images in her mind of the fire-fight and of the Orphan vehicles, concentrating on them long enough to upload them into the *Messenger*'s computer banks. It only made sense that if information could be pumped into a human mind, it could be pulled out of it.

Most people opted never to embrace this function; their subconscious thoughts were far too likely to drift in order to glean a coherent image. Worse, should they have a 'deviant' mind, they might perhaps upload something inappropriate - even condemning! In fact, such risks were so great that some officers chose to use special implants and attachments to their data-ports that could activate and de-activate a straight recording from their visual memory, based on pre-set and supposedly-secret protocols. Say, an older officer having lustful thoughts for younger ones: If the better fantasy crept into a recording, the filter would immediately cut the transfer, as well as "remind" the user of the lapse.

Of course, such technology was highly experimental, and therefore highly prone to errors.

Lahira, on the other hand, had learned how to send an image into a computer while exploiting the mental lens of a symphony. Some people visualized the music they heard, instead, as a musician might start seeing the notes they would play to create the tune; but by linking the orchestra into the images she wanted to upload, she exploited a selective memory to allow crescendos to match impacts, and to allow crashes to meet up with silence. The data flowed into the Human fleet's collective memory for study, much like a professionally-produced movie overlayed by a sound-track.

After successfully submitting the files, she closed her eyes (and her recorder) and allowed the symphony to overtake her completely. She relaxed so terrifically that she even hummed a few bars. Sure enough, she was interrupted by a picture in her visual field; an electronic communication. It was from Ensign Trusaunt, and his deep voice echoed off of her skull as he spoke. "Admiral Owens is en route, Captain. He wants to take care of things immediately."

*****

The Admiral's shuttle was heavily protected, given what a short span of space it was covering. The Human fleet's leader was only crossing a few dozen miles, between his *George Washington* and Lahira's *Messenger*. Not surprisingly, as they were in hostile territory, the shuttle-craft had dopplegangers; not one, but three shuttles flew! Each had five fighters surrounding it as a defensive measure in the event that the Orphan world in the system had the audacity to send its scattered, broken fleet of short-range ships toward the Human armada.

Once the vessels had safely docked within the *Messenger*'s landing bays, Lahira severed her connection with her ship and gave its bridge a swift, final survey. All three of her remaining executive officers had finished (or, at least, put on hold) their business, and made their way back to the command center. The Admiral certainly took his sweet time moving through the ship's lifts, and as the doorway to the bridge opened the entire assembly of soldiers saluted.

The old man walked in without much pomp-and-circumstance, saluting his soldiers in return before he walked over toward Lahira and, quite warmly, shook her hand. "Captain," he greeted in a pleasant tone, "its always a pleasure to see you well."

"The same to you, Admiral," Ocean responded, glancing around the chamber slowly. Computers were running constantly, with vessels always moving and updates coming regularly, and as soon as the rules of decorum allowed them, the bulk of the bridge's residents were back to work on the Fleet's networks. Everything was as it was supposed to be.

The old man, of course, grinned and took a nearby chair, notably not the Captain's. "As you were, Captain." She hesitated, remaining standing, so Owens continued on as he'd planned. "I trust that Ensign Trusaunt has provided us with an excellent security plan for this meeting?"

Nodding softly, the dark-skinned Magellaner advanced and produced a small manilla folder. It was labeled with a stereotypical, red "confidential" stamp, and was placed carefully in the hands of the fleet's commander. He opened the briefing, one leg folding over the other, and thumbed through it quickly. He nodded as he did, humming to himself softly and pointing to two or three clauses.

"I'd like half of our guns hidden, during the meeting, if

that's possible?" the Admiral finally broke the unofficial moratorium on speech-while-reading.

Gavin blinked his eyes; as the head of security, he had been responsible for determining how much firepower was present. "Admiral, the standard is to have twenty-four armed officers. We have already conceded to permitting four of the Speaker of Stasis' guards to attend with loaded weapons. Two in, two out." The old man's eyes showed he already knew how this would play out, but he seemed more than happy to allow it to develop. Gavin, if he recognized his role in the game, continued with it admirably. "It would be beyond foolish to take half of our soldiers out of the room."

"Oh, I want the soldiers, Ensign Trusaunt - I most certainly do." His sudden change in pitch made it clear that the lack of manpower was a comical misinterpretation of his directions. "And I want the guns, and more than just twelve. I fully intend to have my side-arm with me," he said in a reassured tone, "but I want the guns out of *view*. The more triggers with fingers on them, the more likely a round will be fired." He let his explanation hang for a moment. "Once *that* sort of mess begins, our hopes of gaining information from the Orphans has been cut more than in half. I want enough guns in here for every one of us - but I want only a few of them at the ready."

Gavin nodded his head slowly. "Understood, Admiral," the Ensign answered reluctantly, walking toward his area of the bridge and plugging his head into the *Messenger*'s computer. He was presumably ordering the proper ordinance.

Lahira seemed to have far more faith in her superior's viewpoint. Nevertheless, there were certain questions which were expected of a high-ranking officer, certain cliched caution-centric queries. "If this is a trap? If this is all some sort of Orphan gimmick?" she was asking more out of curiosity than actual concern.

Owens' tone was not exactly cold, but far from caring - at least, caring about the scenario he painted. "You have them separated from their vehicles, and we have bomber squadrons all over them. Only their small-arms are going to be circulating, and I'm not terrified of them." She shrugged as the old man paused. Both set eyes upon a number of security officers who were bringing cases of firearms into the Bridge and concealing them as best as long-arms could be concealed in a sterile, clutter-free environment. "At worst," he continued, "perhaps they will try to assassinate us. If so, that is why Ensign Travares is on the *George Washington*."

It hit Lahira like a truck; the old man wasn't just looking for a reliable substitute to govern his ship; he wasn't even proposing that Lucas was the next one to get promoted! He'd placed the Ensign in charge of the fleet, if the executive staff of the *Messenger* was to be annihilated, as the next-in-line to command it! It was a wise decision, indeed. After all, once the weapons were properly (and furtively) stored, the Orphans would be making their way to their location for what was, hopefully, going to be a fruitful talk.

By the time the meeting was scheduled to begin, the Humans were nestled comfortably in the bridge. The firearms were in position, the guards were briefed, and the Speaker of Stasis was on his way. As agreed, he walked with four of his personal guards as an escort - Two would remain outside of the *Messenger*'s bridge, and two would join him inside. All were armed, and they shambled in something resembling a Human silhouette; they had clearly formed arms, but no heads or legs. They moved by shifting the gravel of their feet from front to back - they were, in effect, amorphous!

As for their choice of weaponry, their guns resembled Human rifles, save that they had much larger caliber barrels and suitably large spirals within. It was unclear exactly *what* those weapons were intended to shoot; creatures made mostly of sand weren't going to fare well in the face of high-recoil weaponry, since their firearms would blast right back through them, but then again it was hard to anticipate what would even harm them, other than perhaps flames baking them, or water eroding their bodies!

The four guards formed a sudden, unexpected lock-step

with their Human caretakers as they were guided through the halls. They were so coordinated that only one of them actually found himself off-beat with the rest of his entourage! A mistake quickly corrected. Eventually, though, the *Messenger*'s control room came into view. Two of the alien soldiers stood next to the two Human guards, while the Speaker and his two remaining cohorts were led in.

Every soldier on the bridge was at attention, and the Speaker was saluted as a foreign dignitary might have been. He was silent, as if perhaps not understanding the measure that the Humans had put forth. Then, his body shifted; he grew, or so it seemed, a head and arms, much like the appearance he had taken during his first, impromptu meeting with Lahira. A deep rustling emerged from within him, and a computerized voice piped through his thoughts.

"Captain Ocean," he rumbled, his concealed megaphone serving as his communications device. "It is a good thing to see you again. I honor you for your hospitality." The gesture of a salute was returned to the *Messenger*'s residents.

It was a damned odd phrase to the Humans; then again, this was a damned odd alien. Lowering his arm from its cocked position, James Owens approached the alien and stretched his hand out. The creature looked at it for a moment before patting the back of it gently in what was clearly a misunderstanding of Human greeting patterns.

Owens accepted the gesture freely and took his concealed cross into his left hand, adjusting his uniform in the process. "Speaker," he began without one hint of fear or trepidation, "my name is James Owens. I am the Admiral of the Human's Second Fleet, and our peoples' representative here. I'd like to thank you for your ear towards diplomacy."

The creature was hesitant, translating - or at least letting his built-in computer translate - the Human tongue. A collection of clicks and clacks escaped his interior, and that computer responded. "Admiral. It is not certain. We must discuss where our Code brings us."

"Yes," the old man answered with a deep, sagely nod, in spite of his total lack of knowledge as to what that Code was. "I understand what it means to have faith. It must be kept in mind, with all decisions." As one of the very few religious - deeply religious, at least - Humans aboard the ship, his voice rang with a particularly striking authenticity. It seemed to appeal to the Speaker. "I believe we must nourish our faith with what we see around us, as well, because our faith is our own; and it will grow, given time, into new and greater forms."

The amorphous Orphan did not growl or grumble; nor did his cohorts, who stood across from the Admiral in an arcane, still fashion. They did not seem to engage in respiration, at least not visibly, and their silence did little to inspire confidence in the itchy trigger fingers of the Human security guards. Before long, however, a dull and grim rumble escaped the Speaker's entrails, ready to be translated into Human speech!

"Admiral Owens, you are correct," it conceded, contrary to the grumble that its method of speech might have entailed. "Faith can grow. We can discuss our code. We may find improvements."

Once diplomacy was considered an acceptable path, the alien appeared more inclined to explain just what in the hell had guided his kind's actions, and its pursuit of war. "Our creator," offered the Speaker, "commanded that we find him. We were told to be pure. Purity meant that we may grow very rigidly, and may not add others. Others do not understand. They do not follow. They are not what we are. They were created in other means."

The Admiral was forced to choose his words carefully; these creatures were xenophobic to the extreme. They were religious, as was he, but their faith was so very different from his own; instead of forgiveness, there was only the pursuit of this perfection. "Others may *help* you, Speaker. They may share their knowledge. They can aid your search."

"I have wondered this," the alien answered in what might have passed for a contemplative tone, "but purity is a command.

If we are helped, we do not discover, and we must discover."

Owens thought fast, seeking a loophole. "But you *discover* the help, no?"

The Speaker was silent. The Admiral, sensing he had a lead, continued his train of thought. "Lets suppose you bring your code before a new species. They have seen signs of your creators, and they let you work there. Isn't that a discovery that *you've* made?"

"Yes!" the Speaker agreed; but, if the robotic translator could have held emotion, the creature would have come off as upset. It was clearly a conflict that had gone on for some time within his mind, if not his culture. "But purity is a command!"

The Admiral smiled politely. "You do not need to destroy other worlds to keep yours pure, Speaker. You have encountered the ones we call Automatons, no?" At the lack of a response, he nodded. "They are machines, the robots you may call them."

Now, the creature practically snarled. "Yes, we know them. They were created as well. They destroyed their creator, we know. They are the worst sort of impurity."

It was a response James should have anticipated, but he didn't. Wincing internally, he managed to keep his face plain. "They had a very different creator than you. Yours must have loved you - theirs was cruel and evil." It was a complete bluff, since he only had the Automatons' own words to go on. For all he knew, the truth was that their creators were one in the same - and a war between the two was not only inevitable, but desirable for both sides.

"Creations are always loved," the Speaker answered firmly.

The old man sighed and rubbed his forehead. "I know many times that is true, but I have seen creations be abused. Sometimes things are created to serve, and love is a tool used to control."

The Speaker was, again, silent. It was contemplating the meaning of the Admiral's sentiments, and when it rumbled once more its translator converted the words flawlessly. "I understand.

Our creator was greater than other creators. Our creator must be found. That is our destiny. We must find our creator, and we must be pure. Those are our commands. That is all we must do."

Slowly the Admiral nodded. "I know you do not like them, but the Automatons do not interfere with us. They are neutral; and even helpful, sometimes. They stay out of our affairs. They are pure, in their own way, but they do not fight us over it."

Orphan or not, there was a clear recognition of one's right to exist in the Speaker's form. It was something the Admiral only dawned upon at that moment - that he took the trouble to at least attempt a Human figurine. It was a measure of comfort and mutual identification, and one that brought the Speaker up a level of diplomacy from where the Admiral had originally figured him to be.

"Correct." It was a one-word answer. The Speaker of Stasis seemed to sigh internally, waging a psychological conflict. "But my people do not agree. There is no agreement. Even the Speakers of Stasis do not agree. The ones of Hell-fire are less generous. The ones of The Search are even less. We do not agree."

Admiral Owens gave the Speaker a look of reassurance, while privately figuring out which castes the "Hell-Fire" and "Search" speakers might be. It wasn't a tough deduction. "I understand. I hope that one day, your people will agree that they do not need war to pursue the Code. One day, I hope we can search side-by-side. Until then, we - the Human fleet - will protect anyone in your civilization that wants to follow *your* path."

"*My* path?" The alien sounded confused, now. Clearly, the Speaker was not a proficient diplomat, and clearly he didn't recognize - nor reject - the subtle trap Owens had set for him. The set-up. The suggestion of how to get his will accomplished. "I am Stasis," he reiterated firmly, "I maintain the faith and its people, but I do not lead its ideas. The past is my study, my guide."

Slowly, the old Human shrugged. "Perhaps you are not just stasis? Perhaps you are change? Its hard to say." He sounded more as if he was talking to himself, ruminating on the philosophy of the alien's name. It was not entirely understood by the creature, and what was?

"I do not agree." The Orphan seemed to be weighing it far too heavily, but before the Admiral could explain that it was more of a joke than anything, the alien continued, "I do not like that name. Stasis cannot be change. Change comes through the Search. I do not like th--"

The sudden screech of alarm bells indicated that someone, somewhere else didn't like it, either.

As the dull roar of the *Messenger*'s alarms echoed off of Lahira's skull, she turned her eyes toward Ensign Trusaunt, the ship's defense officer. While she wasn't the highest ranked sailor aboard her ship at this moment - the Captain was outranked by her visiting superior, Admiral Owens - the woman didn't hesitate in barking one swift order. "Report!"

"Gunshots reported in the holdin--" Gavin's voice was interrupted by a new intrusion. The dull thud of weapon impacts punctuated the otherwise bland barking of the alert system. The Captain counted a pair of two shots each; just enough to take down the two Human guards outside of the ship's Bridge, and to leave it secured in the hands of their matching two Orphan soldiers.

Speaking of Orphans, the pair of guardsmen protecting the Speaker of Stasis immediately and expertly turned the barrels of their large-caliber weapons...Towards the doorway in question, prepared to protect their Speaker from the new threat - one which clearly lay outside of the room. Human crewmen and security officers immediately readied their own rifles, with half aiming toward the Orphans in the room and the second half positioning in a defensive arrangement, guns on the bridge's door. No matter how fast the soldiers could react, it wouldn't be fast enough. Even Lahira, who was merely pulling a pistol from her hip, hadn't quite leveled the weapon before it was destined to be needed.

The bridge door didn't explode; it was opened with the Human guards' retinas, as per procedure. Surprisingly, to say the least, there was a small squadron of rogue Orphans invading the command center! More surprisingly, only one of the Speakers' two guards was lying dead on the floor alongside of two of her comrades; the other one seemed to be leading the rabble!

A massive, sudden crash emerged from the very depths of the Speaker's gravely body. "What is the--?!" he shouted mechanically. He, too, wasn't able to finish his statement; the loud, staccato thud of firearms being discharged echoed across the bridge, and some force or another knocked him to the ground. Lahira's eyes widened as the two Orphan soldiers were sliced into ribbons - and the Humans fared little better.

It turned out that the Orphan guns didn't fire bullets, like the Human weapons did. They instead ejected large, spinning knives with multiple edges built around a circular, disc-like projectile. It seemed like a frisbee shot sideways, relying on sharp blades to act like trauma-inducing stabilizing fins. This lethal collection of cutlery cleaved into their targets, intended - or so it seemed - to fully shred an Orphan. For the defending Humans, there was some mercy in this circumstance; these shotgun-like devices fired incredibly slow projectiles, so the cutting tool itself was prone to evasion.

Of course, that was little consolation, because evading the shots at close range was just about impossible, and range was always an issue when circumstances got grave.

The two Orphan guards were dead; the Speaker, perhaps, wounded by the traitors among his group. Admiral Owens? He was pinned on the floor, and a bleeding Gavin Trusaunt lay atop him protectively. Lahira unloaded the clip in her pistol; an unwise decision, since her eyes were taking in her wounded colleagues while she did so. It was blind fire, and while she was far from the only one peppering the doorway with bullets, she was also one of the least effective. Never mind that if any Humans stepped in the way, she'd never have a chance of sparing them.

Her eyes took in the other two commanding officers

aboard her bridge - Kelly Grant, still not fully recovered from her injuries during a previous battle, was hiding behind a computer terminal and firing a shotgun. In what came as a total shock to the Captain, the usually cool-tempered Kelly was screaming in rage, rapidly cocking the gun and unloading on the portal, reloading, and unloading again.

Jackie Quan, on the other hand, was no amateur in firefights. While Lahira and most of the staff on board had only been in one or two, Jackie's life as a pirate gave her plenty of gun-play experience. She held a sub-machine gun tightly to her shoulder, and her eyes were fixed down-range; any time a hint of movement came from the bridge door, she unloaded a swift, three-round burst that actually managed to hit its target on occasion!

The problem, of course, was that even when she connected with the dead center of one of the Orphans, it didn't seem all too inclined to stop discharging its deadly disks. The Human weapons seemed ineffective; and as long as that was the case, they could advance right down the hall and right into the Bridge. Even when Jackie's fire connected with what should have been load-bearing limbs, any damage they suffered was temporary. Yet the Orphans who were slaughtered by their own kind weren't recovering, they were just plain dead - scattered, even! Suddenly, Lahira's mind made the connection.

"They've got some kind of core that they can move!" she screamed to her troops, "Its why they have such big weapons!"

Suddenly, random panic fire seemed almost to be as effective as Jackie's precise, effective shots. Panic-fire was bad, but shooting at random parts of a target? It was counter-intuitive, but they had no way of predicting where their targets truly were! As Human sailors were nicked and sliced, however, the crew of the *Messenger* faced some difficult odds; and as Lahira glared up at the aggressive horde of Orphans threatening to storm the *Messenger*'s control center, she reloaded her pistol and prepared for another harrowing turn of exchanging shots.

Lahira peeked over the slab of cover-renderedunrecongnizable she was hidden behind. Her ship's bridge was already damaged severely, and the Orphan invaders threatened to take the vessel over from within - a serious enough loss before even considering, of course, the fact that the Human fleet's Admiral lie pinned down under her wounded chief of defense; or that the one Orphan left who might align with Humanity would be quickly taken and executed for his orthodoxy-defying open-mindedness.

No, she was in a great deal of trouble, with the burden of her species' future riding on her shoulders, and she knew it. On the plus side, despite staring a crippling defeat in the eyes, Lahira knew that there were ways to get out of her jam. "Quan!" she shouted to her chief engineer, a former pirate who was deftly suppressing the Orphans with a standard Human sub-machine gun. The girl glanced up at her for just a moment, just long enough to let it be known that she was listening. "I need you here, now!"

"A little busy, boss!" she shouted over the sound of her weapon's rapport. The short little bursts of gunfire she let loose upon her enemies hardly seemed to pose a serious threat. Dull little thuds resonated against the gravely amalgamations of sandy stones as each bullet struck. Some rounds passed clean through the creatures, while others got caught within. None seemed to be fatal, although it seemed that the more they were wounded, the less mobile they became. If any were dying, they were being rather swiftly replaced by those who decided to join in the treasonous slaughter.

The Captain bore her teeth. "Now, damn it, now!" Lahira roared, rising above her cover and unloading her entire clip of high-caliber rounds in a matter of seconds. They were a potent little threat, seeing how large the bullets were, but they were only so effective against creatures without a standard central nervous system. While she fired, Jackie scrambled over and hid next to her Captain.

"So what's this meeting about?" chirped a third voice, the unexpected tone of Kelly Grant, the chubby chief navigator of the ship. She still had bandages on her head from her most recent injuries - yet she held a still-smoking shotgun and wore a look of hateful determination on her face. Even as other Human survivors exchanged fire with the Orphans, these three carried the bearings of leadership.

Lahira gestured to the fallen Speaker of Stasis - and to the two guardsmen who had died to protect him. "The same guns, ladies. We need them."

Jackie snapped off a quick laugh. "Fuckin' right. What's the plan? Who plays decoy?"

"You grab two of them, Quan, and I'll keep them under!" Kelly ordered, raising her gun above her head and blindly firing toward the door. Resting her back against their cover, she quickly slipped a few more shotgun shells into the built-in magazine. "...Under fire! They won't have a shot at you." Her eyes leveled at Lahira. She took a deep breath. "Get me one of those guns!" she demanded, meaning that the Captain, who was reloading her pistol with one of her last clips, would most certainly be the odd woman out.

"Fine. Ready? Go!" Lahira roared reluctantly. She lifted a nearby shard of glass and threw into a wall, momentarily distracting whoever's duty it was to keep the ladies' heads down. She heard at least one shot deflect off of the walls in response; and that's all Kelly seemed to need. The chubby girl poked her bandaged head up over the cover just long enough to assess who'd fired from where, and she tucked her shotgun into place and began to fire rapidly. The wide spread of the slugs wasn't an effective threat at long range, but it was just worry-some enough to keep the Orphan zealots from lifting their heads - or whatever they'd consider heads.

Lahira poked her head up and began to take more precise shots; whenever one of them dared to turn the corner of the bridge's door and gain a glance, a pair of rounds would ring out as they were fired, and would smack into whatever scrap of Orphan sand-flesh they could find. As soon as the second, precision layer of suppression was in place, the pirate made her move.

She fired her SMG at the door's general vicinity as she took three quick steps. Kicking her own feet out from under her, she slid along the floor; her mind blotted out the sound of her pants shredding on broken glass, especially as some of those tiny shards made their way into her thighs and rear. She screamed in fury, unloading the rest of her clip and immediately slinging the emptied weapon around her shoulder. She'd reached the trio of dead Orphans lying on the ground, fully prepared to raid the corpses of those who had sought to forge a treaty with her kind.

The first of their firearms was almost instantly freed; she lifted it, quickly dissected where its trigger was, aimed down the sights of the weapon and applied a gentle pressure to it. It was in that last minute that she realized it could be a trap! Caught in the rush of adrenaline, she had completely forgotten that it was possible for the alien device to have biometric scanners - after all, plenty of Human guns had them! Electrocution, explosion, or blades-in-the-hands; all such devices existed to keep a warrior's weapons out of the wrong hands, and Jackie had plenty of experience with defusing and evading them. It was the mistake of an amateur she'd just made, and - worse - the other officers wouldn't figure out what had gone wrong until it was too late.

That didn't really matter to Jackie anymore. "Son of a bitch," she thought, "Gavin would never have let me..." she thought as the trigger found its housing and her life flashed before her eyes at the overwhelming force that hit her.

Until wielded by a Human, it really wasn't too easy to tell how powerful an Orphan gun's recoil was. The large, sand-composed creatures nullified the kickback by virtue of bulk and their pseudo-fluid nature. Captain Ocean stared with wonder at her chief engineer as the girl was thrown from her knees to the floor by the force of one single shot from the long, heavy-barrelled rifle.

"What the *fuck?!*" Jackie bellowed, her face thoroughly pale. She looked at the gun - at her finger on the trigger - a finger still attached; not electrocuted, not burned, not bombed. She wasn't given much time to think, because with her body splayed about on the floor she could just feel the Orphan zealots zeroing in on her - and a similar loud thump, accompanied by the crashing sound of steel striking the floor near her, caused her to scramble back to her knees. Her mind grew fuzzy, causing her to bark, "Fuckin' Gavin!" She immediately tossed the heavy weapon toward her comrades and set about fumbling for the second alien gun. This one was pinned between two of the Speaker of Stasis' deceased guards, and the former pirate had to use the device's barrel as a lever to shift the first dead guard off of the second.

　　　　She only stopped when she heard a dull, robotic groaning sound emanating from underneath the pile of bodies. The Speaker! Her eyes immediately locked upon the aliens' sketchily defined areas of sand which seemed to define its visual input region. Needless to say, this was a vague assumption at best. "Signs of life, there, Speaker?" she asked in as quiet a tone as one could manage in the midst of a gun-battle.

　　　　"I am wounded. I am well enough. Are you...?" It was a quickly aborted expression of concern. It was immediately replaced with a mechanically voiced, "Thank you, Human," with just a hint of reluctance.

　　　　Jackie smirked to herself, suddenly the hero of the day. "Keep yer head down, or whatever your head is, and you'll be fine. Lemme just grab this guy's..." she tugged, she tugged, and it came free! The force she used to earn its release *nearly* lifted her to her feet - a mistake that would instantly have been fatal with all of the lead flying around. She secured the strap of her SMG to the back loops of her belt, ignoring the warm moisture which came from the lacerations she'd opened up earlier.

　　　　"Now, now, now!" the former pirate roared, rising to her feet and taking a few deft steps. This time, she managed to take a more cautious, rolling approach to her descent behind cover. She used the handle of the Orphan rifle in her arms to grasp that of the one lying halfway between her and her captain. Pulling it close, she nestled behind the destroyed bits of masonry and mechanics and gestured to the two weapons.

　　　　"Fuckin' have fun with 'em!" Jackie shouted hatefully as

she swung her smaller, less overwhelming weapon back into position. With a quick press of a button she ejected her spent clip and deftly slapped a second one into its place. It was clear she'd grown to prefer her much smaller sub-machine gun.

Lahira was the first to empty the remaining rounds in her pistol, and she swiftly mimicked the ex-pirate's reloading procedure before holstering her weapon. "I saw!" This was hardly audible, as Jackie rose up and sprayed the doorway with another burst of fire. Already the number of shots being unleashed toward the Orphans was diminishing - much as the number of defenders, as well as attackers, had likely dropped.

Ensign Quan's presence allowed Kelly Grant to unload the final shells in her shotgun. She cheered boldly as she spotted a large chunk of pulverized gravel burst from the arms of one of the attackers - a direct hit! She was quickly muted when the same alien returned fire, causing the Human to duck her bandaged head under cover, lest she have it lacerated.

"Outta shells, anyway!" the resignation, fused with hatred, in Kelly's voice was impressive. "Lets try these big boys out!" the Ensign remarked, offering a grin to her commanding officer and former arch-rival.

The Captain looked to her chief navigator and cocked a small grin of her own. Just as Jackie dipped her head to reload, the two Humans looked toward the cover above them. Sure enough, it was still capable of supporting some weight. The loud crackle of gunfire continued, and when it grew particularly loud - and when it was the Human weapons turning up the dial! - Jackie stood again and began to fire in short, deft bursts.

At the same time, the other two women rose up and took the long barrels of the purloined Orphan weapons, positioning them against the remnants of their cover and leaning into it. They arched their hips back, positioned their centers of mass forward, and grasped the weapons with both hands. They were ready for the final onslaught; their enemy's effort to break through the assault.

To begin with, Lahira and her two subordinates had used

the Orphan cannons to round out a fairly impenetrable barricade near the bridge's main doorway. Behind a cobbled together mess of heavy objects, the three officers made access to the *Messenger's* main targets - Admiral Owens and the Speaker of Stasis - virtually impossible. Others Human soldiers remained alive and fighting, peeking out from their cover when they could in order to lay suppressive fire upon the invaders.

     The flow of Orphans reinforcements, on the other hand, slowed down to a trickle. That was good news and bad - it was good because now the Humans had an idea of just how many guns they were up against. It was very, very bad, however, because they could only confirm five or six kills; they had no idea how badly any stricken Orphans might have been wounded. Human weapons dealt them very little damage, and the aliens could easily wait until they had exhausted their ammunition and charge in for the kill. Hand-to-hand, Humanity was a much weaker target; so without bullets, it would all be over. At this rate, if help didn't come, that wouldn't take much longer.

     It was a delicate balance. A tactical team *had* to be on its way to hit the alien insurgents from behind, even without the direct command of Ensign Trusaunt. The chief military officer of the ship had left behind very detailed instructions on how to handle such a situation, but the unfortunate soul himself was lying atop Admiral James Owens, protecting the wounded commander of the Human Fleet from firearms, while bleeding unconsciously all over him. In the back of Captain Ocean's mind, she truly hoped Gavin had no blood-bourne pathogens to spread to the old man.

     Lahira's time to consider this was cut short when she felt her chief engineer pat her on the head. That could only mean one thing, in a trend carried over from the WWII Bazooka troopers - fire. Her body rocked backwards as she unleashed one of the disk-blades remaining in the Orphan rifle she'd come into possession of. The kick-back was incredible! But the force that she'd served to off-set threw a heavy steel circle out in the air, one laced with barbs and blades intended to cleave a target into multiple pieces.

Her shot missed, but a second round fired by the trigger-happy Kelly Grant caught one of the Orphans clean in the chest. Sand and dirt sprayed out of its back and it fell, limp and dusty, to the floor.

"Move forward!" Lahira cried, waiting until she saw something she could shoot at. Suddenly the Orphans were *very* hesitant to stage an advance. Instead of bodily turning the corner and firing, they were tilting the muzzles of their rifles around to take blind shots at where they thought they remembered the Humans to be hiding. It was almost as if they were no longer invincible in the face of this firefight.

This allowed the remaining crew of the *Messenger*'s bridge to come forward and find new, safer locations to hide. And what's more, it gave Lahira time to come up with a plan.

"Quan!" she hissed. Jackie sat down and nodded, listening as she checked her weapon's magazine over; about half a clip left. "I'm guessing Ensign Trusant put a few grenades in the stock-pile?"

"I think so, but frags aren't gonna be much help!" the ex-pirate answered briskly.

Lahira kept her eyes downrange. "Hold on--" she whispered, taking aim and firing. She thought she might have clipped an outstretched Orphan limb. "Okay! Go look and see if we have any flash-bangs or stun grenades. I'm sure we do."

Jackie nodded, offered a signal, and bolted to the back of the room, far from the lethal arcs of the Orphan guns. Almost instinctively, Gavin's security officers knew to provide additional covering fire for their superiors' trip. She returned with much less haste, and while Lahira didn't see what she'd brought she was able to make a reasonable guess from the loud thud of a crate hitting the ground.

"Pay-dirt!" Quan remarked with a grim cheer. "Want me to start throwin'?"

Lahira mused on it for a moment. "Take a concussion grenade. One!" She was quite clear on this point. "Pitch it as deep as you can into their ranks."

Jackie blinked, taking a moment to process where the strategy was going, then obeyed the command and hit the deck. Concussion grenades just aimed to throw their victims to the ground; they were often used in conjunction with flash-bangs, weapons that blinded and deafened their foes. If one wanted to capture one's prey alive, that was the combination to leave them defenseless just long enough to enter a room.

A tremendous thud echoed off of the walls of the control room. Nobody had a chance to get to their senses and even begin to assess the damage before Kelly muttered to herself, "Well, that'll need to be repainted."

After the powerful stun grenade went off and shook the bridge of the *Messenger*, Lahira poked her head up over the remnants of her cover. She nearly lost it when a loud *bang* accompanied the firing of an Orphan rifle round. Those jagged shards of steel were deadly to both Human and Orphan alike, as she'd found out from the other side of the barrel, but their slow flight made it just barely possible for the vessel's commander to save her neck - literally.

"Looks like it ain't done much good!" chirped the ex-pirate, Jack-O-Lantern Quan. She tucked the muzzle of her submachine gun over the bulwark before her and fired off a quick barrage against the doorway into her ships bridge.

The covering fire offered by the reformed crook allowed Kelly, the erstwhile navigator, to poke her head over their barricade with minimized risk of decapitation. "Holy..." she trailed off. "I count at least eight of them splattered against the wall!" She ducked as another shot was fired; it hit the ceiling, hardly well aimed. "Captain, its--"

More gunfire emerged, suddenly! The navigator popped her head down and hid, but none of the rounds fired seemed to aim for their position - or any of the Human ones! They didn't even make it into the bridge. Recognition dawned. "Woah, its over, alright," Lahira groaned softly. "Those are assault rifles, right?"

Jackie grinned, raising her gun (only what was above her hand, of course!) in victory. "AR-88-S's, sound-suppressed and all. Heard a lot of them fired in my time, that's our counter-intrusion force. Any minute now..."

The engine expert was dead on. The dull slapping sound of boots stealthily striking the floor entered the *Messenger's* bridge as the Captain let out a soft sigh of relief. "Its over," she stated sorrowfully. Then, her voice elevated sharply. "All clear?!"

As the Human reinforcements swiftly swept the command center clear, they repeated their superior's question as statements of facts. "Alright," Lahira stated, rising to her feet and moving over toward where those closest to her - and highest above her, in rank - lay. "Ensign Trusaunt! Admiral Owens!"

Gavin was a bloodied, wounded mess; he had tremendous lacerations on his arms, and he ultimately needed to be physically removed from atop the Admiral he was protecting. What came as something of a shock was the one moving him - Jackie Quan. The two had tremendous differences over the short course of their stay together, but the former pirate looked enraged as she shook the man. The once-violent jerking came to a screeching halt as she realized, in light of the myriad lacerations on Gavin's body, that she might well rip off a limb. "You ain't dyin' on me, frou-frou!" she cried out, slapping him in the face and earning a weary moan in response. "You're too tough a bastard."

A dull cough escaped from the momentarily forgotten space next to the chief security officer of the *Messenger*. "He took..." muttered the wounded Admiral Owens. The old man's uniform had been torn to shreds, and he too was bleeding - though it looked far from fatal. He had his hand clenched around a thick, wooden cross that shone with the blood of his soldiers' reflecting red light over dark varnish. "At least three shots for me."

"Sir, you just relax," Lahira whispered as she knelt down near him. She began to assess his injuries more clearly; she wasn't a medic, but she knew the basics of medicine well enough to treat some cuts. "Everything will be fine. Its over."

The Admiral laughed, his wizened eyes taking in the scene of Kelly Grant as she helped to organize the treatment of their fellow wounded space-farers - and, it was unfortunate, the half-dozen dead Humans. He shook his head. "No," he said with a sigh. "It is not over. It is only beginning. The Speaker, his men - one betrayed them."

"Sir, no, stop," Lahira whispered, reaching down and grasping her superiors' hand.

"Oh, please, Lahira," his tone was sad; reassuring. "I'm not dying, for today" he added somewhat grimly. "See to the Speaker. He might...Might be the key to this thing."

Biting her bottom lip, she pressed her hand to his face. "Alright, fine, but you are *not* allowed to follow that man on the cross you wear. Understand me?"

Smiling, now, the old man merely nodded. "Noble deaths aren't for men to have. He volunteered for a mission I...I never could bear..."

"Yes, I've read," Lahira answered, fighting back a hint of disdain for the ancient ways, before standing and walking over toward the deceased Orphan guards and, more importantly, to the wounded pile of dirt and gravel called the Speaker of Stasis. He had already managed to find what resembled a seated position, and he looked up at Lahira.

A robotic crackling escaped his chest; his vocalizing box might well have been damaged. Slowly, and with what looked like agony on his not-quite-face, he reached inside himself and removed a large lump of metal. Loud clacks and clicks came from his figure, and the machine sputtered as it tried to translate its input.

Sure enough, the mechanical translator was ruined, leaving Lahira only access to the stones that served as eyes for the semi-organic Speaker. He closed them and nodded twice, as if to reassure the Captain that he would live to see another day; and a primal sadness entered into its eyes, as if it was facing something it had never quite believed real, before.

Epilogue
Resolutions

It had taken Jackie about an hour and a half to fix the Speaker of Stasis' voice-box. Re-implanting it seemed much, much easier than removing it had; although it was hard to tell, because Orphans didn't seem to experience pain in the same way as Humans. It was probably because they were made out of a strange type of silicone, and had amorphous bodies used to delicately-executed changes.

Ensign Gavin Trusaunt, recovering on the *Messenger*'s sick bay, was given plenty of awards. They did him little good, mainly because he didn't know he'd gotten them! His blood-loss had mandated a medically-induced coma, and while he was certain to survive his rude awakening, Lahira privately wondered just how well he could recover from such damage - body, mind, and soul. His limbs were in question; not that they would be lost via ex-sanguination, but that nerve damage would render them inoperable. Jackie checked on him often enough, between stints repairing the ship's bridge and working on its engines. She was otherwise silent; she seemed determined to fix anything in her path, including Gavin.

Admiral Owens was faring much better than the one who had protected him. He resumed command of the *George Washington,* and Humanity's second fleet as a whole. The *Messenger* got its chief communications officer back just in time for the Speaker of Stasis to fully recover from his wounds. Once Lucas ran through some diagnostics with the alien and his translating device, and once he'd had a chance to be thoroughly astonished at just how ruined his ship's interior had been, he was ready to play his part in the *Messenger's* next mission.

"Alright," Kelly Grant, the ship's chief navigator stated, "We're in orbit around PX-31's inhabited planet." This wasn't news. "We've gone through all our star charts to pick out likely recipients, and I've plugged a list of all known Orphan worlds that have open transceivers into the comms network. If you're good," she said to Lucas calmly, "I'm good."

Slowly, Travares nodded. "Alright!" He began to toggle the various controls of his computer. He did this by hand, mainly because doing it in a data-stream was likely to leave his ears ringing in a minute. "We're set to broadcast on every channel. Speaker, it is up to you." He flipped a final switch on his console.

Lahira and James stood behind the alien as he stepped forward. His words were mere grumbles and collisions of stone, easily understood by his intended audience, but they were translated by the newly rebuilt device he'd had implanted into his chest so that his new-found friends knew what he said.

"I was the Speaker of Stasis for Grim Promise," he declared proudly, providing Humanity with PX-31's formal name for the first time. "I have lived to uphold our Search for our Creator. I have not found him. I have found friends who will help us look! The outsiders do not have to be our enemy. But the Speaker of The Search and the Speaker of Hell-Fire refused to listen. They refused to improve our Search. To not improve it is to not follow it."

"The Laws of Stasis are forever. The Search is forever. Not following the Search is against the Laws of Stasis. Not improving the Search is against the Laws of Stasis. The Laws of Stasis demand death by Hell-Fire." He sounded as if he would frown, in spite of not having a face. "The Laws *are* Stasis. The laws are cruel."

Slowly he took a step forward. The exact translation of his language could never convey the true meaning of his intent. "I will *not* be cruel. We have killed our own. We have killed the outsiders. These newest outsiders, they say they are Human. I will call them that. They are not part of Stasis. I will *not* be cruel. I will not follow the laws of Stasis. I can not *speak* for Stasis."

"I call myself anew. I am the Speaker of Vision. Vision is seeing outside of the Stasis, seeing ahead of the Search, and seeing something besides the Hell-fire. I declare this Speakship and ask for others to join it. We shall be called Visionaries."

Finally, he seemed to growl - a victorious sound, indeed! "I no longer Speak Stasis for Grim Promise. I Speak Vision for New Hope, the capital of the Visionaries!"

Lahira and James applauded and the broadcast faded to darkness. The Humans were wholly aware of the fact that their new-found friend had just begun an insurrection that the Humans would be expected to support. Earth's government hadn't yet agreed to do so, but how couldn't it? On the other hand, they had just no idea how much of a violation of the religious codes of the Orphans this was, and Lahira knew how such insurrections in history tended to turn out.

Across dozens of worlds, small political groups began to form. Peaceful protests, when tried, were quickly shut down under the charge of heresy. The Speakers of Hell-Fire, and not The Search, would become the first to put down the rogue Orphan's attempt to create a new sect. Even the lay folk of the Stasis, who worked to fuel the Orphan wars, tended to side with maintaining the status quo. Only a few radicals took up arms, finding ways to contact the Human fleet for help - extraction, often.

It often came only in the form of promises to help build that revolution up; to help keep them safe, to extract the Orphans who wished to be Visionaries from harm's way. As battles raged across the border between Human and Orphan space, the few extracted Visionaries helped to improve their own world, New Hope, with Humanity providing some of the raw minerals to get the job done.

It would not be long, Lahira realized, until Admiral Winters had perfected Orphan laser technology. New armors would be placed on her ship as Orphan metallurgy was reconstructed. Even, one day, carbon-fusion rockets would be designed to be used by Humanity against its invaders. And those invaders, some day, would win a battle - would threaten Earth, and Magellan, and Cortes, and Hudson, and more. Human history had shown the outcome of crusades starting - and ending - in many ways. Her reverie, however, had only one fate.

"One way or another," the Admiral declared long after the screen had gone dead, gazing to his starry-eyed subordinate, "You and your ship have met your destiny."

Lahira saluted the old man, who returned it, but her eyes remained perplexed. "Sir, I'm not sure what you mean, Sir?"

He laughed, and quite overtly patted that concealed, blood-covered cross. "Captain Ocean, of the *Messenger*," he announced dryly, "They say Jesus was a messenger, sending people a story of redemption. Well, you've certainly sent our enemies one, just now. A chance for them to yield, a chance for mercy and peace to reign." The old man gazed out of the ship's display screens, at the fleets surrounding New Hope, and at the surface of the all-too-alien planet. "And now, its up to them, whether they accept it, or not."

Lahira Ocean will return, with popular demand, in...
Protostar: Rampant Robots!

or...
Protostar: Revenge of the Orphans!

or...
Protostar: ...Something!

In the meantime, here are some titles of other books by Protostar's author, Jesse Pohlman!
- Physics Incarnate (2012)
- Pillars of the Kingdom (Series)
- Chronicles of Alleron
(http://www.chroniclesofalleron.blogspot.com)